BLANE'S TURN

BLANE'S TURN

A COMPANION NOVEL IN
THE KATHLEEN TURNER SERIES

TIFFANY SNOW

Montlake
Romance

Text copyright © 2013 Tiffany Snow

Published by Montlake Romance, Seattle

www.apub.com

Amazon, the Amazon logo, and Montlake Romance are trademarks of Amazon.com, Inc., or its affiliates.

ISBN-13: 9781477830659
ISBN-10: 1477830650

Printed in the United States of America

For all the readers who love Blane, Kade and Kathleen.

Prologue

Seventeen Years Ago

Blane Kirk stared up at the forbidding structure in front of him. It was a somewhat dilapidated building whose prime had long since passed, but which now housed the city's forgotten, lost, abandoned, and abused children.

And his brother.

The brother he'd never known he had, at least not until four years ago. With the death of the boy's mother had come the revelation that Blane had a half brother. His father's infidelity aside, Blane had been overwhelmed at the news. He'd always wanted a brother. His own mother had a difficult time conceiving and Blane had been the lucky product of many years of failed attempts. Blane had assumed his brother would come to live with them. He'd assumed wrong. Yet again, he thought back to the day four years ago when he'd tried to discuss the matter with his father . . .

"Don't be ridiculous," William Kirk said, his scathing disdain making fourteen-year-old Blane flinch. "You're my son. He's just an accident that was never meant to be. The son of a white-trash whore. That's all."

"But what'll happen to him?"

"The state will see to him," Blane's father said, sorting through a stack of papers on his desk. "And I don't want to hear another word about it. You shouldn't have been eavesdropping."

"If I hadn't, I wouldn't know I have a brother."

His father pinned him with a glare, his green eyes a mirror of his son's. "You don't. And one word of this to your mother and you'll regret it."

Blane choked down the angry bile in his throat, knowing from past experience that his father meant what he said. "Yes, sir."

Blane had hated that there was nothing he could do, that he had no way to help his half brother, foisted on the dubious protection of the state. He'd thought about him often over the next four years. Blane had buried their mutual father two months ago and had immediately set about finding what had become of Kade Dennon. Only his mother's illness had prevented him from coming sooner, her death following quickly on the heels of his father. Now Blane was as much an orphan as the brother he'd come to take home.

The inside of the building was slightly better than the outside, clean, although a dank smell of decay and mildew seemed to permeate everything. Blane gave his name to the waiting social worker and followed the woman up two flights of stairs to a wooden door that wouldn't fit quite right on its hinges.

"This is his room," she told him. "He shares it with four other boys at the moment, though even that is in jeopardy, considering his penchant for running away."

"What do you mean?"

"We just don't have enough resources to pick the kids off the streets when they run off," she said with a resigned sigh.

"How many times has he left?"

"Seven."

Jesus. "How will I know which one is him?" Blane asked. He was unexpectedly nervous at meeting this ten-year-old child, blood kin of his who didn't even know it.

The woman opened the door a few inches and pointed. "That's him. In the corner by the window."

Blane looked and saw a too-skinny boy with a mop of inky black hair. His skin was pasty white from not enough sunlight or a decent diet. He wore a ragged T-shirt that was a size too big and jeans that rolled up at the hem. He was staring out the window, his face turned away from them.

"You realize that we don't often grant guardianship to someone of your age," the woman reminded Blane.

"I don't think that'll be a problem here," Blane said. Yesterday he'd called his Uncle Robert, who'd agreed to help him. The wheels were already set in motion to cut through the paperwork and red tape. "I'll be taking him with me today."

The woman's lips thinned, but she didn't protest. Perhaps even she knew that sending Kade with Blane was a better plan, despite Blane's age, than making Kade stay there.

"Make sure you sign out before you leave," she said. At Blane's nod, she disappeared back down the stairs.

Blane took a deep breath and pushed open the door. Two boys who'd been playing cards stopped and looked at him before resuming their game. Another was sleeping on a bed with well-worn sheets. The fifth boy was nowhere to be seen.

Blane walked across the room to where Kade sat. Even when he was sure Kade had to have heard him, he didn't turn. Looking around, Blane spotted a spindly wooden chair, moved it next to Kade and sat down. Only then did Kade acknowledge his presence, his body stiffening as he drew back slightly, as though he thought Blane might touch him.

"Hi, Kade," Blane said, making his voice as friendly and nonthreatening as possible. His palms were sweating.

Kade said nothing.

Blane tried again. "You don't know me, but my name is Blane. Blane Kirk."

Kade still ignored him with a tenacity that was as admirable as it was disconcerting.

"I'm, well, I'm your brother," Blane said, praying he was doing this right. "And I'm here to take you home."

That got Kade's attention.

He turned from where he'd been staring out the window, studiously ignoring the man who'd walked in and sat down much too close to him, and gave him a quick once-over. Dark blond hair, cut perfectly short, unlike Kade's hair that was always too long and made the other boys call him a girl. Of course, they didn't call him that for long, not after what he'd done to the last one who'd said it.

The man was dressed in clothes that had no holes and didn't seem like he'd worn them more than once or twice. His shoes looked like real leather and were polished to a blinding shine. But it was his eyes that Kade studied most intently.

You could tell a lot from a person's eyes. Their mood, whether they were good or bad, what their intentions were—sometimes before they even knew themselves. You just had to pay attention and never, ever trust what they said with their mouth, only trust what they said with their eyes. That was a lesson Kade had learned the hard way—the bones in his left arm had only just healed.

This guy's eyes seemed . . . honest. He was telling the truth. But there was uncertainty there, too. That's the last thing Kade needed. He'd been in a foster home before where it had been decent, the people nice. Then they'd gotten pregnant and hadn't wanted a foster kid around, so they'd sent him back. That had sucked. Like being returned to the store for a refund.

This guy might change his mind, too, or what if he had a temper? Kade cast a practiced eye over the broad shoulders and muscled arms. This guy could snap Kade like a twig if he got pissed off enough, or drunk. Mean drunks were the worst.

No, thanks, Kade decided. He'd take his chances here or on the streets.

"Fuck off," he said insolently, turning back to stare out the window.

It was only from practice in concealing all emotions from his father that Blane was able to keep the shock off his face. A ten-year-old cursing like that wasn't something in his realm of experience. Well, what had he expected? The kid to greet him with open arms, shouting in glee at his good fortune like Little Orphan Annie?

Okay, obviously he needed to try a different tactic.

"I've got some cool stuff at my place," Blane said, leaning back in his chair. "You like video games?"

Kade shrugged, but at least he didn't ignore him. That was progress.

"I've got a ton of 'em," Blane continued. "And food, too. Good food. Hot, homemade meals three times a day. Pot roast, steak, roast chicken, pies and cake. Too much for me to eat, really."

Kade's throat moved as he swallowed and Blane hid a smile.

"You know," he said casually, "you don't have to stay. Maybe just come visit, see if you like it. If you don't, you want to come back, just say the word. I'll bring you back." Like hell he would. No brother of his was going to stay in a shithole like this. It was bad enough Kade had been here already for four years. Guilt that would soon become an all too familiar, constant companion rose inside of him.

Kade looked in the man's eyes again, and he seemed to know what Kade was doing, staring back unflinchingly.

He was lying, that was obvious. His eyes had turned fierce, but not angry. Interesting. And it didn't matter anyway if the guy was lying about bringing Kade back. If he wanted to leave, he'd find a way to leave and there wasn't fuckall this guy could do about it.

In the meantime, he was hungry. And video games were cool shit. They'd had one at the last foster home he'd been in, but the asshole teenager there had thrown and broken it when he'd lost a game.

To Blane's surprise and relief, Kade said simply, "Okay."

Hopping up from his chair, he went to the one cupboard in the room near the boys playing cards. They were bigger than him and Blane wondered if he'd had any problems being bullied. But strangely, both boys seemed to eye Kade warily as he approached, laying down their cards and shifting nervously on the squeaky bed. However, he ignored both of them, dragging a battered knapsack from the cupboard then walking back to Blane.

Kade's blue eyes were piercing and too old for his years, their depths holding too much pain and knowledge. They fixed on Blane.

"We going or what?" he said, flinging the knapsack over his scrawny shoulder.

"Um, yeah," Blane said, scrambling to his feet. "Let's go."

It took a few minutes to sign all the paperwork for Blane to take Kade, then the social worker handed him a thick manila envelope.

"Here are his records," she said. "You might want to go through them at some point, get the boy some counseling."

The pity in her voice had alarm bells going off in Blane's head, but he just nodded and took the folder, anxious to get Kade out of this place.

Blane was glad to still see his car parked on the street where he'd left it. In this neighborhood, you never knew. He walked toward it, laying his hand on Kade's shoulder to guide him. Kade spun away, shoving at Blane's arm and stopping in his tracks.

"Don't touch me," he snarled.

Blane's step faltered at the vicious look in Kade's eyes. There was fear there, too. His face was a mask of cold fury.

This wasn't the first time he'd said those words to someone.

Abruptly, Blane thought he was going to be sick. He swallowed down the nausea, carefully raising his hands in a gesture of surrender.

"I won't," he said solemnly. "I swear it."

Kade was reading his eyes again, just like he had back inside. Blane didn't move or flinch, and finally, Kade's body relaxed from its fighting stance.

Blane lowered his arms and fished his keys from his pocket, hitting the unlock button on the fob. The Jaguar blinked its lights.

"Nice ride," Kade said appreciatively, the anger gone as though it had never been.

"Thanks," Blane said.

Kade opened the passenger door and got in, immediately checking out the buttons on the console and the stereo.

Blane shut Kade's door and rounded the car. And as he slid into the driver's seat, he wondered if he'd bitten off more than he could chew.

CHAPTER ONE

D amn it, where was that file?

Blane Kirk dug through his briefcase as his clients filed into the conference room. They were representatives from one of the more lucrative accounts the firm handled and Blane had forgotten their file on his desk. Leaving to get it now would make him look woefully unprepared. And even though at the moment he was, he'd prefer to keep that to himself.

"Good morning," he said, setting aside the briefcase to greet one of the men who'd approached him. He dug in his pocket for his cell phone while exchanging pleasantries. "If you'll just excuse me for a moment, I'm going to grab a cup of coffee."

Heading to the table in the far corner where there was a coffee service set up along with pastries for the guests, he sent a rapid-fire text to Clarice, his secretary.

Left Kimmerson file on my desk. Please bring to 3rd floor conf. room.

About ten minutes later, everyone had gotten seated around the table with their coffee or beverage of choice. One of the men, the CFO, was talking when the door opened. Blane glanced over, relieved. It had to be Clarice with the file. Instead, a woman Blane was certain he'd never seen before walked in the room. If he had met her, he would've remembered.

She was petite, her high heels adding a scant few inches to her height but even so, Blane thought she'd barely reach his shoulder. Her hair was long and the color of rose gold. It lay in waves around her shoulders, but it was her face that held Blane's attention.

Delicate cheekbones, full lips, and blue eyes that were wide and innocent met his. She was young and also quite nervous, her tongue darting out to wet her lips and sending Blane's thoughts down a path inappropriate for work.

When he saw that she carried a file folder, Blane refocused. Clarice must have gotten her to bring up the Kimmerson file for him. Not wanting to appear as though he were staring at the girl, Blane glanced away, trying to tune back in to what the CFO was saying, which is why he didn't see what was coming until it was too late.

A gasp made him jerk his attention to the girl in time to see her stumble as she approached him. Hurtling forward, she fell, landing face-down in his lap, papers flying everywhere.

For a moment, Blane was too startled to move, then she did move, but not in a good way.

Her hand pressed somewhere it shouldn't have and Blane nearly shot up out of the chair. Well, he would've, if she'd get off him. He gripped her shoulders to try to stop her moving.

"Oops," she said, her panicked blue-eyed gaze meeting his.

Normally Blane wasn't opposed to a beautiful woman in this position, but then again, he didn't usually have an audience.

Well, there was that one time . . .

She was squirming to right herself again and Blane, not wanting a repeat of her earlier badly placed shove, took matters in his own hands. Picking her up bodily, she weighed next to nothing, he stood and set her on her feet. Her face was a vivid red and she wouldn't look him in the eye as she gasped, "So sorry!" then dropped to her knees and began clambering underneath the table.

Good Lord. Blane took a deep breath, his dignity somewhere on the floor with the papers, then straightened his tie and adjusted his cuffs. He caught the eye of the CFO who was staring, open-mouthed, at him.

The entire table was absolutely silent. Then, as if someone had given a signal, the muffled chuckles began. Hidden behind hands or attempted disguises of a cough, it was still obvious that Blane was a laughingstock.

Blane heaved an inward sigh. This meeting was going FUBAR pretty fucking quick.

James Gage, the son of the managing partner, suddenly dropped out of sight underneath the table as well. Blane's eyes narrowed. James Gage hit all the ticks on Blane's personal list as a complete asshole. Was he trying to ingratiate himself with the girl by helping pick up the papers?

Just about then, the girl crawled out toward him, skirt-clad rear end first, and Blane closed his eyes. That was another image he'd have to not dwell on.

She stood, her face still aflame as she thrust a sheaf of crumpled papers at him.

"Sorry," she mumbled again before beating a hasty, and careful, retreat.

Just as the door was swinging shut, one of the lawyers in the room said, "Now they're literally throwing themselves at you, Blane. What will they think of next?"

Blane fixed the man with a hard glare and he quickly shut up, though that didn't stop the smattering of chuckles. Blane automatically smiled as well, though he was going to tear that guy a new asshole after the meeting.

"I apologize, gentlemen," he said. "Now, where were we?"

～

Blane dropped his briefcase at his desk and immediately headed for the first floor. Clarice had told him she'd asked the new runner to bring the files by the meeting. Blane hadn't told her what had happened and she didn't seem to suspect anything was amiss.

The joke the associate attorney had made about the girl had simmered in the back of Blane's mind all through the meeting.

Surely she wouldn't have done something like that on purpose. Then again, some women didn't seem to care what they had to do to get the attention of a man, especially if he had money.

There was only one way to find out. And if she lied, he'd know it, and she'd be gone. Blane had little time or patience for women harassing him at work.

Blane stopped by Diane Greene's office first. She was the office manager and he needed some accounting issues fixed that the CFO had brought up in the meeting this morning. After he'd finished discussing that, he asked, "Who's the new girl?"

"You mean the new runner? Her name is Kathleen."

Kathleen. Blane turned that over in his head, putting the face with the name. It fit.

"Why?" Diane continued. "Is there a problem?"

"You could say that," Blane said dryly. "Where is she?"

Diane gave him directions to her cube, which was right around the corner. A sharp pang of disappointment hit Blane when he saw the cube was empty, disappointment that had nothing to do with wanting to interrogate her about her "fall" earlier.

But wait . . . not quite empty.

In the reflection from the window, Blane could see her. She was hiding under her desk. How had she even squeezed into that tiny space? But she had and now seemed to be terrified, judging by the look on her face. She was chewing her lip and barely breathing.

Blane was many things, but heartless wasn't one of them, at least not completely. If Kathleen had been aiming for an unforgettable introduction, she wouldn't be hiding from him.

Her eyes squeezed shut and Blane decided he needed to leave her alone. Judging by her actions, she was probably embarrassed and scared she was going to lose her job. She'd obviously heard him talking to Diane, so not exactly an unreasonable expectation.

Blane abruptly turned and walked away. His curiosity about her would just need to be shelved. She was young, way too young, and his employee. End of story.

When he reached his desk, he saw he had two messages from Clarice. His girlfriend Kandi had called. Twice.

Blane sighed and reached for the phone.

∼

Three Months Later

Blane was not in a particularly good mood this morning. The scene Kandi had made at his house last night still had his ears ringing. He'd known breaking up with her was going to be a pain in the ass, it always was, but she'd outdone herself this time. A buddy had called earlier to razz him about something she'd stuck on Facebook about the size of his dick.

Like he gave a shit. She was as ice-cold in bed as she was in person.

His client wasn't making things any easier. A white-collar criminal who had never seemed to come to terms with the fact that his embezzling had gotten caught and he now faced prison.

The judge had granted a recess to Blane until tomorrow so he could hopefully calm his client down. Maybe the prosecutor had some Xanax on her.

"I just really need some air," the guy gasped, tugging at his wrinkled collar. His suit was in sad shape and Blane made a mental note to make sure Clarice had it cleaned and pressed before their next appearance.

"Sure," Blane said, concealing his irritation. "Just give me a moment."

He turned to gather his papers into his briefcase, and when he turned back, his client was gone. Alarmed, Blane glanced around, then heard a scream out in the hallway.

There was a surge toward the door as people wanted to see what was going on and it took a few tense moments before Blane got out into the hall.

It was worse than he thought. His shit-for-brains client had a woman held hostage with a knife at her throat. And it wasn't just any woman. It was Kathleen. His runner.

Well, fuck.

"Stay back!" his client yelled. "Everybody stay back! Or I'll kill her!"

Blane could imagine the lawsuit already.

Kathleen looked terrified, her hands gripping the guy's arm as she tried to keep the knife from her throat.

Blane shut off his emotions, his mind blocking out everything else but the tactical logistics of the scene. He couldn't think about her or how pissed he was at his client. The objective now was to shut it down as quickly and as cleanly as possible.

Glancing around, Blane was relieved to see that Kade was in the courthouse. And if he knew his brother at all, he was armed, metal detector be damned.

Blane caught Kade's eye and gave a tiny nod, watching as Kade immediately dropped out of sight. When he reappeared, Blane saw the glint of metal in his hand.

Cautiously, Blane started moving forward. Kade would take his shot, Blane would grab the girl, and it would be over in less time than it took to tie your shoelaces.

"I want to get out of here," the guy yelled. "I'm not going to jail!"

That's right—he was going to the fucking morgue, Blane thought, taking another step forward and easing between two people.

"Let me out of here or she dies!"

The man's arm jerked toward Kathleen's throat, causing every muscle in Blane's body to momentarily freeze as a bright gash of red appeared on her pale skin. Blane's hands clenched into fists. Sometimes, he really missed being able to bring a gun into the courthouse.

Out of the corner of his eye, he saw Kade raise his weapon to take quick aim—

But suddenly, Kathleen moved, and before Kade could get off a shot, Blane's client had crumpled to the ground, the knife embedded in his side.

Kathleen ran to the far wall as the security guards surrounded the fallen man. Blane gave her a quick once-over. She was okay. In shock, but okay. He saw Kade moving toward her. Blane would have liked to see for himself that she was all right, but he had to take care of his client, the fucker.

Hurrying back into the courtroom, Blane grabbed his briefcase and headed for the judge's chambers. They'd take his client to the hospital and he'd meet up with him there.

Blane wondered if this was the idiot's idea of trying to get an insanity defense. The guy had been harping on Blane for weeks now, no matter that Blane had explained several times that embezzlement wasn't something that could be defended with an insanity plea. And now he'd just added hours of work for Blane to his case, not to mention putting the firm in jeopardy from a lawsuit.

He could use a cigarette, but tamped down the craving, which only put him in an even shittier mood.

~

Hours later, Blane hit the key fob to lock his Jaguar as he headed into the firm. Dealing with the mess at the courthouse from his idiot client had taken most of the day. Needing to blow off steam, since beating the shit out of your clients was bad for business, he'd stopped by the gym afterward to work out. Gladly discarding his suit and tie, he was now in much more comfortable jeans and a black Henley.

The wind had picked up, turning the October evening chilly, but Blane didn't feel it as he crossed the lot, his mind elsewhere. He hoped Clarice had gotten that brief typed up before she'd left for the night, despite him giving her little notice. She was divorced with a couple of kids, though Blane couldn't say how old or if boy or girl. She'd told him at some point, but he couldn't remember. What he did remember was that Clarice had trouble staying later than six or so because of them.

The elevator deposited him on the fifth floor and it was quiet when he stepped out, the only sound that of the grandfather clock ticking in the corner and the quiet clacking of a keyboard as Clarice typed.

Blane glanced at his watch, surprised. It was nearly seven. Damn. Now he felt bad. Clarice had probably had to jump through hoops to get someone to watch her kids so she could work late. Secretary's Day was going to be expensive this year.

But it wasn't Clarice typing at her desk.

Blane stopped a few feet away, staring at the woman concentrating so hard on typing that she hadn't even heard him come in. He knew her without even seeing her face.

It was that girl. Kathleen.

He'd watched her, been aware of her, ever since her unfortunate introduction to him. She left every day around the same time, staying later than she needed to, her long hair blowing in the wind as she crossed the lot to a decrepit Honda that looked at least two decades old. Blane wondered what she did after she left the firm. Maybe she went to night classes. Had a roommate. A lover.

He hadn't allowed himself to find out the answers to those questions. She was off-limits. Not only because of her age and status as his employee, but he'd have been blind not to see how she avoided him like the plague in the months since the tripping-into-his-lap debacle.

If he turned a corner and she was there, she immediately found a reason to go the other direction. If she was talking to Clarice and he came by, she beat a hasty retreat. She wouldn't even look him in the eye, instead studying the floor as though it held a secret code.

Blane had thought about stopping her, talking to her, just so she knew there weren't any hard feelings. But what if she was a ditz? It would ruin the fantasy image of her he had in his head.

It was strange, her being here, especially after what had happened today. Crazy ass clients. Sometimes he wondered if he'd chosen the right profession. Blane was damn lucky, as was the firm, that the guy hadn't done more harm. The liability damages on that lawsuit would've been painful to see.

Blane stepped closer, but Kathleen still didn't look up. Finally, he said, "What are you doing?"

She shrieked, a piercing sound that made Blane flinch. Jumping up, she overturned her chair in a cacophony of noise as she spun around to face him.

"Jesus," he said, shoving a hand through his hair in irritation. "What the hell was that for?"

"You scared me," she snapped, her blue eyes flashing. "You shouldn't sneak up on people."

Was that a reprimand? "I didn't sneak," he corrected her. "And you didn't answer me. What are you doing?"

"I'm typing, obviously."

Her tone oozed you're-a-dipshit and Blane's eyes narrowed. She had spunk, he had to hand it to her. It had been a while since anyone had dared to take that tone with him. Even as he thought it, she seemed to realize she might have overstepped. Her pale cheeks flushed pink and her eyes dropped from his.

Her gaze seemed to give him a slow once-over, taking in his torso, his jeans, all the way down to his shoes. Then she licked her lips and swallowed.

Well. That certainly got his attention. Blane wondered if she did it unconsciously or if she was trying to send a signal. Was she interested?

"Clarice had plans, so I offered to help finish this for her," she said, finally lifting her eyes back to his.

Ah. That explained it. But it was a Friday . . . "Don't you have plans for tonight, too?" She was young, pretty. She had to have a boyfriend waiting for her. No ring, so not married or engaged.

Kathleen turned pinker and shook her head, looking away as though embarrassed. Blane debated saying anything more, but she looked nervous now, her earlier bravado gone. She righted her chair and threw him a quick glance before resuming her work.

Her movements were quick and jerky. Blane frowned as he saw the screen beyond her. Gibberish, it looked like. He hoped she could type. Maybe he was making her uncomfortable. Probably best to just leave her alone.

But he hesitated just a beat longer, watching her. She was very . . . innocent. It was practically stamped on her forehead. With an inward sigh, Blane turned his thoughts away from the direction they'd been heading and went into his office. An unexpected treat, seeing her here and talking to her, but he should keep his distance.

He thought about asking her about today, if she was all right, but he didn't think she'd seen him at the courthouse. If she knew it was his client, would she see dollar signs on the horizon? Best not risk it.

Maybe ten, fifteen minutes later, there was a tentative tap on his open door. Blane glanced up.

"Clarice said to leave these for you," Kathleen said, handing him the file.

"Thank you." The temptation to say something more, to prolong their interaction, was great. But she was his employee. His very young, very pretty, and no doubt very naive employee. And possibly a sexual harassment lawsuit waiting to happen. Blane turned back to his computer.

After a moment, she seemed to realize she'd been dismissed, turned, and left. A draft of air, and Blane caught the slightly floral scent of her perfume. It was fresh and light, reminding him of spring near the ocean. It suited her.

Two minutes later, Blane knew he wouldn't be able to concentrate any more tonight. He had to run that file by anyway. Definitely couldn't ask Kathleen to go there. Besides, it was dark. Shouldn't he head outside and make sure she'd left safely?

That thought had him hurrying to pack his things in his briefcase and lock up the office. Moments later, he was scanning the deserted parking lot as he walked to his car.

There. Blane frowned. Odd she was still here, though his reaction was far from disappointed. He switched directions and headed for her car. When he got closer, he heard what the problem was. A telltale clicking sound when she turned the key. Dead battery.

Approaching the driver's side window, he saw Kathleen bang her forehead lightly against the steering wheel. The sight made his lips twitch.

Blane tapped lightly on the glass and she jerked upright. She seemed less than pleased to see him as she opened the door. "Yeah?"

"Car trouble?" he asked.

She nodded. "Guess so." Her tone was comically miserable. Blane hid a smile.

"Need a lift?" No, she needed someone to jump her car. Even as Blane thought of the jumper cables in his trunk, he still heard the offer come out his mouth.

To his surprise, she shook her head. "No, thanks. I'll just call a tow truck or something."

This was a first. Blane didn't usually have women turn him down— for anything. For some reason, her refusal made him persist in this idiocy. "It's late and it's cold. Let me take you home."

Kathleen was shivering and Blane wished he'd worn a coat just so he could offer it to her. Tiny as she was, it was no wonder that she was cold.

She still seemed to hesitate and Blane decided to take matters in his own hands. She'd freeze to death deciding whether or not he could give her a ride home. He knew she wanted to avoid him, as was her practice, but it was getting ridiculous.

"Come on," he said, pulling her door open the rest of the way. His hand grasped her arm before he realized he'd wanted an excuse to touch her. "I have to run an errand first, but I should be able to get you home before a tow truck would show up here."

It wasn't until she finally acquiesced, grabbing her things from the passenger seat, that Blane realized he'd been holding his breath. She walked beside him to his car, her stature diminutive, and Blane's every sense was focused on her. He didn't release her arm and he wondered slightly at the feeling of satisfaction it gave him to be able to help Kathleen tonight.

He handed her into his Jag, and judging from her sharp intake of breath, his car had made a good impression. As Blane walked around to his side, he realized that this probably wasn't the best idea he'd ever had, but surely he'd spend a few minutes talking to her, assuage his curiosity, and that would be that.

As he settled himself into the driver's seat, she shivered. "Cold?" he asked. When she nodded, he started the car and pressed the button for the heat.

Blane drove south on Meridian, casting glances at Kathleen as he drove. She resolutely refused to look at him; instead her attention was focused on the passing scenery out her window. Maybe he'd been wrong earlier. Maybe she wasn't interested. She wasn't trying to make conversation. Or she was shy?

That would be new. "Shy" was not often an attribute of the women Blane dated. Well, if she was shy, he'd get her to talk. He was her boss. She couldn't very well ignore him.

"Kathleen," he said, rolling the name on his tongue. He liked the sound of it. "What's your last name, Kathleen?"

She seemed to hesitate before mumbling, "Turner."

Kathleen Turner. Like the actress. Her parents must have had a sense of humor. Blane imagined she rarely gave people her name that someone didn't make a comment, so he refrained.

"Do you go by Kathy?" he asked. She'd already looked back to the window, so she had to turn again to face him.

"No."

"Katie?"

"No."

Blane's lips twitched at the disdain in her tone. Yeah, he'd never met a Katie he liked either.

"You prefer Kathleen."

"Yes."

Her monosyllabic answers amused him. A pretty, shy, young thing she was. What was he doing? "You seem to be a woman of few words," he teased, but Blane didn't think she caught on.

She didn't crack a smile as she said, "Sometimes."

Kathleen glanced away and Blane read embarrassment on her face. Thankfully, his job had given him plenty of practice at reading facial expressions and body language, especially if she wasn't going to say much.

"We didn't get off to a great start, Kathleen," he said, hoping to put her more at ease. That plan backfired. Badly. She stared at him, her mouth falling open slightly in dismay, and even in the faint light from the dash Blane could see her face drain of color.

It took Blane just a split second to realize his mistake. Of course she thought he meant her fall into his lap. He hastened to fix that.

"Why don't you tell me where you're from?" he asked. To his relief, she visibly relaxed at the question, releasing a pent-up breath.

"I'm from Rushville, Indiana," she answered, "a small town east of here. I moved here six, seven months ago."

"And what did you do in Rushville?"

"Not much," she said. "Tended bar. Took care of my mom."

"Took care of your mom?" Blane repeated.

"She had cancer."

Her bald reply might have been mistaken for a lack of feeling, but Blane saw the almost imperceptible flicker of sadness cross her face.

"Did she . . . ?" he asked, leaving the rest unsaid. He thought he already knew the answer.

"Two years ago now," she confirmed.

And nice of him to bring that back up, Blane thought she silently added. Not that he blamed her. *"Hey, let me give you a ride home and let's talk about your dead mom on the way, 'mkay?" Good one, Blane. Real smooth.*

"I'm sorry," he said, meaning it not just for her loss.

Kathleen didn't say anything, just turned to look out the window. The lights they passed briefly cast her face in light, then shadow. Blane studied her, his curiosity now working overtime and not at all sated.

"And the rest of your family?" he asked, unable to help himself.

His question forced her to turn to face him again and this time Blane inwardly winced at the pain on her face.

"My dad was a cop," she said. "He was killed in the line of duty when I was fifteen."

And this was officially the Worst Car Ride Ever, Blane decided. He couldn't remember when he'd crashed and burned so badly before. He closed his mouth against the questions hammering inside his head. He wanted to know more about her, to unlock what was rapidly becoming an irresistible puzzle. But he was getting the distinct impression that she didn't like him very much and that she liked his questions even less. Manners had forced her to answer, but Blane didn't particularly want her building up animosity toward him. He didn't question why that possibility disturbed him.

Kathleen intrigued him, an orphan new to Indy. Why had she come to work for him? Where did she live? Did she have friends? What were her plans? What did she do for fun? Who took care of her?

Did she have a boyfriend?

That last thought brought about an unexpected pang of something close to jealousy. Odd. Jealousy was a tiresome, wasteful emotion and not one that afflicted Blane. Ever.

Blane pushed the uncomfortable thought aside as he pulled into a parking lot. Time for business. The puzzle that was Kathleen Turner would have to wait.

Blane got out of the car, thinking she could wait here for him. But on second thought, she was a pretty girl sitting alone in a very expensive car. A billboard sign screaming temptation to criminals. He leaned back inside. "I'd say you could wait inside the car, but it's not the best area," he said.

She didn't bat an eye. "It's not a problem," she replied, immediately getting out.

It was obvious she wasn't into conversing with him, following a step or two behind rather than walking at his side, but Blane didn't push it. He didn't want to draw any attention to her, if he could help it. Though once they were inside and being let into Frank Santini's office, he wondered if that would even be possible. She stood out like a bolt of sunshine on a gloomy day, her eyes round and taking everything in, though she seemed to miss Jimmy in the corner.

"Blane!" Frank exclaimed, coming to shake his hand. "Fantastic that you could get here tonight." His eyes lit on Kathleen, a gleam coming into them that made Blane's teeth clench. "Who is your lovely friend?"

"This is Kathleen," Blane said. "She works for me. Kathleen, this is Frank Santini."

Kathleen's smile was as fake as Frank's dye job. Her smile grew even more forced as Frank pressed a sloppy kiss to her knuckles. After she slid her hand from Frank's, she sidled a bit behind Blane, as though instinctively trusting him to protect her despite her antipathy for him.

And she was right. Feelings Blane hadn't felt since his Navy days washed through him, including the overwhelming need to protect and shield.

"I brought the file with the affidavit summary you requested," Blane said, handing the file to Frank. "I'm not sure why it was so urgent that you had to have it this evening." This entire case had been a mess, and Blane knew the Santinis were behind the recent "accident" of their accuser. He just needed them to screw up. Then he and Kade would have them.

"I spoke with Bill about it," Frank said, tossing the folder onto his desk.

Blane felt that William Gage, a senior partner in the firm Gage, Kirk, and Trent, was a bit too willing to accommodate the Santinis, clients or not.

"We'd like a quick word with you," Richie said from where he still sat. "Alone, if you wouldn't mind." His gaze rested pointedly on Kathleen. "Jimmy can take her outside."

Jimmy slithered forward into the dim light like the snake he was. Blane stiffened even as Kathleen inched closer to him. He had to clench his fists to keep from reaching out and pulling her behind him, out of Jimmy's path. But he knew he couldn't do that, not if he wanted to keep up this charade with the Santinis.

Kathleen looked up at Blane, the alarm in her wide, clear blue eyes causing the conditioned response to again flare in Blane. Protect. Defend.

It was an act of sheer will to give her a quick nod. He didn't know what the Santinis wanted, but he'd make it quick, five minutes, tops.

His eyes stayed on Kathleen as she walked out the door, Jimmy following closely behind.

"This case needs to go away, Kirk."

Blane turned toward Richie, who hadn't moved from his chair, and still puffed on his cigar.

"The witness is dead," Blane said. "It's only a matter of time, now."

"We're not sure if he managed to get the information to anyone else," Richie added. "The election is in two weeks, you know."

"I'm aware."

"See that you don't forget."

The threat was there, behind the words, and Blane stared long and hard at Richie. He didn't appreciate being threatened.

"Listen, Kirk," Frank cut in. "We have a little . . . party coming up, right after Halloween. We'd like you to come."

"What kind of party?"

Frank leaned closer. "The kind people don't talk about, if you know what I mean." He chuckled. "I'll send you what you need to find it and get in. We'd love to see you there."

Blane wanted to question Frank further, but Kathleen was waiting, so Blane gave a curt nod and walked out the door. By the time he reached Jimmy and Kathleen, Jimmy was doing what he did best—being an asshole.

" . . . because I'd hate to have to mess up that pretty face," Jimmy sneered.

"Knock it off, Jimmy," Blane snapped. Kathleen looked terrified, her face white as a sheet. She jumped to her feet as Blane approached, moving toward him as he squared off with Jimmy.

"You got a problem, Kirk?" Jimmy had pulled his trademark switchblade. Word had it, he liked to slit his victims' throats and carve his initials into their skin while they bled to death. He was an ice-cold killer without a conscience or a shred of humanity. It made Blane anxious just to have him in the same room as Kathleen, never mind him knowing her name or anything else about her.

Blane took Kathleen by the arm, tugging her behind him. She came along quite willingly, her frightened gaze on Jimmy's knife. "Stay away from her, Jimmy," Blane threatened. It would be a pleasure to take Jimmy down, but he didn't want Kathleen anywhere nearby when he did.

After a tense moment, Jimmy smirked. "Watch your back, Kirk." The knife disappeared and he backed away, his malevolent gaze still fixed on Blane.

Blane wasted no time in hustling Kathleen out of there. It had been a bad decision to bring her along. He should have just jumped her car and sent her on her way. Irritation with himself made him walk fast and he didn't even realize how tightly he was gripping Kathleen until she said, "You're hurting me."

Blane immediately loosened his grip, noticing that she was nearly jogging to keep up with him. He slowed down, glancing back at the building before opening the car door for her. She didn't speak again until they were pulling out of the parking lot.

"Who was that guy?" she asked.

"He's called Jimmy Quicksilver," Blane answered. "His real name is James Lafaso."

"Why is he called Jimmy Quicksilver?"

Blane hesitated before answering. He didn't want to scare the girl even more than she already was, but neither did he want to lie to her. "Because he's good with knives," he finally said.

He couldn't tell how she took that. Glancing over, he saw her rub her forehead. A stab of guilt pierced Blane. The girl had already gone through enough today without an asshole like Jimmy scaring her even more.

"You all right?" he asked.

Her answer seemed a little dazed. "Um . . . yeah. I guess so."

It had probably been hours since she'd eaten. She was probably hungry. A little thing like her couldn't afford to skip meals.

Up ahead, Blane saw one of his favorite restaurants. Making a spur-of-the-moment decision, he pulled into a parking spot along the street and turned off the car. Kathleen looked around, confused.

"Why are we here?" she asked.

Yeah, Blane, what the hell are you doing? Take the girl home. She's on the Do Not Touch list.

But Blane ignored the voice inside his head. He was close enough to her to get another whiff of her perfume and temptation reared its head. His gaze dropped briefly to Kathleen's mouth before he replied.

"I thought you might be hungry," he said. "And I could use a drink."

Her look of shock would've been comical if Blane didn't feel exactly the same way. He knew better than this, and no flimsy excuse that he just wanted to make sure she got something to eat justified him spending more time with her.

And yet he hurried to get out of the car before she could say no, heading to her side to hold the door open for her. To his relief, she hesitantly got out, looking up at him with those eyes that made his breath hitch in his chest. Reaching for her, Blane took her elbow and led her inside.

~

Seventeen Years Ago

Kade sat in the car, looking up at the imposing mansion the guy had driven them to. Obviously, the guy was rich, and it looked like there were plenty of places to hide in there. If he turned out to be an asshole—and all of them had—he'd have a hard time catching Kade inside there.

"This is my home," the guy said. "It's yours now, too, if you want."

Yeah, right. Whatever.

Kade grabbed his knapsack and got out of the car, instinctively moving to keep a distance between himself and the guy as he approached to stand next to Kade.

"Come on," he said, heading up the walkway to the front door.

Kade followed, trying to ignore the increasing apprehension creeping into his bones. He hated that feeling, hated being afraid. But this house was far away from the streets where he knew all the players and who dominated which corner. Who set the rules here? And what if he broke one without even knowing? His steps slowed without him consciously doing so.

Blane glanced at Kade, concerned but trying not to show it. It was obvious the kid was terrified. His face was pasty white and he clutched that dirty knapsack as though afraid someone was going to take it from him. He was so thin, Blane could see the rapid pulse beating in his neck. His steps grew slower and heavier the closer they got to the house.

"You know what?" Blane said. "I forgot that this door is locked. Let's go around back."

Leading the way around the house, Blane took his time, his feet crunching in the few leaves scattered on the grass. The grounds were covered with oak trees, their wide expanses shading the house while their leaves were a constant source of irritation to Gerard, especially in the fall.

Kade seemed to relax as they walked, his body not as stiff when he moved, and he glanced curiously around.

"Do you have a dog?" he asked.

Blane shook his head. "No, but we can get one, if you want."

"Nah. They just die." He said it matter-of-factly, completely without emotion.

A chill went through Blane. It seemed the only emotions Kade was capable of were anger and fear.

This was what he'd let his brother become.

The door into the kitchen was unlocked and Blane entered first, hoping Mona was there. To his relief, she was. She knew where he'd gone and was anxiously waiting for his return, saying she'd make cookies, since everyone knew kids liked cookies.

Kade entered the kitchen warily, one slow step at a time, his head swiveling to take it all in. Blane looked around, trying to see things through Kade's eyes.

The kitchen was bright and cheery, one of the few rooms in the house that Blane would term "welcoming." Sunlight streamed through the window, bathing the line of plants on the window ledge. A white kitchen table with four chairs sat in an alcove, a vase filled with white flowers at its center. Another beam of sunlight rested on a plump cat snoozing in its warm rays, and the whole place smelled like freshly baked chocolate chip cookies.

Mona, Blane's housekeeper and erstwhile nanny, stepped closer, smiling. A petite woman, she had a bob of brunette hair and kind eyes. She and her husband, Gerard, had been Blane's salvation growing up. She'd heartily approved of him bringing Kade into his home, if for nothing else than to keep Blane company. Mona and Gerard lived adjacent to the property, and now that William Kirk was gone, it was just Blane in the house.

"You must be Kade," Mona said. "I'm Mona. It's so nice to meet you!"

Kade eyed her, but didn't react nearly as suspiciously as he had with Blane, giving her a nod and a mumbled, "Hi." No smile, though, and Blane noticed his knuckles were white again as he clutched the knapsack.

Mona cast a practiced eye over Kade and Blane knew what she was seeing: a dirty, scared little boy who was too skinny for his age. Her lips thinned, but her voice was friendly when she asked, "Are you hungry? I made some cookies. Would you like some?"

"Sure."

Mona placed a platter of cookies on the table along with two plates. "And I know you'll want some, Blane," she said.

Kade seemed unsure whether to stand or sit, so Blane sat in one of the kitchen chairs, slouching in his seat while Mona set two glasses of milk on the table.

"Come sit down, Kade," she encouraged.

Kade approached the table and slid into a seat. Mona reached for his knapsack.

"Here, let me take that—"

"No," he interrupted loudly, clutching the knapsack. "I've got it."

Mona smiled like this was nothing out of the ordinary. "Okay."

"So how's Gerard coming with the garage door repairs?" Blane asked Mona. He didn't want Kade to feel like they were staring at him. Mona seemed to catch on, picking up the conversational ball and telling him all kinds of minute details about the house and Gerard's current projects. Blane listened with half his attention, the other half firmly focused on Kade.

Once Blane had taken a cookie to munch on, Kade had reached out, too. That cookie had disappeared pretty quickly, as had five more in rapid succession, one of which was stealthily slid into his knapsack.

Both Blane and Mona pretended not to notice this, keeping up the patter of conversation until Kade seemed to have his fill and leaned back in his chair after draining the last of his milk.

"Come on," Blane said, getting up from the table. "I'll show you your room."

Kade followed him up the stairs and Blane took him to the first room on the left. It had been serving as a guest room, but Mona had quickly redone the décor in something more suited to a ten-year-old boy than the bland elegance that had been there before.

A queen-size bed with navy and hunter green plaid print bedding took up one corner, the matching furniture in a warm honey oak. The heavy drapes that had dressed the window before were gone, replaced by filmy white ones that let the sunshine in.

"The bathroom is across the hall," Blane said, watching as Kade looked around the room. "And I think Mona put some clothes in the closet for you." She'd guessed at his size and Blane knew everything she bought was probably going to be too big, but maybe after a couple of months of her cooking, the clothes would fit Kade properly.

"I thought you said you had video games?"

"Yeah, I do. They're in the TV room."

Kade followed him back downstairs, still keeping his knapsack with him, and Blane set up the video games. They spent the next few hours playing "Super Mario" on the Nintendo. Blane had never seen someone beat the levels as fast as Kade did. After Blane's Mario died yet again, Kade tossed down his controller.

"I'm hungry," he said.

Blane glanced at his watch, then rubbed his eyes. He couldn't remember the last time he'd spent so long playing video games. "Mona should have dinner done by now. Let's go check."

Sure enough, Mona was just setting the dishes on the table when they got to the kitchen. Blane chatted with Mona and Gerard during dinner, watching as Kade put away a good amount of food as well as sneaking a chicken leg and a biscuit into his knapsack to go with the cookie from earlier.

Blane glanced at Kade, who seemed to be having a hard time keeping his eyes open. "Well, I'm tired," he said. "I think I'm heading upstairs. Kade? What about you?"

Kade nodded and slid out of his chair. He looked at Mona. "Thanks. That was really good."

She smiled at his blunt honesty. "You're very welcome, Kade. Good night."

After a little encouraging, Kade took a shower. Blane got him some pajamas from the bureau drawers while he waited, but Kade came out dressed in the clothes he'd had on before.

"Here," Blane said, handing Kade the pajamas. "I thought you might want something clean to wear."

Kade eyed the clothes before reluctantly taking them. "What'll happen to my clothes?"

"I'm sure Mona can wash them for you," Blane said. Or burn them.

"Turn around," Kade ordered.

Blane obediently turned his back so Kade could get undressed. He faced the mirror now, though he didn't think Kade noticed. Blane was about to glance away to give Kade his privacy, when he took off his shirt.

It was like someone had slammed his fist into Blane's gut.

Kade's skinny torso was marked with a vivid, jagged scar that ran nearly the entire length of his chest. It was still red and puckered; recent, then. Kade turned around and Blane had another shock at the pink pockmarks that dotted his back, the kind that came from cigarettes. Then everything disappeared as Kade pulled the pajama shirt over his head.

"Okay, you can turn around," Kade said.

But Blane couldn't. His feet were rooted to the spot as the horror of what his brother had endured washed over him.

"Dude, I said you can turn around now," Kade repeated.

It took a massive amount of will to compose his features into something resembling normalcy. Blane turned around and forced a smile. Kade had already climbed into the bed. Blane bent down and pulled the covers up over him, noticing the knapsack rested beside Kade in the bed.

"Got everything you need?" Blane asked.

"Yeah."

"Okay then."

Blane headed for the door and turned off the light. In the doorway, he hesitated.

"Kade, I'm really glad you're here."

He couldn't see Kade, not in the dark, but knew Kade could see him in the light from the hallway. There was no reply and Blane didn't expect one. He softly closed the door and went back downstairs.

He could really use a drink.

CHAPTER TWO

The restaurant was quiet, the lighting dim, and Blane immediately relaxed. He led Kathleen to his usual table and watched as she paused for a moment before climbing onto the tall barstool. Her feet didn't touch the floor and Blane hid a smile as he pushed her stool in to the table. She mumbled a "Thanks" even as her cheeks flushed a delicate pink.

Greg came by to take their order and Blane ordered his usual drink, Dewar's and water. Kathleen took him by surprise, ordering a manhattan. A drink like that would probably knock her flat on her ass in about twenty minutes, especially considering Blane had doubts as to the last time she'd eaten today.

He studied her as he sipped his drink while she carefully avoided looking at him. Her poise and complete lack of interest in him only made her that much more fascinating to Blane. She took in the room, her eyes drifting over the other tables and the bar before she finally seemed to sense his gaze on her.

"Why do you keep staring at me?" she snapped, her eyes narrowing.

Blane thought fast, giving her his best disarming smile. "My apologies," he said easily. "I suppose I was just waiting for you to go into hysterics." Which was total bullshit. If Kathleen hadn't lost her shit when a man's knife was at her throat, she wasn't going to lose it because of Jimmy.

"Why would I go into hysterics?"

Blane shrugged. "It's been my experience that hysterics would be the typical female reaction."

"Well, I'm not your typical female," she said, arching a delicately curved eyebrow.

Blane couldn't help a smile now. "I can see that." If she had been typical, he'd have taken her directly to her home.

"Why would Jimmy feel it necessary to threaten me?" she asked.

That protective instinct again. Damn. What was it about this girl that had made that part of Blane go into hyper-mode? "It wasn't anything personal. It was just Jimmy being Jimmy. He's not happy unless everyone in the room is terrified of him."

She frowned at this. "Who were those men anyway?"

"Frank and Richie Santini. They're brothers and they run that local union we're defending against election fraud."

Thankfully, Greg came back just then. Kathleen glanced over the menu before ordering a bowl of soup, and that was all. Was she not hungry? Maybe doing that ridiculous girl thing of pretending she didn't eat? Blane was aware of a pang of disappointment. She'd been so against type until now. He ordered himself a steak, medium rare.

"You sure all you want is soup?" Blane asked her, just to be sure. She nodded and Greg went on his way.

"You've had a busy day," Blane continued, deciding to out himself and the firm. "In one day you've had someone holding you hostage, and someone else threatening you." He couldn't keep himself from reaching across the table to tug open the collar of her shirt to expose the bandage covering the wound at the base of her neck.

Blane was taken aback by the strong, sudden urge to brush his fingers against her throat. His skin was dark against the pale ivory of hers, which only made his thoughts go tripping down a path that imagined what the rest of her looked like.

"Excuse me," she snapped, jerking backward out of his reach. Her blue eyes flashed.

Blane took another sip of his drink, trying to cool the surge of heat in his blood. She had a bit of a temper, which he liked, but now he needed to mollify her, much like soothing a hissing cat.

"Where did you learn to get away like that?" he asked, pretending he hadn't noticed the flash of anger.

"My father," she said, calmer, though her gaze was still suspicious.

Blane waited for her to continue but she looked away, fidgeting a little before taking another nervous sip of her manhattan. Perhaps Blane did have an effect on her after all, though why that produced a surge of satisfaction, Blane couldn't say. He hardly knew the girl.

"What else did he teach you?" Getting information out of her was like interrogating a suspect.

She thought for a moment, then said, "The fine art of making a proper whiskey drink, as any good Irishman knows. How to shoot, and more importantly, how to hit what I'm shooting. Not to trust what people say, but only what they do."

Okay, that was hot, though Blane thought it was unintentional. She was just being bluntly honest. Another unusual trait for a woman. He took another drink.

"How did you find out about today?" she asked.

"I was there," Blane said. "He was my client. On trial for embezzlement. Couldn't handle the pressure. I had no idea he'd do something like that, though, I swear."

His confession had an odd effect on her. Something like disappointment flitted across her face and was gone, then she drank the rest of her manhattan down in one practiced swallow.

Greg arrived before Blane could question her further, setting the food down in front of them. By the longing gaze she gave his plate, Blane realized she was hungry, but just hadn't ordered food. Didn't want to eat in front of him, then? He heaved an inward sigh at the quirks of women.

Blane then had to revise that opinion as she scarfed down her soup as though it might run away any moment. She sat back on her stool and drank the second manhattan Greg had brought, eyeing his steak in such a way that Blane briefly considered offering her a bite.

She seemed content to let dinner pass in silence, but Blane had a thousand questions running through his mind. He'd been tired earlier but now he was wide awake, his mind analyzing everything she'd told him and what she hadn't, creating a picture inside his head of who she was. He was anxious to know how close or far it was from reality.

"Why did you come to Indianapolis?" Blane asked.

"Just needed a change," she said.

Her answer was as vague as he'd expected, though that didn't make it any less frustrating.

"So how's the embezzlement guy?" she asked, unsurprisingly turning the conversation away from herself.

"He's going to be all right," Blane answered, leaving out how close the guy had come to being very far from "all right" if it had gone how he and Kade had silently planned. "We'll press for a psychiatric evaluation once he's recovered."

"The insanity defense," she said. "A bit cliché, really."

"Not something I would have encouraged him to do," Blane said, wondering if she'd realized yet that she could sue the firm. She didn't appear to be dumb. He was sure she'd figure it out, and he wasn't disappointed.

"I'm not going to sue the firm," she said, her tone one of let's-cut-the-bullshit.

"I didn't think you were," he lied. The look she gave him said he wasn't fooling her one bit.

"C'mon," she said with a disbelieving snort. "Like I don't know what this is about."

Blane leaned forward, wondering if she could feel the electricity between them like he could. He watched her throat as she swallowed more bourbon, her eyes locked on his. Her lips shone wetly with a sheen of liquor and Blane had the insane urge to lick them clean.

"I'm glad you're not going to sue the firm," he said, "and we're grateful for your loyalty. We'd like to offer you compensation for what you had to endure today."

She blinked, as though she had to process what he'd said. "Are you trying to pay me off?"

"Of course not," Blane lied again. "It's what I just said. Compensation for hardship endured under our employment."

Her eyes flashed again. "How much?"

Blane's stomach sank and he leaned back. They were all the same, especially when money was involved.

"Five thousand," he offered, though in a lawsuit, she'd probably win four times that.

"Five thousand?" she squeaked.

"Or ten," Blane said with a shrug, "if you feel that would be more appropriate."

Her eyes were wide as saucers and Blane knew what would happen next. She might hem and haw about how she really shouldn't, right before asking how soon she'd get the check.

"Forget it," she said. "I don't want your money."

"What do you mean, you don't want the money?" Was this her version of hemming and hawing?

"I don't want it," she said, even more forcefully, and Blane didn't think she was playing a game. Interesting.

Greg came by with the check and Blane tossed some money down on the table, though the focus of his attention was on Kathleen. A flash of relief crossed her face as she noted him paying the bill and realization struck Blane. Ah. That's why she hadn't ordered much to eat.

Now Blane felt slightly chagrined at having taken a woman to dinner without making it clear he was *taking* her to dinner. His mother would have been sorely disappointed in his manners.

The urge to make it up to Kathleen made him reach a hand toward her to help her down off the too-tall stool. She seemed reluctant to take it, but finally did. The bones of her hand felt fragile inside his grip. She was breakable, too much so.

Blane opened the car door for her and she slid inside. When he got behind the wheel, he asked, "Where to?" She gave him an address and he headed that way. He was as excited as a kid at Christmas that he finally got to see where she lived.

Unfortunately, his excitement waned as he neared the address Kathleen had told him. The area of town they were in was one often reported on the news, and not in a good way. Did she live alone? She said she could shoot, but did she own a gun? Maybe she had a live-in boyfriend who kept her safe. That thought made Blane's hands tighten their grip on the steering wheel.

He opened his mouth to ask her, but noticed she'd fallen asleep. The streetlights cast an orange fluorescent glow on her face every few seconds.

Warmth spread from Blane's stomach outward. She trusted him enough to sleep, knowing he'd get her home safe and sound. Even when he pulled into her parking lot and turned off the car, she still slept.

The opportunity to observe her undetected was irresistible to Blane. He moved close to her, studying her in the faint light.

She was beautiful, in a classic, elegant way. He took in the arch of her brows, the delicate tilt of her nose and full lips, parted a fraction in sleep. Her hair tumbled in waves over her shoulders and Blane's fingers itched to touch it. This close, he could smell her perfume again.

Blane hadn't ever felt drawn to a woman, not like this. Appreciating the shape of a woman enough to take her on a date or two and fuck her was different. This was deeper, like something inside him recognized a kindred spirit and wanted to latch on.

Before he realized what he was doing, his palm was cupping the velvety softness of her face, his thumb brushing over her cheekbone.

This was bad. Very, very bad.

Her bleary eyes fluttered open while he was touching her, and he froze.

Awareness struck and she jerked upright. Blane's hand fell away.

"Sorry I fell asleep," she said breathlessly. "Thanks for the ride." She practically fell out of the car in her haste to get away.

"I'll walk you," Blane offered, though he didn't consider it optional.

Watching her hips gently sway as she walked up the stairs made Blane feel like a horny teenager, but he couldn't help it. His eyes were riveted to her ass until they reached the top floor of her two-story building. She walked toward the door on the left, which was also the closest to the street.

Blane glanced around, taking in the scene. His arousal was forgotten as he assessed her apartment's location and probability of being breached. The second floor was better than the first, but there were bushes and trees planted next to the building and stairs, giving a possible haven to criminals out to do her harm.

He didn't like that. Not a bit.

She unlocked the door and turned to face him. Obviously an invite to come inside would not be forthcoming. Blane looked over her head into the darkened apartment, wishing there was a light on so he could see inside.

"Do you live alone?" he asked. He was worried about her safety, that was all.

Right.

"Yes."

She'd begun nervously fiddling with her keys, the metal jangling loud in the night.

"What are you going to do about your car?" Blane asked. She might not remember, but she had no transportation.

"I guess I'll call a tow truck," she replied with a shrug.

"Do you have any family here?" Maybe she had a brother who looked after her, kept her car running, and made sure men like Blane didn't get too close. But she shook her head.

"Boyfriend?"

Negative, Ghostrider.

This was going from bad to worse. She had no one to take care of her, and no one to protect her from . . . him.

Blane moved closer, forcing Kathleen to tip her head back to look at him. Her eyes widened and her keys jangled faster. Blane hid a smile. Closing his hand over hers, he stilled the keys. The pulse at the base of her throat was beating wildly. Blane reached up, doing what he'd wanted to do in the car, and traced a long lock of her hair, curling its soft wave around his finger. He could swear she stopped breathing for a moment.

"I'll take care of it," he said.

"Take care of what?" she breathed, her gaze dropping to Blane's mouth.

He nearly groaned. The urge to kiss her, back her into her apartment and show her how very, very well he could take care of her, was nearly overpowering.

But instead, he smiled. She was his employee. She was off-limits. He could no more sleep with her than he could sleep with his sister, if he had one. Blane reached for his sadly lacking self-control.

"Your car," he said. "I'll take care of your car."

Her eyes jerked back up to his and Blane could see her blush in even this faint light.

"You don't have to do that," she weakly protested.

"It would be my pleasure," Blane said, wishing he was just talking about the damn car. His gaze dropped unwillingly to her mouth. She licked her lips and he nearly forgot his resolve not to touch her.

Time to go.

"I'll need these," he said, slipping the key ring from her fingers. "Good night, Kathleen."

She seemed too dumbfounded to say anything, though her throat worked as she swallowed. Blane stepped away, reluctant to leave. But if he stayed, he knew what would happen. He'd have her naked and in bed before she could slip off her shoes. But he'd regret it tomorrow, and likely she would, too.

He felt her eyes on him as he walked down the stairs.

~

It was the matter of a phone call to get someone out to tow Kathleen's car and replace the battery. The cost wasn't much, a couple hundred dollars, but Blane thought that might not have been a paltry sum to Kathleen and he was glad he'd happened to be around when her car broke down.

Blane agreed to meet the towing company at the firm, which was fine with him because although it was a Saturday, he still had work to do in the office.

He didn't know why he suddenly swung into the hardware store as he drove by, having them make another set of keys from the ones he'd taken from Kathleen. It was early, the store had just opened, and Blane was the only one there. He stood by, impatiently waiting, wondering what the hell he was doing.

Blane was briefly tempted to take the car to her himself once it was fixed, but he had work to do and really needed to stay away from Kathleen for his own peace of mind. His dreams last night had showcased a woman with blue eyes and strawberry blonde hair, and he'd been doing things to her that he was pretty sure were illegal in at least a dozen states.

With that decision made, Blane got to work, losing himself in his cases until his stomach growled, reminding him it was time for lunch.

He was eating a sandwich one-handed while he flipped through files with his other hand when his cell rang.

He glanced at the caller ID before answering.

"Kirk," he mumbled, swallowing a mouthful of turkey and Swiss on rye.

"Yo, Cap'n, how's it hangin'?"

Blane snorted at his friend Todd's idea of urban slang. "What are you? Fucking fifteen? Talk like a man, for chrissake."

Todd just laughed. "I figured with all the lowlifes you hang with, that'd make you feel more comfortable and shit."

"Fuck off," Blane said without heat, taking a swig of the Coke he'd gotten from the vending machine downstairs.

"What've you got planned for tonight?" Todd asked.

Blane thought a moment. For once, nothing, which sounded just fine to him. God, was he getting old when staying at home on a Saturday night was something to look forward to?

"Nothing," he answered. "I'm at work now. I might stay late."

"You broke up with Queen Bitch, right?"

"Kandi," Blane corrected, not bothering to reprimand Todd's pet name for her. None of his buddies liked her and he didn't see that changing anytime soon. Not that it mattered anymore, he supposed.

"Whatever. She's out of the picture, right?"

"Yeah, why?"

"I need a favor, man."

Blane's eyes narrowed in suspicion. "What kind of favor?"

And that's how Blane found himself on a blind date with Todd, some girl named Jenny, and her best friend Tory. Todd had met Jenny at the grocery store and they'd supposedly hit it off. However, Todd didn't want to do the first date alone in case she was psycho or had their children's names picked out by dessert.

Tory was easy on the eyes with curves in all the right places, shown off to their best advantage in a dress that fit her like it was painted on. Her makeup was bold and thick, her eyes outlined in black while her lips were stained red. Tory said she was an "aesthetician" which seemed to mean she did manicures and pedicures all day with an occasional massage thrown in.

When he'd heard that, Blane had shot Todd a look as they let the girls precede them into the restaurant.

"You should be thanking me," Todd hissed, clapping him on the shoulder. "She was a gymnast in high school."

"And when was that?" Blane hissed back. "Six months ago?"

But Todd ignored him, hurrying after Jenny and sliding into the chair beside her.

Conversation with Tory was mind-numbing, Blane feigning interest in something she was saying about a reality TV show she was obsessed over. He took another sip of his drink, eyeing Todd and Jenny. Todd was feeding her a bite of his pasta, then leaned forward to kiss her.

Blane signaled the waitress for another drink, calculating how much Todd was going to owe him for this. Tory had now slipped off her shoe and was trying to see how far up Blane's pant leg she could creep her perfectly polished toes.

Blane breathed a sigh of relief when the interminable dinner finally came to an end, only to hear Jenny say, "Hey, I know this great bar we can go to!"

Tory quickly agreed and Todd, well, Blane figured Todd was good with whatever gave him better odds of ending the evening in Jenny's bed. Blane thought that was already a done deal, judging by the way the two of them made out in the back of Blane's car while he drove.

The bar was called The Drop, and Blane had never been there before, though he'd driven by a few times. A younger crowd filled the place and it was busy at this hour on a Saturday night. Todd spotted a group leaving and snagged their spot in a booth.

The waitress came by and Blane ordered a round of drinks. It took patience he didn't have to smile down at the woman next to him, who seemed determined to rub every inch of her barely clad breasts against him.

Blane glanced up and time seemed to stutter to a halt.

It was her. Kathleen. Only she wasn't a customer, she was the bartender.

Her gaze was locked on his, their blue depths clear even from this distance, sucking him in as he immediately forgot the brunette squeezed against him.

Then the moment was over, Kathleen turning away as though she hadn't even recognized him, or if she had, then she certainly hadn't cared enough to acknowledge him.

Their drinks were delivered by the waitress and Blane's mind spun as though new life had been breathed into him, the cobwebs of being up since before five a.m. wiped away. Had she gotten her car without any problems? Was she glad to see him? Had she even noticed him?

The answer to the last question seemed to be no, as he didn't see her looking his way again. However, she seemed pretty busy. Blane faked a laugh at something Jenny had said, he had no clue what, but which had the rest of them in gales of laughter.

He kept casting surreptitious glances in Kathleen's direction as she worked, her movements practiced and efficient. She laughed and joked with the customers and the other bartender, some guy who looked about her age.

Blane frowned at that. Kathleen seemed really comfortable with him. Maybe more than a work friend? But she'd said she didn't have a boyfriend.

Which didn't mean she wasn't sleeping with someone.

That thought had him downing his drink. "I'm going to get us another round," he said. Tory moved and he slid out of the booth. Ingrained manners made him ask, "Anyone want anything?"

"I'm getting a little tipsy," Tory said with a flirtatious grin, "but I'd love an appletini."

Blane wanted to roll his eyes at the not-so-subtle hint, but just nodded and smiled at her before heading for the bar. He had to work to keep his steps even and slow. It would not be cool for Kathleen to see how much he wanted to talk to her.

He slid onto an empty bar stool and waited, taking the time to appreciate how cute Kathleen looked in her ponytail. It took a minute or two, but she finally turned to him with a smile on her face—which immediately faded when she saw who was sitting at the bar.

That took Blane aback. He'd thought after last night, the moment at her door, she'd thawed toward him a bit. It seemed he was mistaken.

"So you work here, too," he said, scrambling for something to say in light of her frosty demeanor.

"A few nights a week," she replied. "Can I get you something? Dewar's and water?"

Blane smiled a little. She'd remembered what he drank. For a fraction of a moment, the ghost of a smile hovered over her lips.

"Yes, and something called an appletini, please."

The smile was gone now and she nodded, going to fill his order. Blane watched her move, wondering what he'd do if he were here alone rather than with a date. Sit here and watch her work until they threw him out as a creepy-ass stalker, most likely.

Kathleen set the drinks in front of him, took a deep breath, and blurted, "Thank you for getting my car fixed."

It sounded like the words had been forced from her mouth, and her reluctance to owe him anything amused Blane. He got under her skin, all right.

Good to know.

"No problem," he said, smiling full on now, just to see how she'd react.

Her breath seemed to catch and her eyes widened. She swallowed, her throat moving in a way that drew Blane's eye.

Blane tossed a fifty down, picked up the drinks, and went back to the table. Yes, a horrendously overdone tip, but he hadn't been able to resist. If she worked two jobs, money had to be tight. And he'd rather blow fifty bucks on Kathleen than the two hundred he'd already spent on the brunette tonight.

Speaking of which . . .

Blane was able to hustle everyone out the door not too much later. He thought he'd given Todd enough time to close the deal. If not, then too bad.

Blane dropped Todd and Jenny back off at Todd's car and expected Tory to go with them.

"Hey, man," Todd said to Blane, shoving his head back in the open window. "Can you take Tory home? I think Jenny's going to come over to my place. For a drink."

Yeah, right.

"You owe me," Blane hissed.

"You got it."

Blane drove Tory home and she didn't shut up the entire way there. The warm buzz he'd had going from seeing Kathleen had all but evaporated, giving way to a pounding migraine behind his eyes that had *Drunk Aesthetician* written all over it.

Tory needed help into her apartment—of course she did—and Blane got her inside. Once he was in there, however, she attacked him, pulling at his tie and latching her mouth to his.

Blane disentangled her arms from the grip she had around his neck and gently, but firmly, set her from him.

"It was nice to meet you, Tory," he said, "but I have to go now."

"Don't be silly," she panted, stripping off her dress faster than Blane could have believed possible. "You don't even have to call me tomorrow. I promise." She leaped for him and Blane had to again hold her off, thinking this was one of the most ridiculous things that had ever happened to him.

He was so not in the mood for this shit.

Blane stopped holding her off and kissed her. She tasted of the sickly sweet appletini and cigarettes. Not a thing like how he imagined Kathleen would taste.

"You know what I'd really like?" Blane said against her lips.

"Mmm, what?"

"To tie you up."

She pulled away, looking up at him with a sly smile. "I'm totally into that," she said, leading Blane to her bedroom.

Five minutes later, Blane adjusted his tie as he stepped out of the apartment, ignoring Tory's shrieking curses at him. Once she sobered up, she would realize her purse was close beside where Blane had tied her to the bed. She could call a friend if she couldn't free herself. He'd used her bra, so it probably wouldn't be very hard for her to get out of her current predicament, when she wasn't drunk.

Now the migraine felt like it was going to split his skull.

Blane glanced at his watch. It wasn't yet midnight. The Drop was probably still open—

No. He was not going to stalk her like some love-struck idiot.

His cell phone rang as he was getting into his car. "Kirk," he answered.

Shit. It was one of his indigent clients. Busted again for solicitation.

"I'll be right there," he said with a sigh, shoving the key into the ignition.

Blane took a few indigent cases every now and then. They were usually a pain in the ass, but often those particular people, especially repeat offenders, had all kinds of contacts on the streets and behind bars. That kind of information came in real handy sometimes.

It took nearly three hours to calm Roberta down. She accused the officer of entrapment, yelling at him and anyone else standing around, then crying on Blane's shoulder. He assured her he'd be at the arraignment on Monday and watched as the cops led her back to a holding cell.

And his headache hadn't abated in the slightest.

Blane slid into his car and rested his head back against the seat for a moment. He closed his eyes. Shit, he was tired. He could fall asleep right here, if the cops wouldn't give him a fucking ticket for it.

He started the car just as his cell phone rang again.

"Are you fucking kidding me?" Blane groused to no one. "Kirk." His greeting was curt.

"Sir, it's Clarice. I'm sorry to bother you, but it's Kathleen. You know, the runner? She's in trouble."

Blane sat up in his seat, suddenly alert. "What kind of trouble?"

"There's been a murder."

∽

Seventeen Years Ago

Blane took another drink, the bourbon a welcome burn in his throat. He leaned back on the couch, eyeing the spread of photos on the table in front of him.

He'd been reading Kade's file for the past couple of hours. It had been eye-opening, in a horrifying, sickening way. Pictures of Kade, bruised and bloody. His eye so swollen, it couldn't open. Cracked ribs from a bat. He'd just gotten a cast off his arm a couple of days ago. The marks and scars on his body weren't an aberration of his life the past few years, but a common occurrence, all written in the detached clinical voice of doctors and ER techs.

Blane set down his drink and buried his head in his hands.

He should've done something sooner. Shouldn't have let his father abandon Kade like he had. All of this could've been prevented. No kid should have to endure what Kade had endured, especially not his brother.

Blane pressed the heels of his hands hard into his eyes, wiping away the wetness there.

He would just have to make it up to Kade. No matter what it took or how long.

A noise made Blane lift his head. Mona and Gerard had left for their home hours ago. He heard it again.

Kade.

Blane jumped to his feet, taking the stairs two at a time. He was in front of Kade's door less than ten seconds later, twisting the knob.

But the door wouldn't open.

"Kade!" Blane pushed against the door, but it scarcely budged. He pounded the wood with the flat of his hand. "Kade!"

Panic was starting to hit. Blane braced his shoulder against the door just as he heard Kade.

"Chill. I'm coming."

Blane heard the scrape of wood, then the door opened.

Relief flooded him at seeing Kade, who appeared unhurt. He blinked up at Blane as though he thought he was insane.

"What?" he asked when Blane said nothing.

Blane scrambled to make sense of it, realizing he must have heard Kade having a nightmare. No way was Kade going to admit to that. He'd only known Kade for twelve hours, but Blane knew that much.

"Why couldn't I get in the door?" Blane asked instead, trying to calm the rapid beat of his pulse.

Kade's eyes narrowed. "I don't like visitors in the middle of the night."

Blane looked behind Kade, realizing that he'd pushed the desk chair under the knob, which had quite effectively barred him from entry. And he could see it in the dark because Kade had turned on the closet light. Of course he probably needed a night light or something. Why hadn't Blane thought of that?

"Sorry, man," Blane said. "I, uh, just wanted to check on you."

Kade just looked silently at him, his eyes sleepy but still suspicious.

"Do you need anything?" Blane asked, wanting to offer some kind of comfort but at a loss as to how or what.

"What, like warm milk or some shit like that?" Kade retorted.

"Well . . . yeah. I always thought warm milk tastes like shit," Blane said bluntly, "but if you want some, I can get it for you."

The tiniest hint of a grin twitched at Kade's lips.

"No, thanks," Kade said. "Just stop banging on the door would be good."

"Right."

Blane stood there awkwardly for a moment until Kade cocked an eyebrow at him, then said, "Well, good night then."

Kade didn't reply, just shut the door. As Blane turned away, he heard the scrape of the chair being placed under the knob again.

CHAPTER THREE

It was a matter of minutes before Blane was pulling into Kathleen's parking lot. He'd used the Jag's speed to his advantage, the streets deserted at this time of night. He grabbed his gun from the glove box, checked the clip to make sure it was loaded, then shoved it in the back of his pants. Its comforting weight against the small of his back eased Blane's peace of mind. He hated having to go unarmed.

He knocked on Kathleen's door, waiting impatiently for her to answer. His skin was practically twitching at the idea that she wasn't safe. It was with relief that he saw the door open and she stood there, unhurt.

Kathleen didn't say anything, just stepped back so Blane could enter. He could tell at once she was in shock. Her face was stark white, her eyes barely seeming to focus on anything.

Blane took her arm and led her to the battered couch, sitting next to her and taking her hands in his. They were freezing, and fine tremors shook her, though she seemed wholly unaware of it.

"Your hands are like ice, Kathleen," Blane said. "Tell me what happened." He gently rubbed her hands, trying to ground her before she recounted her tale. Blane had lost count of the times he'd done this with family members and friends of victims of a violent crime. Their reactions were almost always the same. Shock, horror, fear, grief.

She looked up, her eyes wide. Haltingly, she spoke.

"I was asleep. Something woke me. I heard arguing. I thought it was Sheila and her boyfriend, Mark. Then it stopped.

"I couldn't go back to sleep. I was worried about her. So I got up and went over to her place."

Tears started slipping down her cheeks, tracks that spilled from eyes made even more brilliant blue from the saline. She wasn't sobbing or making any noise at all as she told him what happened. She just cried. It was like a punch to Blane's gut, and he was forcefully reminded of the supposed power of a woman's tears over the opposite gender. He'd always thought himself immune.

Guess not.

"The door was open, so I went in," she said. "And she was in her bed. And blood was everywhere—" She couldn't continue. It felt like the most natural thing in the world to take her in his arms while she cried on his shoulder, her small form shaking with the force of her grief.

Blane held her closer than appropriate, but couldn't seem to help himself, running his hands up and down her back and cursing himself six ways from Sunday for enjoying holding her a little too much in a situation such as this. He justified it by reminding himself that she was alone. She needed him.

He liked that. A lot.

When her sobs had died down, he asked, "You went into the apartment by yourself?"

She nodded, her body still clinging to his.

"Did you see anyone?"

"No."

Blane's eyes slipped shut in dismay and the next question was said more curtly than he intended. "So the person who did this could have still been there when you walked in?"

Kathleen didn't answer, but a violent shiver ran through her and Blane instinctively tightened his hold.

Had this been some random thing? Was it a matter of luck, of the capricious whim of fate that the killer had chosen the door on his right rather than the one on his left? Had Blane nearly lost Kathleen tonight, before she'd ever been his to lose?

The thought had him pulling back. The need to make sure she was safe, that no one lurked nearby waiting to hurt her, was riding him hard.

"I'm going to go check things out," he said, unable to resist the compulsion to act.

"No," she said, grabbing a fistful of his jacket. "They might still be out there!" Her eyes were wide with panic.

Ouch. It might take a while for his ego to cope with that direct hit.

"It's all right," Blane said, removing his Glock. Her eyes widened at the sight of the weapon.

"Why do you have a gun?" she asked.

Her naiveté was kind of sweet, refreshing. Blane had seen too much of the world to have any illusions left as to the people he sometimes defended. "Have you met our clients? Don't worry. I know how to use it."

The obvious doubt on her face was another blow to his pride. What, did she think he was some pansy-ass that needed protecting rather than being the one who *provided* the protection? He was definitely losing his edge.

"But . . . how?" she asked.

He was starting to get seriously offended. "Military," he replied curtly. Enough of this conversation. They were wasting time. He stood. "Stay here," he ordered.

She didn't acknowledge his command, but neither did she make any moves to stop him.

The scene next door was one straight out of a horror flick. Blane's lips pressed into a thin line as he took in the woman's naked, battered body. Blood smeared the sheets, pooling now, and dripping onto the floor.

Violence like this left a residual impression. Fear and horror hung in the air like phantoms mourning the unwitting victim. Death always had a certain smell about it, and the tang of blood and other bodily fluids hit Blane's nostrils. If this was what Kathleen had seen of her friend, then she was going to have nightmares for weeks, that was for damn sure.

No one was in the apartment or anywhere in the vicinity. Uncomfortable leaving Kathleen alone for too long, Blane was back inside her apartment a few minutes later.

"No one's around," he said, tucking the Glock away. "They're probably long gone by now."

Sirens screamed in the distance. It was about time. Blane was slightly concerned that Kathleen might be too upset to talk with the police, but she proved more resilient than he'd thought, recounting to the uniformed cop what she'd told him in a calm, steady way. The only time she faltered was when she got to the part about finding Sheila's body.

Her voice cracked and she swayed a little on her feet. Blane quickly slid his arm around her waist. If she passed out, he'd be able to catch her before she hit the ground.

The cop kept questioning her, Blane listening while he carefully watched Kathleen for any sign that she couldn't continue. Then something she said caught his attention.

"She worked as an escort," Kathleen told the cop, who glanced up from his notepad, his eyebrows lifting.

Shit. Of all the fucking coincidences.

"Did she say who she worked for?" he asked.

"No, she never said."

Thank God.

"Did she tell you anything else about this escort service?"

Blane tightened his grip on Kathleen's waist, hoping she was clever enough to pick up on his signal. If this friend of hers worked for whom he thought, then no one needed to know how much or how little Kathleen knew, not even the cops.

Kathleen hesitated before answering and Blane held his breath. "No. That's all I know."

Blane relaxed his hold on her. Smart girl.

The questioning was interrupted by the removal of the woman's body and Blane felt Kathleen stiffen. She didn't need to see this.

He turned her into him, pressing lightly on the back of her head, and she obediently rested against his chest. Tears soaked through his shirt as Blane held her. She was such a little thing, curled into him as though he could protect her from anything. And, Blane thought as the crimson-stained figure was loaded into the waiting ambulance, perhaps he could.

A few minutes later, Kathleen seemed to pull herself together and moved to step away. Blane reluctantly released her. Her eye caught something.

"Tigger!" she cried, rushing forward and picking up an orange cat. One who could use a diet, judging by its rather plump proportions. Kathleen cuddled the overgrown feline to her chest and headed back to her apartment. Blane didn't hesitate before following.

"Why did you want me to stop talking?" she asked him once they were again behind closed doors. She sat on her couch, the cat resting contentedly in her lap while she stroked his fur.

Blane eyed the cat with something akin to jealousy. "You didn't tell me she was a prostitute," he said instead of answering. This case had just taken a very different turn. The last thing he needed, or wanted, was Kathleen asking questions.

"Why should it matter?" Kathleen shot back, her tone one of pique, and misunderstanding Blane's irritation entirely. "She was my friend and someone killed her. It doesn't make her death any more acceptable because of what she did for a living."

The headache was back, though it hadn't really left, the pain like a knife in his skull. "No, but it does make things more dangerous," Blane replied bluntly, sinking down next to her on the couch. God, he was tired. He idly wondered if he shoved the cat to the floor and laid his head in her lap, would she pet him instead?

"What do you mean?" she asked, her tone less combative.

Blane decided to tell her a little, just enough to scare her. "There's only one escort service in Indy, and if that's who she worked for, the last thing they're going to want is for that fact to get out. Or any information on who her johns were." Now for the warning. "I want you to keep quiet about what you know, or else you could become a target."

She seemed to take this to heart, Blane was glad to see, mulling it over while she petted the cat. Blane's eyes narrowed as he watched the animal purr under her touch. Probably would get to sleep in her bed, too. Lucky bastard.

"I don't know if I can do that," Kathleen said.

"What do you mean?" Blane asked, taken aback.

"I can't just pretend I don't know anything," she said.

Oh yes, you can.

"Sheila told me she was seeing some guy that kept requesting her. She'd mentioned him several times. The police should know that information. It could have been him and not Mark that killed her."

Mark. "The computer guy," Blane had heard her tell the cops. Surely that couldn't be the same person—

"You don't know that," Blane said.

"No, but somehow I can't see Mark doing that to her either. He just . . . didn't seem the type."

As innocent and naive as Kathleen was, it was a wonder she hadn't already been taken for a ride by some piece-of-shit guy out for a quick lay and an easy out. She was an honest-to-God good person, kind and loyal.

She'd be fortunate indeed if that didn't get her badly hurt someday.

"Ted Bundy didn't look like a homicidal maniac either," Blane said, trying to reason with her. "If you think this man she talked about might have been involved, then I'll look into it."

"You will?" she asked, finally turning away from the cat to look up at Blane.

"Yes. Better me than you." *Promise her the fucking moon, anything, just put her off and keep her safe.* But apparently he'd said the wrong thing because her eyes narrowed and she sat up straighter, her little shoulders squaring like she was readying to do battle.

"Why is that?" she asked. "Because you're a man?" She said "*man*" like it was a bad thing.

The answer seemed obvious to Blane, whether she liked it or not. Facts were what they were and he was much better equipped to deal with killers than was Kathleen. "Yes," he said, then to placate her pride, "I also have more resources at my disposal than you." *Such as the Glock tucked into the small of his back.*

Kathleen's pale cheeks flushed rose. "Oh," she said. "Well, thank you."

Blane hid a smile at her tone, which was about a mile short of thankful. But considering what she'd gone through tonight and the fact that she'd let the line of questioning go, he could afford to be gracious.

"Are you going to be all right tonight?" he asked. She looked at him strangely. "By yourself. Is there someone I can call to come stay with you?" *Being alone after witnessing your friend's butchered body wasn't something Blane would wish on anyone.*

To his surprise, her cheeks grew even redder and she avoided his gaze. "I'll be fine," she replied with a shrug.

It occurred to Blane then that maybe she *didn't* have anyone to call. She'd been working at his firm for, what, three months? And she'd already told him she had no family and no boyfriend, though the lack of the latter still stunned him. Were men her age idiots as well as blind? He made a quick decision. *No way was he leaving her alone.*

"Look," he said, glancing at his watch, "it's really late. Why don't I just stay on the couch for a few hours? You can get some sleep and I'll leave in the morning." *Yes. Stay on the couch. Couch couch couch. Cat gets the bed, the shit.*

Her eyes filled with tears before she quickly looked away. She cleared her throat. "If you wouldn't mind," she said, her voice husky, "I would appreciate that." She paused, then said, "Um . . . unless you have someone . . . waiting for you?"

Kathleen's face was bright red now and she still avoided his gaze. It took Blane a moment to figure out what she was talking about that would have her so embarrassed.

The aesthetician from tonight. What was her name? Blane had already forgotten. Apparently, Kathleen figured she was waiting in his bed. Or he'd just left hers.

"No," he said. "Not tonight." Or any night, with that particular woman. Kathleen, on the other hand . . .

Blane shut that thought down right away, though his gaze lingered on the expanse of leg revealed by the little cotton shorts she wore.

"Can I get you anything?" she asked politely, standing and picking up the cat. At least the way she held the pet concealed her breasts that strained against the thin fabric of her T-shirt. She seemed unaware of her state of undress, which was hardly her fault, considering. Unfortunately, it hadn't escaped Blane's notice.

A cold shower, Blane thought. Good God, could he be any more inappropriate? He blamed it on his exhaustion and the ache pounding in his skull.

"I'm fine," he said, wanting her to go to bed before he did something colossally stupid. He pulled out his cell. "Just going to make some calls." Who the fuck would he be calling at this hour? But she seemed to buy it, giving him a tiny nod before disappearing into her bedroom.

Blane sighed, tossing his cell down on the battered coffee table along with his keys, wallet and gun. He stood, discarding his jacket and tie, idly folding back the cuffs of his shirt as he surveyed Kathleen's apartment.

Her furniture looked to be family hand-me-downs, which was expected, given her age and background. The couch had definitely seen better days, the fabric worn and the cushions flattened from years of use. An old patchwork quilt was folded neatly over the side. A ghastly orange recliner sat in the corner, the faded print screaming nineteen seventies.

After kicking off his shoes, Blane briefly considered turning on the television, but he didn't see a remote. Besides, his head was still killing him. He should've asked her if she had any medicine.

The sofa was too short for him to stretch out on, so Blane rested his head against the back and closed his eyes. He'd learned a long time ago to sleep wherever and whenever he could, despite the inconvenience or discomfort. It was a trick that served him well, and he was asleep within moments.

～

The sound of a scream woke him. Blane was instantly alert, on his feet with his gun in his hand before he'd even processed where the scream had come from.

Kathleen.

Blane glanced at the front door, but it was still firmly shut and bolted. No one had entered.

Of course. Nightmare.

Setting the gun back down, Blane hurried to Kathleen's bedroom, hesitating only briefly before opening the door.

A dim glow from the streetlight outside filtered in through the blinds on the windows, illuminating the figure on the bed. Kathleen thrashed, kicking the sheets and covers away, and the cat leaped to the floor. She screamed again, a sound that tore through Blane the way a baby's cry would affect its mother.

Grasping her shoulders, Blane tried to wake her.

"Kathleen!" he said, but the word didn't seem to penetrate. She began fighting him.

Blane sat on the bed and wrapped his arms around her, hauling her upward and imprisoning her against him. "Kathleen!" he tried again. "Wake up! You're okay. It was just a nightmare."

This time, she seemed to hear him. She stopped fighting, going abruptly still. Her chest heaved and she shook like a leaf.

Blane relaxed his grip as another hard tremor shook her. A pang of sympathy made him turn so he sat with his back to the wall, pulling Kathleen onto his lap. He remembered very well the first few times he'd seen what war could do to the human body, to his friends. Nightmares had been par for the course until, God forbid, a man grew accustomed to the horrors.

Kathleen didn't protest, just curled against him as though wishing she could crawl inside his skin. It felt good to be able to help her, bring her some kind of comfort. No one had needed him, at least not in that fashion, for a long time.

He needed to get her mind off it. Blane thought for a moment, remembering a particular story from when he had taken Kade diving. "My family used to vacation every summer at a lake in New Hampshire, Lake Winnipesaukee," he said. "We had a summer home there and every May I couldn't wait until school was out and we could go. The days were filled with things young boys love to do. Hiking through the woods, hunting, tracking bears."

Blane made it sound much more idyllic than it had been. He left out the part where his father had worked nonstop, completely ignoring Blane and his mother. But Blane had still loved the place, and had taken Kade there, hoping he'd love it, too.

"I still went after my father died, taking my brother with me. We used to take our boat out on the lake. We'd water-ski or dive. The water was always cold, but we didn't care. The trees were deep green, the sky a brilliant blue, and the water ice-cold." Kade had taken to diving as though he were part fish.

Half of Blane's attention was on talking, the other half on Kathleen.

She'd stopped shaking, his story effectively distracting her. He rubbed her back lightly, wishing it was her skin he touched rather than cotton.

"One time we were diving and I wasn't paying enough attention to my brother," he continued. "He wandered away. I was frantic, trying to find him in the dark water. Nearly exhausted my air supply." The little shit. It hadn't been the first time and wouldn't be the last that one of Kade's close calls would terrify Blane. And those were just the ones Blane knew about.

"What did you do?" Kathleen asked when he didn't continue.

Blane pulled himself out of his thoughts. "Found him, finally. He was only twelve, maybe thirteen, at the time and since I was older, I was responsible for him. We made it up with moments to spare and then I wanted to kill him for scaring me half to death, though really it was my own fault. I didn't lose track of him again after that." Not even when Kade wanted him to.

"Where is he now?" she asked.

Good question. "He lives here in Indy," Blane answered. Which was sort of true.

"It must be nice to have family close," Kathleen mused, reminding Blane of how very alone she was.

"It can be," he said.

She was quiet then and Blane fell silent, too. It was nice, nicer than he would have expected, to be with her. Kathleen wanted nothing from him except his presence, a novel experience. Blane tried very hard not to think about how little she was wearing. Even the tiny shorts she'd had on before had been discarded. The way she was situated on his lap, she'd know very quickly if his thoughts turned carnal.

"When were you in the military?" Kathleen asked.

Blane answered automatically, his concentration focused on keeping control. "Six years ago." Maybe if he resituated them . . .

He moved, which was a bad idea. His arm brushed her breast and she shivered. Kathleen's telltale response to the touch sent Blane's imagination careening off into a decidedly non-platonic direction. If an accidental brush had caused that reaction, how responsive would she be to a more purposeful seduction?

"Which branch?" she asked.

Blane tamped down his wayward thoughts. He was acting like a horny teenager with nothing but sex on the brain, though to be fair, he was in bed with a nearly naked woman sitting on his lap. "I was a Navy SEAL," he answered, though the past tense wasn't really correct. Once a SEAL, always a SEAL.

She was quiet at that and Blane thought he knew what she was thinking. "Surprised?" he asked.

"A little."

She really knew how to take his ego down a few notches. "And why is that?"

"It's just that not many men like you join the military."

Ouch. "And what are 'men like me'?" Blane was almost afraid of her answer, since she obviously thought so little of him, and perhaps his tone clued her in because she didn't answer. He sighed. "I guess I can't blame you for thinking that. My father was furious when I told him I was going to join the Navy. But he and I had come to a parting of the ways long before I decided to sign up." And he'd died before they'd ever reconciled, not that Blane knew if they ever would have.

Thinking about his father was an exercise in futility, and Blane leaned his head back against the wall with another tired sigh.

Kathleen moved to sit up and Blane tightened his arms around her, hoping she'd take the unspoken hint. He liked her on his lap and he wasn't keen to let go. She hesitated, then tentatively relaxed against him. Her body was warm and soft, the faint scent of her shampoo lingering in her hair.

Blane stayed awake for a short time, just to make sure her nightmare didn't resume where it had left off. But her breathing became deep and even, her limbs utterly relaxed. Carefully so as not to wake her, Blane shifted, turning so he could lay her down on the bed.

The thought crossed his mind that he should probably go back to the couch. Blane slowly slid his arm out from beneath her.

Kathleen immediately frowned in her sleep, murmuring something. She shifted restlessly and Blane curved his arm in the dip of her waist as he lay behind her. She became still, a soft sigh escaping her lips.

It looked like he was stuck. Blane's lips curved in a sardonic half smile. Oh, what a terrible thing—he had to cuddle a sexy, half-naked woman in her bed so she could sleep. Yes, he led a difficult life indeed.

Her shirt had twisted, exposing the warm planes of her stomach down to the tops of her little bikini panties. Blane's hand rested on her belly, his iron control all that kept him from exploring the possibilities, though his fingers did lightly brush her skin, smooth and soft to the touch.

His headache was gone now and he closed his eyes, realizing before he drifted off to sleep that this was the first time he'd ever slept with a woman and *not* had sex with her.

～

Blane didn't know what woke him, but he lifted his head off the pillow, listening for a noise.

Nothing.

Where the hell was he?

Oh, yeah. Kathleen.

Last night came back in a rush and he laid his head back down. He felt much better after a few hours of sleep and was glad he could function on less than the ideal eight.

Of course, the warm curves of Kathleen's body against his might also have something to do with his current good mood. That was until he abruptly realized that a) he had a raging hard-on pressed against her ass and b) his hand was under her shirt and cupping her breast. Her naked, gorgeous, mouthwatering, perfect breast that fit in his hand like it'd been made just for him.

Blane closed his eyes, sending up a quick prayer that maybe she was still asleep, that he could extricate himself from this fuckup without any damaging repercussions. God, all he needed was her accusing him of rape or sexual harassment or some other such shit. She didn't seem the type, but he hardly knew her and sometimes you just couldn't tell.

The nipple of her breast grew taut and Blane's cock twitched. He didn't move. Every instinct inside him wanted to take this to its natural conclusion, which would only be adding a huge mistake onto what was rapidly becoming a pile of mistakes where Kathleen was concerned.

His lips by her ear, Blane breathed in a nearly silent whisper. "Are you awake?"

She gave a tiny nod.

Fuck.

But this was also interesting. She was awake, but not moving. Neither encouraging nor discouraging him. If she was upset, she'd have started yelling by now, Blane was sure, slapped him or jumped up or *something*. But she hadn't. Of course, neither was she doing anything to signal she wanted him to continue.

Hmm.

Still, better to think with his head and not with his dick.

Regretfully, Blane removed his hand, but he couldn't resist the slow slide of his skin against hers from her breast, down her stomach to the tops of her panties, then up to the gentle curve of her hip. He stopped there, his thumb whispering across her skin as his fingers settled into the bend of where her thigh met her hip. He could hear her breathing, fast and shallow. Did she want this?

One last try. "I'd better go," he rasped. All Kathleen had to do was say one word, make just one hesitation, and Blane would do all he could to convince her that she wanted to wrap those legs around his waist and let him give her fabulous breasts the undivided attention they deserved.

To his disappointment, she nodded, still without moving any other part of her body or speaking.

It suddenly occurred to Blane that she might be afraid. Maybe her breathing and rapid pulse weren't from arousal, but from fear. He was just as much a stranger to her as she was to him, and here he was touching her without her permission. Yes, she'd been amenable to him entering her bed last night, but he had been comforting her. Maybe she was thinking he now believed she owed him this. And he was her boss. Did she think he'd fire her if she turned him down?

That certainly had a dousing effect on the heat in his blood, propelling Blane up and out of the bed. In the living room, he grabbed his jacket and tie, glad the sobering thought that he might have scared Kathleen had taken care of his hard-on. Nothing like the idea that a woman feared she was moments from being raped to take the wind out of those particular sails.

She'd followed him, he saw as he pocketed his wallet and cell. Thankfully, she'd put on a pair of shorts first. Or maybe that was a shame? Her arms were crossed protectively over her chest, which definitely was.

"Thanks for coming," she said as their eyes met.

Blane shoved his gun into the small of his back and picked up his keys.

"And for staying," she added. Her fair skin was flushed, turning even rosier as he looked at her. Her hair was tousled in a just-fucked way that most women could only achieve after an hour and an entire can of hair spray.

At least it didn't sound like she was going to sue him. "It wasn't a problem," Blane finally said. "I'm sorry about your friend. I'll let you know if I find out anything."

She nodded.

"If the police contact you, call me," he continued. "Don't talk to them without me there."

"Okay."

Blane hesitated. Should he say something? Apologize? Or just pretend it hadn't happened?

He went with the latter, heading out the door and down to his car. She was still outside, watching him leave, when he pulled out of the lot.

~

Kade was waiting for him when he got home.

"Decided not to stay for breakfast?" he asked with a smirk and a cocked eyebrow when Blane walked into the den.

"Says the man who never bothers to learn their names," Blane retorted, tossing his jacket and tie onto a nearby chair and heading for the sideboard. Was it too early for a drink? Without a doubt. But he wanted to burn away the feel of Kathleen's body pressed against his, the weight of her breast in his palm, the trust in her clear blue eyes.

Kade was sprawled on the leather sofa, his long legs stretched out in front of him, ankles crossed. He wore his usual black boots, jeans and black shirt, and had tossed his leather jacket over the back of the couch.

"Did she try to sink her claws in?" Kade joked, eyeing Blane's drink. "Or was it so bad you're trying to forget?"

Blane shook his head, taking another swallow. He didn't want to talk about Kathleen. Best to just forget about last night, or this morning, really. "It's five o'clock somewhere, right?"

Kade just snorted.

"There was a murder last night," Blane said. "I think the victim might have been someone related to Mark."

"The snitch?"

"Yeah."

"Is he still alive?"

"No clue. I'll try to get a hold of him," Blane said. "In the meantime, can you see what you can find on James Gage's possible involvement?"

"I'll have to break into his office."

"Fine. Just don't get caught."

"Please," Kade scoffed. "You forget who you're talking to."

Blane half smiled. Kade was good, he had to give him that.

"So what are you doing here anyway?" Blane asked. "We have to keep me and you on the down low, especially if I'm being watched."

"No one saw me come and I promise, no one will see me go," Kade said, rolling his eyes. "Mona texted me, said she was making waffles." He grinned. "So I came."

Blane huffed a laugh. "She always could bribe you with food."

"Damn straight."

～

Monday was cloudy and cold, not that Blane noticed. He buried himself in work and tried not to think of Kathleen. That hadn't worked out so well yesterday, when he could still smell her on his clothes.

He wasn't about to hunt her down. He'd already made too many mistakes with her. Staying away was the absolute best decision.

And then he turned the corner and saw her sitting in a chair, talking with Clarice.

His memory hadn't done justice to how pretty she was. He was abruptly reminded of her body pressed into his.

Then he heard what she was saying.

" . . . James asked me out."

"James?" Clarice asked. "James Gage?"

"The very one," Kathleen answered. "We're going out to dinner tomorrow night."

Blane stepped into view. Both women glanced up at him in surprise.

James Gage was bad news. Blane knew it, even if Kade had yet to find the evidence. And now Kathleen was going on a date with James? No way in hell.

Whatever the look on his face was, it must not have been very friendly because Kathleen immediately jumped to her feet.

"Did you have any deliveries for me?" she asked Clarice, her tone switching from friendly to no-nonsense.

"No, not today, thank you," Clarice answered, turning back to her computer.

Kathleen made to pass him by, but Blane reached out to grasp her arm. "Can I see you for a moment, Kathleen." It wasn't really a question.

"Um . . . sure," she said.

She followed Blane into his office where he closed the door behind her. Even as he tossed the files he was carrying onto his desk, Blane wondered what the hell he was doing. Hadn't he been berating himself all day for getting involved with her? He had to stay away, and instead, here he was ordering her into his office.

Leaning against his desk, Blane crossed his arms over his chest and surveyed her. She wore a bluish sweater today that made her eyes seem two shades darker. The soft fabric clung to her curves, the demure turtleneck only serving to make her innocence more tempting. A headband pulled back the long strands of strawberry waves that brushed past her shoulders, accentuating her youth. Blane wondered how she'd gone this long without attracting James's attention.

"How are you doing?" Blane asked, hoping she hadn't had more nightmares last night.

"I'm fine." Her stoic reply belied the sudden brightness in her eyes, but her gaze didn't waver from his. "I was wondering if you'd been able to track down anything on the person Sheila had been seeing."

As if he was going to tell her. "No, I'm afraid not," Blane replied with a shake of his head.

Kathleen's face fell, her disappointment obvious, as if she'd thought it would only take him a day to solve her friend's murder. Her faith in him was astounding, and an aphrodisiac.

Blane couldn't resist coming closer, her soft scent drifting to his nostrils as her head tipped back to look him in the eye. Her pupils dilated and the pulse underneath her jaw jumped.

"I'll keep trying," he said. Reaching out, he snagged a long, wavy lock of her hair, the silky strands sliding through his fingers. Her throat moved as she swallowed.

"I managed to get Sheila's cell phone," she said. "I was wondering if maybe the person who killed her might have called her. Or, at least, there should be a call on there from the person she worked for. Maybe I could get in touch with her. Or him."

Shit. It was just Blane's luck that she'd have a brain. It'd been so long since he'd bothered with caring what a woman had between her ears, he'd nearly forgotten what it was like to be with someone who didn't just do as he told her. This one wouldn't. He was sure of it.

"Why don't you bring it to me?" he suggested, careful to phrase it as a question. "I can get the numbers run to see who they are." Logic should work. Kathleen wasn't stupid.

She hesitated, seeming to consider his offer before replying. "I'd better put the phone back," she said, "but I'll write down the numbers first and bring them in."

She was lying. Blane could tell. But he didn't call her on it. He was much more interested in *why* she was lying to him.

"Okay. Good idea. Bring them to me tomorrow."

Blane stepped a bit closer, wanting to test a theory. Judging by how she was looking at him and how shallow her breathing had become, his nearness was having an effect on her. The same effect he'd had on many, many other women. Kathleen was attracted to him, which meant she might be amenable to breaking her date with James.

"What's tomorrow night?" Blane asked, his tone more seductive than curious.

She looked completely befuddled. "Um . . . Tuesday?"

Obviously she was so looking forward to her date with James that she couldn't even remember having made it. Blane couldn't help the smug twist of his lips. "Yes, Tuesday," he said. "I meant, what were you telling Clarice about tomorrow night?"

Her eyes dropped as though she were embarrassed. "James asked me on a date."

Blane waited until his silence forced her to look up. "I don't think that's a good idea," he said, hoping his influence and opinion would persuade her to ditch James. *In favor of me,* he thought. But her response wasn't anything he would have guessed.

"I'm not good enough for him, right?" she retorted, stepping away from him.

Okay. Hadn't seen that one coming. "I didn't say that—"

"You didn't have to. You think I don't know that you see me as some hick that's far beneath the notice of someone like him?" Her blue eyes flashed with anger and hurt.

Blane bit back the words he wanted to say, that James wasn't good enough to lick her shoes, because if he said that, she'd know. She'd know she'd gotten under his skin, that this was personal. That he wanted her.

"James at least respects me enough to ask me out on a date! You just groped me in my bed and left!"

Sometimes Blane hated being right. He'd known that would come back to bite him in the ass. He should've apologized . . . or had sex with her. Though it didn't look like either of those was really an option right now.

Turning on her heel, she was through the door and out of his office before he could even think of what to say, how to rectify the situation.

"Kathleen, wait!" he called, but she was already at the stairwell door and didn't look back. It clanged shut behind her.

Well, fuck.

Blane's gaze fell on Clarice, who was staring at him with her mouth hanging open in shock. He gave her a "Don't ask" look, then went back into his office, slamming the door shut behind him.

Seventeen Years Ago

The place wasn't bad, Kade had to give him that. He'd never been in a house like this. The guy had so much shit, no way he'd miss a little of it.

Kade inspected his haul so far, pulling the items out of his backpack, munching on the apple he'd smuggled at lunch. A heavy, silver paperweight, a gold-plated letter opener, a men's watch he'd seen on the kitchen counter and pocketed when no one was looking. All of it would be easy to sell.

He didn't entertain the thought even for a second that they'd let him stay here for long. The novelty of "saving" the long-lost little brother would wear off soon and the guy would want to get back to his picture-fucking-perfect life. It was a good idea to be prepared for when it did, because no way was Kade going back to that orphanage. He'd decided that the moment he'd left to come here. He'd rather live on the streets than go back.

You knew what you were getting on the street. Kade had managed to disappear for a while when he'd run away before. It was everyone for himself and no one made any bones about it. Not like at the orphanage where childless couples came to scrutinize him, warily eyeing his worn clothes, too-long hair, and unsmiling face before deciding that maybe they weren't cut out to adopt an older child after all. As much as he fought it with everything he had, each time a tiny spark of hope would light in his mind, only to be extinguished again and again.

No one wanted him? That was fine with Kade. They could all go fuck themselves. He'd take care of himself.

The last item Kade pulled from his bag was the switchblade. He'd seen the guy empty it out of his pockets along with his keys and wallet, dumping everything on a desk. That knife would come in handy, that's for sure. Too bad he hadn't had it at the last foster home he'd been in. He'd have cut that fucker's dick off for what he did to Branna—

His memories of the little girl with the jet-black hair and sad, sea-green eyes made Kade go still. She hadn't been there long, just a temporary thing, but the mom had gone out of town to visit family, leaving Kade and Branna with her husband, Joe.

Kade had seen the way Joe eyed Branna, had seen that look before in the gazes of men who looked at little girls when they thought no one was watching. Had seen that look aimed at him, and knew what followed. Kade had watched him all week and so far he hadn't done anything. The wife was coming back the next day, thank God.

Branna had been oblivious, even that night as she sat eating her bowl of macaroni and cheese in front of the television. She'd only been there two weeks and Kade didn't think she'd said more than ten words the entire time.

Kade hovered that night, sitting on the couch while Joe drank too many beers and yelled at the game on TV. Branna eventually got up, taking the worn doll that never left her side and disappearing upstairs into the bedroom set aside for her and Kade.

"Make yourself useful, kid," Joe slurred to Kade. "Get me another beer."

Kade did as he was told, hoping he'd get drunk enough to just pass out. He'd never called Kade by his name, he was just "kid." When Kade came back from the kitchen, he looked Joe in the eye as he handed him the beer.

"Leave the girl alone," Kade said.

Surprise flitted across the guy's face, followed quickly by shame, then anger. "What the fuck are you talking about, you little shit?" he snarled, giving Kade a hard shove. "You're lucky I even let you live here, you creepy-ass kid."

He backhanded Kade, who'd expected just such a reaction and braced himself. It still knocked him to the floor. It took a moment for the room to stop spinning, then Kade got to his feet. Joe was ignoring him, drinking the beer while he watched television.

Kade resumed his seat on the couch, pulling his skinny knees to his chest. He wished with a longing born of desperation that he was bigger, stronger. His head throbbed and his cheek ached, but he said nothing, did nothing. So long as he sat here, maybe Joe wouldn't do anything to Branna.

Eventually, Joe fell asleep, his snores vying with the television for dominance. Kade's head drooped, but he kept jerking awake. He had to stay awake, had to keep watch. But finally, the hour proved too late and exhaustion overtook him.

A sound made Kade's eyes pop open and he realized with a start that he'd fallen asleep. In the next instant, he realized Joe was no longer passed out in the chair.

Kade heard the sound again, faint but unmistakable. Branna.

He launched himself off the couch and ran upstairs, his heart in his throat. The door to the bedroom where Branna lay was half open and Kade pushed inside, then nearly threw up.

Joe was lying half on, half off Branna's bed, his pants down around his ankles, the light from the hallway falling onto his bare ass. Kade couldn't see Branna, but he could hear her muffled whimpers.

Kade flew at the man in a blinding rage, hitting him as hard as he could and yelling. Joe threw him off, but Kade just came back. His fists were too small to do any real damage, so Kade picked up the lamp off the bedside table and slammed it against the guy's head. That got his attention and he finally released Branna. Kade saw her crawl to the far corner where the bed met the wall and huddle there.

"You fucking piece of shit," Kade snarled. "What's the wife gonna say?"

As he'd hoped, that got Joe's attention and he jerked his pants up before turning the full extent of his fury on Kade. Kade had endured beatings before and he focused on surviving the next few minutes. The important thing was to draw the guy away from Branna.

A blow to the side of his head sent Kade careening into the wall. Tears stung his eyes, but he bit his lip until he tasted blood. He would not cry. He never, ever cried.

"You tell my wife anything, it'll be the last thing you ever do," Joe threatened.

Kade turned to see Joe was holding a baseball bat. He swung and Kade narrowly dodged, the bat hitting the wall and knocking a hole in the sheetrock. Backing out of the room, Kade watched with bitter satisfaction as Joe followed. He leaped for Kade and this time Kade wasn't fast enough, the guy's fist colliding with his face and pain exploded in Kade's eye.

He couldn't see the next blow as the bat landed in his ribs and this time Kade couldn't help crying out. His knees gave out and he collapsed to the floor. Joe advanced on him and it took everything Kade had not to crawl away. He wouldn't show fear, even though he was terrified.

The man towered over him, his eyes bloodshot, his pants buttoned but unzipped. "That real clear, you little punk?" Joe stepped forward, placing his foot in the middle of Kade's forearm as he lay on the floor. "Just so you don't forget." He put all his weight on Kade's arm and the bone cracked. Kade screamed this time, the pain too much to take, and he lost control of his bladder.

"You're a loser and a pussy, kid," Joe scoffed. "You peed yourself like a little girl."

Kade barely heard him, shame engulfing him along with the pain as tears he couldn't stop poured down his cheeks.

Joe shoved Kade out of the way with his foot and stepped over him. As he started down the stairs, Kade used his good arm to pull himself forward. With the last of his strength and his impotent rage, he kicked out, his foot connecting with the back of the guy's knee.

Joe cried out in surprise as his leg collapsed underneath him. His arms flailed and he seemed suspended for a moment. Kade watched in satisfaction as he fell, his body toppling down the wooden stairs. The noise was horrendous, and then it was over. Joe lay at the bottom, his neck at an odd angle, and didn't move.

Kade lay there, fighting the pain, and tried to breathe. His chest hurt where the bat had hit, every breath a stabbing pain. Worry for

Branna drove Kade to his feet. He stripped his soiled jeans off in the bathroom, digging in the dirty laundry for his other pair and painstakingly pulling them on.

Branna wasn't in the bed any longer, making Kade's worry ratchet even higher. He finally found her hiding in the closet.

"It's me," he said, once he realized she was in there. "Don't worry. He won't be back."

Kade could barely see her, huddled in the far reaches of the closet, but it didn't look like she'd be coming out anytime soon. Crouching painfully down, Kade crawled inside the closet.

He couldn't see out of one eye and it still hurt to breathe, but the pain in his arm seemed detached somehow, and he wondered if he was in shock or something. Being careful not to jostle the arm, he settled inside the closet, leaning back against the wall with a sigh. He closed his eyes.

"You okay?"

The words were faint, barely discernible, and Kade opened his eyes. "Yeah," he replied to Branna. She'd inched closer and now watched him with fearful concern. "You?"

She shrugged. Kade knew the feeling. "Okay" covered a lot of shit. They were breathing, that was the important part. He wondered if this had been the first time something like that had happened to her. Or maybe, like him, the hell that they endured was the tenor of their lives, the difference being only in the gradation from day to day.

Branna moved to sit next to him on his uninjured side. Tentatively, she leaned into him. It took effort, but Kade put his arm around her. The doll was clutched tightly to her chest and her thumb was in her mouth. Eventually, she fell asleep, sinking down until her head lay on Kade's lap.

Kade stayed awake until the dawn sent streaks of light across the sky, then he, too, couldn't resist the need for his exhausted and abused body to rest.

A cop found Kade and Branna hiding in the closet the next day, when the wife had come home to find her husband dead at the foot of the stairs. The look on the cop's face when he saw Kade was one of horror that dissolved into pity. They'd taken him to the hospital, and he hadn't ever seen the girl again. An autopsy showed the husband had been at three times the legal limit for intoxication, so no one questioned the conclusion that he'd fallen down the stairs to his death.

Now, as he turned the switchblade over and over in his hands, Kade knew that if he'd had a knife like this against Joe, the sonofabitch wouldn't have had the opportunity to break his arm. A gun would be better, but it looked like they were all kept inside a safe here, so the knife would have to do.

Now he just had to figure out when to leave.

CHAPTER FOUR

After Blane had calmed down, he decided to use what resources he had to find out all he could about Kathleen. She was lying to him about the phone, didn't seem at all inclined to let the murder of her friend go, and had a date with a man Blane knew was rotten. There were plenty of excuses to rationalize digging into her life, and none of them were personal.

Right.

"Clarice," he said, standing by her desk. She looked up from what she'd been working on. "You're friends with Kathleen, correct?"

"Yes," she said, somewhat hesitantly. Blane ignored the question in her eyes.

"For how long?"

Clarice shrugged. "Since she started, I guess. A few months ago."

"What do you know about her?"

"Um, well, just the usual stuff. She's twenty-four, just moved here from Rushville. Single, no kids or anything. I think she's real sweet, seems to be a hard worker."

"Did she go to college?"

"I think she went for a while, then her mom got sick and she had to quit."

Yes, Blane knew about the deceased parents, thanks to the disastrous car ride with her last Friday.

"Is she seeing anyone?"

"Well, she told me she has a date with James tomorrow night," Clarice said, then added in a conspiratorial whisper, "I don't like him."

"Neither do I," Blane said. "Has she been out with him before?"

"I don't think so."

"Has she dated anyone else at the firm?"

"Not that I know of."

Blane stared off in the distance, thinking.

"So, what's this about?" Clarice asked, drawing Blane's attention back to her. "These don't seem like the type of questions that have anything to do with the murder next door." The knowing grin on Clarice's face had Blane schooling his own expression into one of indifference.

"Just looking out for one of my employees," he said.

"Uh-huh. She's so pretty, don't you think?" Clarice asked, all innocence.

"I hadn't noticed." Blane's dry reply only made her chuckle. He turned away to head back into his office.

"I think she'd go out with you, if you asked," Clarice called after him. "I've seen the way she looks at you."

Blane paused. He shouldn't, but couldn't seem to resist asking, "What way does she look at me?"

Clarice's eyes twinkled as she said, "Like she thinks you're dreamy," she teased in an exaggerated sigh.

Blane rolled his eyes, though he was secretly pleased, and disappeared back inside his office.

He had tried multiple times yesterday and today to reach the snitch he'd mentioned to Kade. His name was Mark and Blane had a suspicion that it was the same "computer guy" that Kathleen had said was dating her neighbor. Blane had been trying to get him to come forward and testify. Mark had tentatively agreed, but then had gotten spooked and had refused to return any of Blane's calls. Blane left another message for him, not holding out much hope that he'd hear from him.

Blane didn't see any reason why Mark would have killed his girlfriend. It was much more likely that whoever showed up at Sheila's place had taken him and killed her, or just killed her to send a warning. *Keep your mouth shut.* Which also meant they had no reason to go after Kathleen.

Unless she kept poking her nose in and drew their attention.

He'd have to talk to her again and *make* her listen. She couldn't get dragged into this. The bastards wouldn't hesitate to kill her if she got in the way or found out too much, just as they had Sheila.

And Blane wasn't about to let that happen.

~

Blane let himself into Kathleen's apartment with the key he had copied. If she wouldn't bring Sheila's phone to him, he would get it from her. The less she had to go on, the more quickly she'd give up. He hoped.

The cat, Tigger, purred and wound its way around Blane's legs as he glanced around the apartment. There. A cell phone sat on the kitchen counter. He pocketed it and turned to go, but paused.

A neat stack of envelopes sat on the kitchen table. Blane hesitated. He shouldn't look, that would be invading her privacy.

But then again, he was standing in the middle of her apartment, without her knowledge, in possession of a key she hadn't given him. The "invading her privacy" ship had sailed.

Thumbing through the opened envelopes, Blane saw they were all bills. Several were from medical places such as a hospital and a cancer treatment center. Those were in the thousands and were past due. From the history, it seemed Kathleen sent in sporadic payments of varying amounts, he guessed whatever she could afford when she could afford it.

A couple of utility bills were there, too, their amounts piddling and yet they were close to being overdue.

The phone rang in her apartment and Blane automatically glanced toward it. She had a machine. He replaced Kathleen's bills, careful to arrange the stack just as he'd found it, when he heard someone start speaking at the beep.

"Ms. Turner, this is Alfred Lloyd and I'm with the credit collection department for Mission Cancer Treatment Center. We need to speak, please return my call at—"

"Hello," Blane said, picking up the phone.

"Oh, hello," Alfred said, sounding surprised. "I'm looking for a Ms. Kathleen Turner. Is she available?"

"Not at this time," Blane said. "I'm her attorney, Blane Kirk. How may I help you?" He'd be damned if some creditor was going to start harassing Kathleen, the vultures.

Alfred seemed taken aback. "I see. Her attorney?"

"Correct."

"Well, Ms. Turner has been woefully neglectful of the amount she owes this facility," Alfred said. "I was calling to speak to her before we begin action to place a garnishment on her wages."

That wasn't going to happen.

A few minutes later, Alfred had been informed as to exactly what would happen if they tried to do that to Kathleen. When Blane hung up, he was relatively certain they wouldn't be contacting her in that fashion again. Reaching over, he erased the message on her answering machine.

Okay, that privacy thing was a distant point in the rearview mirror now. Blane locked up behind him as he left.

It was at the end of the day when he saw Kathleen's car back in the firm's parking lot. He knew she stayed late most nights, so he didn't rush outside. The sun had nearly set by the time Blane dropped his things off at his car and crossed the lot to Kathleen's.

As he'd predicted, her car was unlocked. She came from a small town, but her dad had been a cop. She should know better. Anyone could just get inside and lie in wait for her.

Including him.

Blane didn't have to wait long. About twenty minutes later, the shadows had deepened and he saw Kathleen walking toward the car. Her shoulders drooped and her steps were slow, her body language saying she'd had a long day. She didn't look around at the lot, completely oblivious if someone had been following her, and didn't even check the backseat before opening the unlocked door and sliding behind the wheel.

It took a split second for her to see him, then she jumped about a foot, biting off a scream. She recovered quickly, though, and Blane was left staring at a highly pissed off female.

"What the hell are you doing?" she yelled. "You nearly scared me to death!"

"You should lock your doors," Blane said automatically, his eyes narrowing as he studied her. Her sweater was ripped. Correction. Not ripped. Cut. "What happened to you?"

"I had a run-in with your friend Jimmy," she snapped. "He had a message for me."

That fucking asshole. Blane kept a tight grip on his temper. If Jimmy had harmed a hair on her head—

"I'm supposed to keep quiet or else I'll get sliced to ribbons," she continued. "Any idea what he was talking about?"

The accusation in her eyes stung Blane, as if she thought he was behind Jimmy's threat. As if he would ever hurt her. "What are you implying?" he asked.

"I'm implying that you're the only one I've said anything to about who Sheila was seeing and who I think might've killed her and now, suddenly today, Jimmy's telling me to keep my mouth shut! Do you want me dead?"

Blane took the opportunity Kathleen had offered. If she wouldn't listen to him as a protector, maybe she'd listen if he was a threat.

In a flash, Blane had her by the throat. His hand easily held her neck in his grip, the delicate bones just under the skin reminding him of how terrifyingly fragile she was.

She choked on a gasp, her hands pulling at his arm, but he barely felt them. Seeming to realize the futility of struggling, she squeezed her eyes shut and went still.

Her pulse beat wildly as Blane leaned to place his lips by her ear. "If I wanted you dead," he whispered, "you'd be dead. And I wouldn't need Jimmy to do it for me."

A shudder wracked her body at his threat and Blane felt a wave of self-loathing. He'd never deliberately tried to scare a woman before, and it didn't sit well now, despite the fact that he was doing it for her own good.

His hold loosened and her eyes opened, their gazes colliding. But it wasn't fear he saw in the blue depths of her eyes. It was something else entirely, and it called out to him as though she'd spoken aloud.

Her lips were parted slightly, just enough for Blane to see a hint of gleaming pearl beyond. The rose-tinted skin was moist and begged to be tasted. Unable, or maybe unwilling, to resist, Blane lowered his head and brushed her mouth with his.

At first she didn't respond, out of stubbornness or fear, he didn't know. But her lips were pillowy soft and he teased them gently, brushing his tongue against the tender skin in a silent request. She made a noise at the touch, her mouth opening fully beneath his, and Blane couldn't stop a groan from escaping as his tongue surged inside to stroke hers.

Kissing Kathleen was like having his first kiss all over again. Her innocence was immediately apparent, her hesitation slowly evaporating as Blane kissed her. It was like she was giving him a gift, something precious and special, and not something bestowed just for a fleeting moment of carnal pleasure.

Blane's hand moved to cup the back of her neck, his fingers sliding through the silk of her hair. The tentative exploration of her hands as she touched his chest made Blane wish she was wearing a skirt, the need to touch her nearly a compulsion.

In another time and place, Blane knew he would've seduced Kathleen without a second thought. The chemistry between them could easily ignite into a raging inferno and it would be very, very good.

But the front seat of her car in the middle of his firm's parking lot wasn't the place. Reluctantly, Blane pulled back, the sweet taste of her still on his tongue. Her eyes were liquid pools of desire, her lips reddened and full.

God had to be keeping score because Blane deserved a damn gold star for not taking this further. His cock was hard as a rock, which was uncomfortable as hell. Blane consoled himself by knowing that at some point, he'd have her. Just not yet.

Kathleen shivered and Blane realized the confines of the car had gotten cold. The heat in his blood would serve to keep the chill away and he shrugged out of his suit jacket, wrapping it around her. As he lifted her hair from under the fabric, his fingers brushed her skin and she trembled again at his touch.

A blush bloomed in her fair cheeks, discernible even in this low light, and Blane was struck anew at the sight.

"You're blushing," he said, brushing the backs of his knuckles against the soft satin of her cheek. "So young and innocent." Which he would do well to remember, in spite of the heat between them. She wasn't a wham-bam-thank-you-ma'am. He'd need to go slow, be gentle. He ached just imagining it.

Kathleen wouldn't look at him so Blane forced her chin up until her gaze lifted to his. He wanted to make sure, despite the kiss, that she understood the danger.

"Be careful," he said. "Don't get involved any further in this." Blane brushed her lips once more in a fleeting kiss. Her eyes were still closed when he got out of the car and walked away.

Maybe she did think he was dreamy.

~

The burning impatience to see Kathleen didn't abate, his curiosity about her overwhelming, and Blane knew he had to see her again. Unfortunately, after their kiss last night, she seemed even more determined than usual to avoid him.

Blane found an excuse to loiter by Clarice's desk around the time Kathleen usually came by, but she never appeared. Frowning and avoiding Clarice's sideways glances, he went to get a cup of coffee. When he returned, she was on the phone. Blane took up his position loitering again, listening with half an ear.

"Um . . . yes, Mr. Galloway, we do have those files you requested," Clarice said.

Blane closed the file he'd been fake-reading. He knew for a fact that Galloway was in London this week, which put him at having dinner right about now. She had to be talking to Kathleen.

"Absolutely," Clarice continued. "You're correct about that, sir."

Blane held out his hand, giving Clarice a look that said he knew what she was up to. She sighed, realizing she'd been caught, and handed the phone over in time for Blane to hear Kathleen say, " . . . interference for me, Clarice. He's the last person I want to see right now."

"I assume you mean me and not the aforementioned Mr. Galloway," Blane said, careful to keep his voice flat, as if he was angry. "I'd like you in my office, Kathleen," and about a dozen other places just off the top of his head, but who was counting? "You have three minutes." He hung up the phone.

"Don't scare the poor girl," Clarice gently admonished.

"I'm not scaring her," Blane protested.

Clarice just looked at him until he sighed. "Fine. I'll be nice. I promise. Send her in when she gets up here."

Blane was too keyed up to sit, so he stood behind his desk, staring at some papers on his desk, but not seeing them. It was ridiculous how much he wanted to see Kathleen. He wasn't a high school teen with a crush. He should take a step back, regain his usual aloofness.

Which was all well and good until a light tap on the door made his pulse jump. He glanced up, as if he didn't already know who was there.

Kathleen.

She looked nervous, Blane noticed as he waved her into his office. "Close the door behind you," he said, and she obeyed.

Blane walked toward her, thinking. He had to have some excuse for making her come see him, right? And somehow he doubted "Because I can't get you off my mind" would go over real well.

Kathleen stopped when he got close, her eyes wide and unsure. Well, he had threatened her last night. Blane heaved an inward sigh.

"Did you bring that list for me?" he asked. He knew she hadn't. She couldn't. He'd taken the phone.

"No," she said.

He waited for an explanation.

"It was gone when I got home last night," she said.

Blane frowned, playing dumb. "What do you mean?"

"Just what I said. I left the phone on my kitchen counter yesterday and when I got home last night, it was gone." She looked at him strangely, and for a moment, Blane thought she suspected him.

"Was your apartment locked?"

"I always lock my apartment."

Just not your car, he thought but didn't say.

Kathleen cleared her throat. "Is that all?"

Blane wasn't ready for her to leave. "I don't like the idea of someone breaking into your apartment," he said. In his defense, he hadn't broken in. He'd had a key.

"Yeah, you and me both," she retorted.

She was so feisty. He liked that.

Moving into her personal space, he said, "You're so combative. Are you this way with everyone or just me?"

Kathleen looked like she didn't know what to say to that, stammering an "I . . . um" without saying anything more. Blane lifted a hand, eager to touch her again and see if the silk of her skin was as soft as he remembered from last night. His knuckles brushed her cheek and jaw.

"I like that color on you," he said softly. The deep crimson set off her eyes and the red tones of her hair and her lips. Desire flared. He wanted to kiss her again, see if she had the same effect on him today as she had last night, and he on her.

But she took a step back, blurting, "I have to go. I have a date tonight."

James. Jealousy spiked, the emotion unwelcome but perhaps not unexpected.

He stalked her, Kathleen retreating until she came up against the wall which was, coincidentally, right where he wanted her. Blane trapped her, bracing his hands on either side of her head as he leaned into her.

"So you said." His voice was low and quiet, forcing her to listen closely. "Though somehow I doubt James will be to your liking."

"What do you mean?" she asked, the breathlessness in her voice giving Blane a surge of satisfaction. "James is a nice man."

A pathetic defense, especially when said as she had, almost as an afterthought. Kathleen's eyes dropped to his mouth and Blane smiled. She was as ready to be kissed again as he was eager to kiss her.

"Maybe," Blane murmured, "but I don't think you like nice men."

"That's ridiculous," she sputtered. "Of course I do." Her gaze dropped even lower to his neck. She licked her lips and Blane nearly groaned. But he had to take it slow. Slow seduction would get Kathleen into his bed. He'd get under her skin until all she could think about was him, building a slow burn that would consume them both in the best possible way.

Blane placed his lips at her ear. "But I'm not a nice man," he whispered, "and I know you like me." His mouth grazed her neck in the lightest of touches.

A knock sounded at the door, shattering the spell he was weaving over her. Blane ignored it, capturing her jaw in his hand. His thumb caressed her lips, moist and trembling at his touch.

The knock came again and Blane wanted to shout at whoever it was to go away. But the damage was done. Kathleen ducked under his arm and hurried to the door, throwing it open to reveal Derrick Trent, another senior partner in the firm.

"I'm sorry, Blane," he said, glancing from Kathleen to Blane. "I didn't realize you were in a meeting?"

"I was just leaving," Kathleen said, hurrying away down the hall.

Where the fuck was Clarice and why hadn't she stopped Derrick? Blane shoved a hand through his hair and blew out a sigh.

"It's fine. Come on in," he said to Derrick.

Blane had been hoping to have a chance to persuade her not to go with James, but to spend the evening with him instead. Now all he could do was sit and stew, wondering how Kathleen's date was going to go.

Blane locked his car and pocketed the keys, checking to make sure his Glock was firmly wedged in the holster under his arm. It was fully dark now, the neighborhood where Mark lived was quiet and still. An occasional dog barked and lights were on inside houses, but the carpet had been rolled up for the evening.

Keeping to the shadows, Blane crossed the lawns from where he'd parked down to where Mark lived. A few other cars were parked on the street and he took a moment to watch until he was sure no one was inside them.

Blane's approach to Mark's house was silent, his training as a SEAL second nature. He melted into the shadows and crouched under the door in the back, listening.

A television was on inside and Blane heard a floorboard squeak. It was a matter of a moment to pick the lock on the door, then he was inside. Blane reached for his gun, its familiar weight reassuring in his hand.

He found Mark in the living room, and though the TV was on, Mark was staring off into space. Blane holstered his gun.

"You haven't returned my calls," he said.

Mark leaped to his feet, knocking over a glass that had been sitting on the coffee table.

"Blane, you scared me to death," he said, breathless. "What are you doing here?"

"Like I said, you haven't been returning my calls," Blane replied. "You told me you had evidence against TecSol. Proof that they're trying to rig the online election voting."

Mark was already shaking his head. "I'm sorry, man, but I don't have anything."

Blane took a few steps toward him. Mark was six inches shorter than him and about eighty pounds lighter. "You lied to me?"

"No, I just don't have it. I was wrong." He swallowed heavily as he eyed Blane.

"I think you're lying now," Blane said. "I think someone got to you, that you're scared, and now you're going to run out on me."

Mark looked terrified, his gaze darting to the windows. "I don't know what you're talking about," he said.

Blane tried his hunch. "Is this about Sheila? Are they sending you a message?"

"You've gotta go," Mark said. His face was sickly pale and shone with sweat. "If they see you—"

"Who is 'they'?" Blane asked. "Who threatened you? Who killed Sheila?"

"None of this would've happened if I hadn't come to you!" Mark burst out. "You told me no one would find out who I was, that you'd make sure of it!"

Blane flinched inwardly. All of that was true. He just hadn't expected there to be a mole in his own firm. "I can protect you," he said to Mark. "Just give me what you have—"

"Screw you! Why should I trust you? For all I know, you'll kill me as soon as I hand it over." Mark's eyes were crafty now, his cheeks becoming a mottled red.

"I promise you—"

Mark bolted for the door. Blane lunged, catching hold of his shirt, but it ripped. Mark grabbed something off a nearby shelf and flung it at Blane, who ducked. It shattered against the wall.

Mark headed for the kitchen, grabbing his backpack before flinging open the door and running outside. Blane was just steps behind. He had to stop that kid. Mark would get himself killed, or worse, and it would be for nothing.

But the kid was fast, staying out of Blane's reach and ducking into a neighbor's yard. It was a moonless night, pitch black except for the patches of light cast from the street lamps. Mark seemed to know the area a lot better than Blane did, and after chasing him through several backyards, Blane had lost enough ground that he could no longer tell which way Mark had gone.

Cursing under his breath, Blane stood still and closed his eyes to listen, but heard nothing. The kid was gone and Blane knew he wouldn't dare come back to his house again.

It was getting late when Blane pulled into his driveway. He headed to the den to pour himself a drink. He was mulling over possibilities of where Mark might have gone when Kade came in.

"Find out anything?" Blane asked as Kade went to the sideboard.

Unlike Blane, Kade preferred vodka to bourbon, a choice Blane never could understand. The stuff had no flavor.

"Junior's in it up to his eyeballs, if that's what you mean," Kade replied, taking a seat opposite Blane. "I was in his office, but then he showed up and I had to ditch."

Blane's brows rose. Guess the date hadn't gone very well with Kathleen if James had gone into work afterward.

"He had the case file on TecSol," Kade continued. "And he was talking to someone, but I couldn't tell who."

"What did they say?"

"Something about the timing being bad, but I didn't get much."

"He's not on the TecSol case. There's no reason he should have that file," Blane said.

"Is Mark's information in there?"

Blane nodded. "Yeah, but the files are locked and only the senior partners have access."

"Then it looks like one of your senior partners is working for the opposite side."

Yes, that's the same conclusion Blane had drawn. He heaved a sigh.

"Mark got away from me tonight," he said.

Kade frowned. "You mean the snitch?"

"That's the one. Found him at his house, but he grabbed his backpack and ran. Little shit lost me in the dark."

Kade laughed. "Losing your touch there, brother," he teased.

Blane just gave him a look which only served to broaden Kade's smirk.

"Can you put a trace on his phone, see if he calls anyone? His credit cards, too."

"Consider it done," Kade said. "I'm getting close to figuring out where TecSol gets their money. It's buried, but I should be able to track it down."

"Okay. Just keep me posted. And here." Blane handed Kade Sheila's phone. "The dead girlfriend's phone. She worked as an escort. There may be something in there that can help us."

"Got it." Kade tossed back the rest of his drink and stood. "I'll be in touch."

Blane gave him a nod, watching as Kade disappeared from the room, but as hard as he listened, he couldn't hear when he left. A smile tinged with pride tugged at the corners of his mouth. His little brother was good. They made a damn fine team.

~

The first call Blane made while driving to work was to the florist he had on speed dial. When they had been seeing each other, Kandi had demanded flowers for every infraction, real or imagined. It had ceased being a pleasure to give them to her and had become a chore. This occasion had him feeling quite different and he was clear to the florist about his specifications.

There wasn't a woman Blane had met who didn't have a weakness for an elaborate floral display, the more expensive, the better. He wondered when the last time had been that Kathleen had received flowers. This should work to get her back into his office, and from there . . . well, Blane would just let things take their natural course.

By noon, however, he still hadn't heard from her. He called the florist, who confirmed delivery, leaving Blane wondering if Kathleen was stubborn enough to not even acknowledge the gift. Well, what had he expected? Her to come falling into his arms because he bought her some roses?

Well . . . yeah. Sort of.

"Shit," he muttered, grabbing his jacket and briefcase. He had to be in court this afternoon. It had been so long since Blane had needed to exert himself in pursuit of a woman, it seemed he was rusty. It was a bit demoralizing.

His cell rang as he was leaving the building.

"I found Mark," Kade said.

Blane slid behind the wheel of his Jag. "Good. Take him to my place."

"Can't. He gave me the slip."

"Are you serious?"

"Don't be judgy," Kade retorted. "It was either follow him or his backpack, I picked the backpack."

"So you have that?"

"Not yet—"

Blane interrupted him with a disgusted snort.

"—but I will."

"And what exactly am I paying you for?" Blane asked as he started the car's engine.

"You're not," was Kade's dry response before he ended the call.

Blane smiled. Kade hated looking incompetent. Come hell or high water, Blane was positive he'd have that backpack and its contents within the next forty-eight hours.

Court seemed to drag this afternoon and afterward Blane had dinner with a potential client. Wining and dining was his forte so William Gage often sent Blane to win new business.

While part of his mind was focused on the conversation, another part was solely occupied with wondering about Kathleen. Blane couldn't help the niggle of worry in the back of his mind. Yes, he'd taken away Sheila's phone and hopefully distracted Kathleen from thinking there was anything else she could do with this case, but from what he was quickly learning about her, she wasn't the type to be dissuaded easily.

His smile was automatic as he listened to the man sitting across from him, impatiently waiting for the dinner to be over. Finally, the tab came and Blane paid before walking the guy out to his waiting car. With a final handshake, he sealed the deal and sent him on his way.

Now to go check on Kathleen.

He was close to home so he stopped there to change into jeans, throwing on his leather jacket to conceal his gun. Ten minutes later, he was pulling up to her apartment.

The windows were dark and no one answered his knock. Blane stood there, wondering if she was on another date. He had no way of knowing, no way to track her down, and not enough of a relationship with her to be informed of what she was doing, and more importantly, whom she was doing it with.

Shoving a hand through his hair in frustration, he turned to go just as her new neighbor stepped outside. Her eyes widened slightly when she saw him.

Blane immediately smiled. People always responded more positively to a smile. "Hi," he said. "I'm looking for Kathleen. Do you know where she went?"

The girl was young with dyed black hair and black clothes. Her eyebrow was pierced and she had a lit cigar in one hand.

"What's it to you?" she asked.

"I'm her boyfriend," Blane lied. "Wanted to come by, surprise her." His smile turned slightly sheepish. "I thought she'd be home tonight."

The girl still looked suspicious, but said, "She left hours ago. I thought she was going to work or something, the way she was dressed."

Of course. Her bartending thing. "Thanks," he said before heading back down to his car.

Sure enough, her car was at The Drop. Blane checked his watch. On a weeknight, they'd be closing soon. He briefly considered going inside, but then decided against it.

At closing, a few of the workers left, but Kathleen wasn't among them. Blane waited a bit longer, then got out of the car, leaning against the side as he waited for her. If he knew her like he thought he did, he'd lay odds she'd been the one who'd offered to stay behind, clean, and lock up.

Blane's patience was rewarded when the door opened once again to reveal Kathleen. She didn't even see him, preoccupied as she was with holding onto a sack and her purse while trying to lock the door.

The sight of her, alive and unharmed, eased a tightness inside Blane's chest that he hadn't even been aware was there. That surprised him. Yes, he was attracted to her and yes, he wanted to seduce her. But he hadn't realized that keeping her safe had somehow become personal in the last forty-eight hours.

Distracted by these thoughts, Blane didn't immediately say anything to alert her to his presence. Something he regretted when she turned around and he saw a flash of fear in her eyes before she saw just who was standing in the shadows, watching her.

"If you could stop scaring me half to death when you show up, I'd appreciate it," she snapped at him.

Her obvious pique was adorable. "Did you get the flowers?" Blane asked.

Blane thought he saw guilt in her eyes as she said, "I did, thank you. They were beautiful."

Yeah, she sounded real thankful. She was as prickly as a kitty cat, pretending aloofness while taking in every move he made. Even now she took a small step away from him, which was like waving a red flag at a bull. Or perhaps more like a tiger, the way the instinct to pursue her grew within him.

Blane's lips twitched as he thought of what she'd say to that analogy. "Is it just killing you to thank me?" he teased, just to watch her get her back up, and he wasn't disappointed.

"Of course not," she denied in a huff. "I just don't know why you sent them, that's all."

She didn't know? Hadn't figured it out yet? Yes, he was indeed too rusty at this if his wanting her wasn't blatantly obvious by now.

Blane pushed away from the car and stalked her as he'd wanted to. She took another step back, coming up against the wall behind her. The predatory feelings inside Blane seemed directly linked to his arousal, which notched upward with each step he took. When he stopped, he was directly in front of her, their bodies nearly touching.

"How was your date?" Blane asked, reaching out to snag the long braid she wore. He had a burning desire to see her hair long and loose again and didn't think twice about slipping off the band holding the strands together.

Kathleen was breathing faster, he noticed, her eyes wide and her cheeks flushed. It took a moment before she responded. "Fine, it was fine," she said.

"Sounds thrilling," Blane replied, immediately dismissing James as a rival. Her hair was slowly unfurling under his hand. The light from the street lamp made the long tresses shine as they slid like silk between Blane's fingers. He imagined how that hair would look spread upon a pillow with him above her . . .

"Wh-what are you doing?" she stammered.

"Touching you," he said, pitching his voice even lower. If she only knew the thoughts going through his mind right now on exactly where he'd like to touch her, she would blush an even deeper rose.

"Stop," Kathleen said, but the tone of her voice said something else entirely.

"Do you want me to stop?" Blane asked. His fingers combed up from her neck to the base of her scalp before sliding again through her hair. Her eyes fluttered closed at the touch, as though his petting would make her purr. Blane's hand moved to her hip, its curve fitting perfectly in the palm of his hand.

The electricity between them had all of Blane's senses on high alert. He could smell the scent of her perfume, the fragrance of her hair as he combed through it. He heard the small sounds of her breath, quick little pants that went straight to his cock.

Her eyes opened and focused on his. "Did you find out anything with those numbers on Sheila's phone?"

Blane froze.

"I know you're the one who took it," she continued. "Which was really low of you, you know?"

Fuck. Well, it looked like he'd been right about her tenacity, damn it. "How do you know I took it?"

"I don't . . . I mean, you could've . . . but maybe not," she stammered. "I guess anyone could've broken in and taken it. Hey, what do I know?" Kathleen seemed to realize she was just babbling now so she stopped, her lips pressing tightly closed.

Blane thought fast. Should he tell her? He couldn't tell her all of it, that would only put her in danger. But she was clever, she'd figured out he took the phone. Usually, he'd just lie, but for some reason he was reluctant to do that to her.

"You're right," he admitted. "I did take the phone."

Blane assumed she'd be relieved to know a stranger hadn't been in her apartment, but his words seemed to have the opposite effect. She swallowed hard, her eyes glancing nervously past him to the empty street. When his fingers unconsciously combed through her hair again, she jerked back, a tremor running through her small form. Blane abruptly realized she was afraid.

Of him.

His hand cupped the base of her skull, forcing her to look at him. "I'm not going to hurt you," he said. "I took that phone because I'm trying to protect you." She still looked skeptical. "The people who killed your neighbor, they wouldn't think twice about doing the same thing to you." But first, they'd have to get through him.

"You know who killed Sheila?" she asked.

Of course she'd leap on the one thing he didn't want her to focus on.

"Stay out of it, Kathleen," Blane said firmly. "Or you'll end up the same way."

"Is that a threat?" she retorted, fire in her eyes.

Blane closed his hand, pulling her hair and forcing her head back. She made a little gasp that sent Blane's pulse into overdrive. Snagging her around the waist, he gave in to temptation and pulled her fully against him, lifting her feet off the ground. She dropped the bag she'd been carrying, her hands coming up to try and push him away, but it was a futile effort.

"You're like a cornered kitten, Kathleen," Blane said, his eyes intent on hers. "Still hissing and pretending you can fight your way out. I'm trying to protect you. Let me."

She stopped fighting, her brow knitting in confusion as she stared at him. The blue of her eyes was as deep as a midnight sky.

"But . . . why?"

Why indeed, Blane thought. How to explain that he couldn't stop thinking about her, couldn't stop fantasizing about her?

Her body felt right against his, the curve of her hips, dip of her waist, swell of her breasts, all of her so very feminine and fragile. Blane touched his lips to her jaw, gratified at the choked breath she took. He tugged her hair again, forcing her head farther back so he could trail his mouth down her throat, the scent of her more potent at her neck. Blane breathed it in like the aphrodisiac it was.

"I don't know," he murmured against her skin. She shivered in his arms and this time it wasn't from fear. "I can't seem to stay away."

The taste of her was like a fine wine, her skin satin against his tongue. Blane buried his head against her neck, licking and kissing the tender skin. She was making those panting noises again, causing his dick to go hard as a rock. Her body melted against his, her little arms sliding around his neck. Her nails scraped lightly against his scalp, a gentle pain that caused Blane to briefly wonder who was seducing whom. He fastened his mouth to her neck and sucked.

"Ma'am, are you all right?"

The voice made Blane react on pure instinct, releasing Kathleen and pulling her behind him, putting himself between her and the unknown threat.

But it was just a cop.

"Ma'am, do you need some help?" he asked again, giving Blane a jaundiced glare.

Kathleen stepped out from behind Blane. "I'm fine," she said to the officer. "Just heading home for the night."

She glanced at Blane, who was too busy trying to rein in the desire to tell the cop to fuck off so he could toss Kathleen in his car, drive her home and talk his way into her bed. From her responses to him so far, he didn't think it would take much talking.

"I'll see you later, Blane," she said before heading to her car. She gave him one last glance before driving away.

"Better luck next time, buddy," the cop chortled before turning away and ambling down the street.

Asshole.

Blane shoved a hand through his hair again, heaving a heavy sigh. He glanced down and something caught his eye.

The bag Kathleen had dropped. She'd forgotten it.

Frowning, Blane picked it up and peered inside. His lips twitched in amusement, his bad mood forgotten as he pulled out knee high socks, a tiny, black schoolgirl skirt, a white tank, and a white blouse. It took a moment before he realized it was a costume. Then there was another moment as he imagined Kathleen pulling off the naughty schoolgirl thing.

This should come in handy.

~

Seventeen Years Ago

It was four days after Kade arrived when Blane woke up to find Kade's bedroom empty. It wouldn't have been that big a deal if he hadn't also noticed his backpack gone. Kade never went anywhere without it.

Blane stood in the front entryway, keys in hand, as he tried not to panic. If he panicked, he couldn't think. Where would Kade have gone?

He should have listened to Mona. She'd told him last night that Kade was sneaking food again. Blane didn't think much about it, but it seemed Kade had been preparing. The question was, why? Why would he leave?

Blane ran to his car, wondering how long Kade had been gone. Had he left last night? Or early this morning? Blane had told him good night, seen him go to bed. Why would he leave? What had Blane done?

Acid churned in his stomach as he drove, slowly making his way to the heart of the city. That's where he'd go, right? Blane was guessing. He had no idea. He just knew he had to find him. Allowing Kade to live on the streets wasn't an option. And whatever it was Blane had done that had set him off, he'd apologize, swear to never do it again, anything so long as Kade agreed to stay.

Blane drove to the police station, telling the guy at the front desk what had happened, asking what he should do. Though the cop looked sympathetic, he also wasn't too positive about Blane's chances of finding Kade.

"You can try down off New York Street," he said. "Sometimes the runaways gather there, banding together for protection, work, that sort of thing."

Grateful for a lead, any lead, Blane took off. He found a spot on the street and parked, opting to hoof it as a better means of looking for Kade. God, what was going to happen to him? He was just a kid. Worry ate at Blane, anxiety making his palms sweat as he searched alleys and walked the streets.

It wasn't until dark that he finally came across a group of kids. Teenage boys—they were huddled near the mouth of an alley smoking. Blane approached them. They eyed him warily, their gazes raking him from head to foot.

"I'm looking for a boy," Blane said. "About ten years old, dark hair."

The one who seemed to be the leader spoke up. "We got Johnny over there, he's the youngest, but he's blond. It's fifty bucks up front." He dipped his chin toward a smaller child huddled in the shadows.

Blane felt the blood drain from his face as he realized they'd misunderstood why he was there. Bile rose in his throat and he choked it back down, dragging his gaze away from Johnny's haunted eyes.

"No, I'm not here for . . . that," he rasped. "I'm missing someone. My brother. I was hoping maybe you'd seen him. Dark hair. Blue eyes. His name is Kade."

"Sorry, man, can't help you," the boy said, turning away.

Blane didn't know if he should be relieved these boy prostitutes hadn't seen Kade, or disappointed that he still didn't have a lead on him.

He kept going, ducking in and out of homeless shelters, Laundromats, anything that was open all night. Finally, he sank onto a dilapidated bench, the despair he'd been fighting all day overwhelming him. He rested his head in his hands, swallowing the lump in his throat that felt as though it might choke him.

"Blane?"

Blane's head jerked up, hope flaring in his heart. Kade stood on the sidewalk, staring at him in utter astonishment.

"Kade," he choked out, relief making his eyes water. "Thank God." He jumped up and had nearly grabbed Kade in a hug when he remembered how much he hated to be touched and stopped himself at the last second.

"What are you doing here?" Kade asked.

The utter relief at finding Kade unharmed faded to anger, the emotions of the day taking their toll on Blane. "What do you mean, 'What am I doing here?'" Blane bit out. "Why the hell do you think I'm here? I've been looking for you all goddamn day!"

Kade's expression shuttered. "Well, you found me, so now you can go home." He turned to go.

Blane grabbed his arm and Kade spun around, jerking it from his grasp. "I told you not to touch me," he snarled.

"You're coming home with me," Blane said. "And I don't care if I have to drag your ass there by your neck."

"Man, I'm doing you a favor," Kade sneered. "You did your good deed, brought the orphan home for a while. Now you go your way and I'll go mine."

The anger abruptly drained from Blane. He was going to lose Kade. He could feel it.

"Please, Kade, come home with me. Whatever I did to make you want to go, just tell me. We can make it work."

Kade studied Blane. He couldn't believe Blane had come looking for him. Kade had left in the middle of the night, hitched a ride downtown, and been going back to his old haunts all day, lining up a place to crash. The last person he'd expected to see sitting on the street was Blane.

"Why are you here?" Kade asked. He honestly didn't know why the guy had spent what looked like the whole day and night looking for him. He hadn't shaved, his hair was in disarray, probably from his habit of shoving his fingers through it. It was hot, the end of July, and his normally immaculate clothes were stained with sweat and dirt.

Blane's throat moved as he swallowed. "You're my brother. I want to take you home, to our home. We can talk about it, change whatever set you off—"

"Nothing set me off," Kade interrupted. Frustration at the guy's inability or unwillingness to just let it go edged his voice. "I just left, okay?"

"But . . . why?"

"God, do I have to spell it out for you?" Kade burst out. "You think I want to wait until you throw me out? Fuck that shit. You can go to hell for all I care."

Blane felt like he'd been kicked in the gut. Of course. Kade didn't trust that Blane wouldn't want to get rid of him at some point. After all, hadn't that been his experience for the past four years?

"I'm not going to throw you out," Blane said. "I swear it. I'm not lying to you."

He could tell by the suspicion on Kade's face that he didn't believe him.

"If you stay out here," Blane said, "then so do I."

Kade's lips twisted. "What?"

"I mean it. If you live on the streets, then that's where I'll be, too. I'm not leaving without you. I refuse to be at home, in my house, knowing you're out here. You're my brother. We stick together. No matter what."

Kade glanced away, his shoes scuffing the dry pavement as he considered. Should he take a chance? Staying longer with the guy wouldn't hurt, he guessed. There was no way Blane would last long on the streets, that was for sure, not even with Kade to protect him.

"All right," Kade finally said. "I'll come."

"And you'll stay?" Blane persisted. "No more running away?"

"Man, what the fuck do you care?" Kade asked in exasperation.

"You're my brother," Blane said evenly, despite Kade's outburst. "And you may not like it or believe it, but I love you."

Kade struggled not to let his astonishment show. The guy looked completely serious, his gaze unblinking as they looked at one another. It had been years since Kade had heard those words, and he reeled from hearing them now. Instinctively he knew that if he did believe them, the guy so determined to keep Kade with him would have the power to hurt him more than baseball bats or bottles ever had.

Kade approached Blane until he stood right in front of him. "So you say."

Blane looked down at Kade, stark anguish in his eyes. "So I swear."

To Blane's relief, Kade followed him as they walked back to the car and got in. They didn't speak on the way home or as they headed inside.

Mona and Gerard were waiting, Mona nearly bursting into tears when she saw Kade. He allowed her to give him a hug, then she hurried into the kitchen, dabbing at her eyes.

Blane felt ready to drop, the emotional toll and physical exertion of the day exhausting him. Even so, it was a long time before he fell asleep, his senses constantly alert for any sound of a footstep in the hallway or the creak of a door.

He knew in his bones that Kade would try again, and he just prayed he'd be able to find him when he did.

CHAPTER FIVE

Blane had court the next morning, leaving him no time to check in on Kathleen. By the time he finally got to the office, he had a stack of messages of calls to return. One on top caught his eye.

"What's this?" he asked Clarice, who'd followed him into his office with several folders in her hands. He held up the message. "The IMPD called?"

"I guess you gave the police your name the other night at Kathleen's?" Clarice asked. When Blane nodded, she continued, "Well, they called to speak to you. Said they wanted her to come downtown."

"Did they say why?"

"No, sorry."

Blane sighed. It seemed everything he was trying to do to separate Kathleen from the murder of her friend was in vain. The universe was aligned against him.

"Do you want me to tell Kathleen?" Clarice asked. "She could probably go by herself."

"No, I'll take her," he said. "Clear my schedule this afternoon."

"Got it." Clarice left, closing the door behind her.

Blane's pleasure at being given the opportunity to again see Kathleen warred with his reluctance to put her in harm's way. If the police were still interested in what she knew, or what they thought she knew, then she wouldn't escape the notice of the dangerous people who would want to hurt her.

Leaving his briefcase in his office, Blane grabbed his keys and headed downstairs. It took him only a few minutes to find her again.

Kathleen glanced up in surprise as he stepped inside her cubicle. Her cheeks flushed pink, making Blane wonder what she was thinking about, and if it was the same thing running through his mind, namely their encounter last night. Blane dragged his thoughts back to business.

"We need to go downtown," he said.

"Why do we need to go downtown?" she asked after a moment. Her eyes did a quick path down and up his body and her blush deepened. Blane really wished he could read her mind.

"The police want to meet with you," he said.

"What for?"

"They wouldn't say." Blane turned away. He didn't want to discuss anything further here where they could be overheard. He held the door for her as they left the firm, letting her precede him before walking her to his car. A few moments later, they were heading downtown in his Jag.

"You didn't have to come," Kathleen said. "I could have gone by myself."

As if Blane would have let that happen. "I'm your lawyer. It's my job to go with you."

"Then I need to pay you," she replied.

Her stubbornness made Blane's lips twitch. He billed his time out at nearly a thousand dollars an hour. She probably didn't know that information if she was offering to pay. A wicked image inside his head made him say, "You can pay me by wearing what's in the backseat." It would be well worth the money.

Kathleen turned to see what he was talking about and when her eyes lit on the bag she had dropped last night, she groaned, causing Blane to laugh softly.

"I'd hoped I'd lost it," she said, her voice forlorn.

"Dare I hope it's an example of your usual taste in non-working-hours apparel?" Blane teased. The image of Kathleen dressed as a naughty Catholic school girl made his mouth water.

"No," she retorted, "it's not. The staff at the bar are all dressing as pop divas Friday night." She hesitated before adding, "I'm supposed to be Britney."

Blane couldn't help the laugh that burst out. She was obviously none too happy about her predicament and her childlike grousing was amusing. Searching his memory, he seemed to recall some music video with Britney Spears dressed in that outfit.

"Gee, thanks," she mumbled, crossing her arms over her chest, precisely like a disgruntled toddler.

Blane stifled his laugh, but was still smiling as he said, "I just can't imagine you pretending to be Britney. You don't seem the type." The type to show off so much skin in so public a venue. Even now her fair skin was flushed with embarrassment. Modesty, something so rarely found in women her age, was incredibly sexy.

"Hey, she's very successful, especially for how young she is," Kathleen defended Spears, as if Blane gave a shit about the singer.

"I'm not saying she isn't," he replied, amused all over again at her loyalty. "I'm sure she's a very talented young woman."

This seemed to appease Kathleen and she settled back in the seat, her ruffled feathers soothed.

Blane decided he really needed to make sure he went by the bar tomorrow night.

After pulling into the police department's parking lot, Blane turned to Kathleen.

"Let me do the talking in there," he said. "I'm your lawyer, so trust me, okay?"

She swallowed hard and nodded. Taking her elbow, Blane led her inside. He straightened his tie and buttoned his suit jacket as they walked. Once inside, he spoke to the cop on duty at the desk. A few minutes later, a cop who introduced himself as Detective Frank Milano came up to them.

"What's this about?" Blane asked after the introductions were made.

"We'd like Miss Turner to help us identify a body," Milano said.

"A body?" Kathleen burst out.

Blane shot her a look.

"Yes," Milano continued. "We think we may have found the person who killed your neighbor, Sheila Montgomery, but need to make sure. We thought you might know him. We'll need to take you down to the morgue."

Kathleen looked surprised, but said, "Okay."

Blane and Kathleen followed the detective. In an undertone, Blane asked her, "Have you ever seen a dead body before?"

Kathleen nodded.

Blane didn't think she understood, not really. He tried again. "Have you seen a dead body that hasn't been prepared by a mortician?"

"I'm not going to get sick or pass out, if that's what you're wondering," she hissed back, her irritation obvious.

Did she just roll her eyes at him?

Blane bit back the retort that was on the tip of his tongue. He'd lay odds she'd be eating those words soon.

Kathleen held together right up until the tech pulled back the sheet to expose Mark's body. He'd been shot in the head with a high-caliber weapon, the exit wound taking out a big chunk of the rear of his skull.

Shit. He'd been afraid of this.

Kathleen stumbled backward, her hand flailing as though searching for something. Her knees gave out and Blane caught her in his arms just as her eyes slid shut. She was out cold.

The sight of her, helpless next to Mark's lifeless body, struck Blane as being morbidly prophetic. If he didn't do something, it would be Kathleen on the next slab and Blane would be the one identifying her remains. Fear made him angry and he lashed out at the detective as he turned around, holding Kathleen's limp body in his arms.

"You're a piece of shit, Milano," Blane bit out, brushing past him on the way out the door. Kathleen didn't need to see Mark's body again when she woke. Her head lolled limply on her neck, her arms dangling at her sides as Blane carried her.

The detective followed Blane, whose long strides ate up the floor. They'd passed an employee break room earlier and that's where Blane headed.

"I don't know what the fuck you think you're doing, detective. Some warning would have been nice." Kathleen had no doubt never seen anything like that before and Blane regretted the fact that it was another horrifying image she'd have to live with. She was innocent and good. She should be coddled, protected, and never be touched by that kind of gruesome reality.

The break room had a couch and Blane laid Kathleen gently on it just as her eyes fluttered open. Blane shrugged out of his jacket and covered her, the paleness of her face worrying him as did the shivers that wracked her. He crouched down next to the couch.

Her confused gaze met his. "Didn't I hit the floor?" she asked.

Kathleen's innocent question softened the edge of Blane's anger. She had no idea that somehow, between waking up next to her in her bed and stalking her outside of her work, she'd wrapped Blane completely around her little finger. She couldn't get rid of him if she tried. It was a revelation to himself as well, but now wasn't the time to dwell on it. Blane simply accepted the fact and moved on.

"You think I'd let you fall?" he asked, trying to keep it light. He didn't want her dwelling on Mark's body. "I have to keep you uninjured so I can remind you that you were quite sure you wouldn't pass out."

Blane's teasing was rewarded with a faint smile, but it was gone quickly. She sat up and turned her gaze to the detective as Blane swung his jacket over her shoulders.

"Why didn't you tell me it was Mark?" she asked Milano, her eyes flashing with anger.

"We weren't sure he was the same person as the one you said was Sheila's boyfriend," Milano said. "We needed you to identify him as the same man."

"What happened to him?" Blane asked, moving to sit beside Kathleen. The need to feel her, be right beside her, was overwhelming and he didn't fight it.

"Neighbors found him," Milano answered. "He wrote a suicide note confessing to the murder before he shot himself."

Which was utter bullshit.

Kathleen wavered slightly and Blane was immediately concerned that she'd pass out again. Sliding an arm around her back, he held her close. "Breathe slow," he said into her ear. "Breathe deep."

She closed her eyes and did as he said. It seemed to help because soon she was firing more questions at the hapless detective. "You're saying he killed himself?"

"That's how it appears."

"You've got it wrong. There's no way he could have murdered Sheila, and he didn't kill himself either. He was murdered, too."

Milano looked skeptical. Kathleen must have seen it, too, because she persisted. "Believe me," she said. "You've got to find whoever did this. They killed Sheila and now Mark."

And soon Kathleen herself, if Blane didn't protect her.

"I'm sorry," Milano said, "but the case has been closed. Mark was her boyfriend. You yourself said they argued that night, which places him at the scene of the crime. His note was his confession."

"But you're wrong!"

Blane pulled her closer to him, worried that she was becoming hysterical.

"I'm sorry," Milano said, sounding somewhat regretful. "There's nothing more I can do."

After he left, Blane glanced down at Kathleen, huddled against his side. She was crying.

"Are you all right?" he asked.

She swiped angrily at her eyes. "Fine. Can we go?"

Blane stood and helped Kathleen to her feet. She handed his jacket back to him, though Blane would have preferred she keep it. He didn't say anything, though, until they were in the car. She shivered in the cold and Blane reached for the heat controls.

"Don't you ever wear a coat?" he asked. Little things like her were usually cold even when it was seventy-five degrees outside.

"Not usually," she said.

Blane headed in the direction of her apartment. There was no point in taking her back to work and he wouldn't have allowed it anyway.

"Why are you taking me home?" she asked after a few minutes.

"You've had a shock," Blane said. "You're taking the rest of the day off. You need to rest." And he could work just as well sitting in her living room as he could in his office.

Blane knew she'd have something to say about that and sure enough, he shot her a look just as she opened her mouth. After a second, she seemed to think twice about arguing.

At her apartment, Blane made sure he had his Glock before rounding the car to open Kathleen's door. He followed her up the stairs and waited while she dug in her purse for the keys. He briefly considered offering her his copy to use, but didn't think that would go over real well, so he held his tongue.

Finally, she found her keys and started to unlock the door. Then she froze.

"What is it?" Blane asked.

"I always lock my door," she said, her eyes wide and fearful.

Blane's gun was in his hand in the blink of an eye. He pulled Kathleen behind him. "Stay here," he ordered. She nodded.

Blane carefully eased open the door, the gun leveled in front of him. There was enough light still to see that Kathleen's apartment had been completely wrecked. His gaze took in the damage even as he searched the shadows, listening intently for any sound.

After clearing the living room, he checked the bathroom, then the bedroom. Everything had been torn apart. It was obvious whoever had done this had been intent on finding something. Blane was just thankful Kathleen hadn't been here to greet them. He could imagine only too well what they would've done to her.

As he emerged from the bedroom, Blane saw Kathleen standing in the living room, looking shell-shocked. Of course she hadn't waited like he'd told her. One glance at the look on her face, though, had him biting back chastising her.

"Did you find Tigger?" she asked, frantic.

Shit. The cat.

"No. We can keep looking, though." Blane didn't want to say that the cat was probably long gone, though it didn't seem he had to. Kathleen's eyes filled with tears as she stepped over the broken shards of glass and ceramic in the kitchen to look inside the bedroom. She stood there for a moment, taking in the shredded bedding and clothes.

A knock at the door had Blane reaching again for his gun, but it was just the neighbor he'd spoken to the other night. Thank God, she was holding the cat.

"Tigger!" Kathleen hurried to take the cat from the girl. "Thank you so much. How did you find him?"

"He was wandering around outside," the girl replied. "I thought he might be yours. So, what the hell happened in here?"

Blane holstered his gun. "Did you see or hear anything unusual today?" he asked.

The girl shook her head. "Nah. I work at night, so I sleep during the day. Didn't hear a thing. Sorry."

Kathleen thanked her again and the girl left. Blane watched Kathleen as she turned in a slow circle, surveying the disaster. He made a decision.

"Come on," he said, heading toward the door.

"What do you mean?" Kathleen asked. "I can't leave. I need to call the cops and start cleaning this mess up."

That wasn't happening. She wasn't staying alone in this apartment for another night, not until Blane had these guys arrested or killed. And with the way he was currently feeling, his preference was for the latter.

"No, you're not," he said. "We'll call the cops from my place. You're staying there tonight."

"I don't think so," Kathleen said. "I can go stay with Clarice or something."

As if she had a choice in the matter. "You can come willingly or unwillingly," Blane said baldly. "But like it or not, you're coming with me." Throwing her over his shoulder seemed a little caveman, but at this particular moment, Blane didn't give a shit. He'd do what he had to do and she could just be pissed later. At least she'd be alive.

To his relief, though, she gave in and followed him out the door.

The drive to Blane's house was done in near silence, the only sound in the car that of the purring cat. Kathleen had a death grip on the animal, but it didn't seem to mind.

Blane was well aware of what it felt like to have someone break into your house and mess with your possessions. It was a feeling of violation that few understood unless they'd experienced it firsthand. Home was supposed to be a place of safety and comfort. It worried him enormously that Kathleen was now in the crosshairs of some very dangerous people. If he didn't miss his guess, he'd say Jimmy Quicksilver's fingerprints were all over the break-in.

Kathleen didn't seem to snap out of her stupor until he opened the car door for her. As they walked, Blane lifted the strap from her shoulder, carrying her worn purse.

Mona met them at the door and Kathleen hesitated, necessitating a quick explanation from Blane.

"It's all right," he said. "It's just Mona, my housekeeper."

Blane wondered briefly how Mona would take to him suddenly bringing a woman home to stay with him. The women he dated rarely saw the inside of his home and none had ever stayed the night. Even with Kandi, they'd stayed at her house, not his. Blane had always felt the need to keep his home sacrosanct. For some reason, he found himself now anxious about whether or not Kathleen would like it, if she'd feel comfortable. He wanted her to feel welcome and hoped he could count on Mona to read between the lines since he'd given her no forewarning.

But he needn't have worried. Mona didn't bat an eye as Blane introduced Kathleen, chatting with her about her cat and seeming to put Kathleen at ease.

"I'm putting Kathleen in the Garden Room," Blane said to Mona. "Is it suitable?" Knowing Mona, she kept the linens fresh and the room aired out despite the fact that no one had stayed in it for years. His mother's favorite room in the house, Blane had always felt her presence most strongly there. The décor seemed to suit Kathleen and he didn't think twice about his decision to put her there.

Mona's surprise showed this time, but she only responded with "Quite."

"This way," Blane said, taking Kathleen's elbow and leading her upstairs. "Mona and her husband Gerard take care of the house and grounds," he explained. "They live in a house that adjoins the property. They decided to come with us when we moved here from back East when I was a child."

"How long have they worked for you?" Kathleen asked.

"As long as I can remember. Mona was also my nanny when I was a child."

Blane found himself holding his breath as he showed her into the room. After a moment, he had to ask. "Do you like it?"

"It's . . . amazing," she said, gazing around the room with rapt awe.

Blane let out the breath he'd been holding. "My mother was an artist," he explained. "She decorated each of the bedrooms in a different style. This room she painted herself."

Kathleen turned to face him. "Your mother painted this?" she asked, her brows lifting.

Blane nodded with a smile. "She was quite talented." An understatement, though his father had never appreciated the extent of his wife's artistic ability. "There's a bathroom through there," he continued. "In case you want to freshen up before dinner."

"Blane," Kathleen said, "I don't know how to thank—"

Blane placed his finger on her lips, halting her thanks before she could finish the sentence. Now that she was here, in his home, the possessiveness he'd felt earlier was amplified tenfold.

"Don't thank me yet," he said. "When it comes to you, my motives aren't exactly . . . altruistic." Now the trick was to go slow and keep his hands off her, but he was making no promises to himself. He wanted her too badly to be anything but pragmatic as to how this evening would end.

"I'll be back to get you shortly," he said, exiting the room while he still had an ounce of chivalry.

As he'd expected, Mona was full of questions when he reappeared downstairs after changing clothes.

"Kathleen works for you?" she asked as Blane opened a bottle of wine.

Blane eyed Mona while she prepared dinner. He poured two glasses of the merlot before he spoke.

"Yes, and it's not what you're thinking," he said.

"What am I thinking?" she asked, all innocence.

"She's in trouble," Blane said. "She's not safe in her apartment, so I brought her here."

"So you *personally* need to see to her safety? It's not something Todd or Rico could do?" Mona named a couple of Blane's SEAL buddies who ran a private security firm in Indy.

Blane took a drink of his wine, handing Mona the other glass. He didn't answer her question. She knew him too well to pretend.

"She's . . . different," he acknowledged.

Mona's teasing grin softened. "I'm glad to hear that," she said. "She seems very sweet and quite pretty. Young, though, don't you think?"

Blane nodded. "A bit. Is that a problem?" He was being serious. He valued Mona's opinion, always had. But she shook her head.

"I don't think so. She seems older than her years."

"She's been through a lot," Blane said, explaining about the death of Kathleen's parents.

"Yes, that'll certainly make one grow up in a hurry," Mona said with a sympathetic sigh. "Poor thing. Do be careful, though. It sounds like she's not your usual one-night-stand kind of girl."

Blane acknowledged this with a nod. Mona had never passed judgment on how he chose to conduct his private affairs and he knew the statement wasn't intended as such.

Blane made some calls in the den while Mona finished making dinner. Kathleen's apartment needed to be cleaned up and her things replaced, preferably as quickly as possible. Although technically it was after business hours, money made all the difference in how fast some things could be done. Another phone call to the man who did his suits, and Blane had someone willing to be a personal shopper for Kathleen. Her sizes were easy enough to guess and the man assured Blane he'd take care of it.

A short while later, Mona informed him that dinner was ready. Kathleen hadn't yet returned so Blane went upstairs for her. Perhaps she was shy and needed a little encouragement.

He tapped lightly on the door and waited. When there was no answer, he cautiously pushed it open a crack.

Kathleen was sound asleep on the bed. She hadn't even removed her shoes, she'd fallen asleep so fast. The emotional turmoil of the past few days had to be taking a toll on her.

But she'd felt safe in his home. Safe enough to sleep so soundly she hadn't even heard him enter the room.

Blane carefully removed the flats she wore, then grabbed a blanket from the closet and gently covered her. She sighed softly, burrowing deeper into the pillows. Blane brushed his knuckles against her cheek, his touch feather light.

What was he going to do with her?

The thought preoccupied him through dinner and after he'd retired to the den for a drink. Blane had asked Mona to do some shopping for Kathleen; she needed groceries, linens, that sort of thing. Mona had been happy to comply, taking the key and the address to her apartment.

Blane hadn't heard from Kade about Mark's backpack but knew better than to call him. Kade hated being nagged. He'd call him when he had it.

It was late when he heard Kathleen creeping down the stairs. Someone else might not have heard her, but Blane was attuned to every sound this house made and he knew immediately when she woke and began moving around upstairs.

Soundlessly, Blane followed the noises to the kitchen. Kathleen was sitting at the kitchen table, eating what looked like ice cream. She hadn't spotted him yet.

"I see you woke up," he said, moving closer until he could lean against the counter and crossing his arms over his chest.

She started at the sound of his voice, her hand immediately moving to smooth her hair when she saw him before seeming to catch herself. When she said nothing, he nodded to the nearly empty container in front of her. "Ice cream?"

"Sorry," she said, sounding a little embarrassed. "I've eaten nearly all of it."

That was fine with Blane. He hadn't even realized Mona kept ice cream here.

"It's rocky road," Kathleen added.

"Rocky road?"

"Chocolate-covered nuts wrapped in marshmallowy goodness in chocolate ice cream. What's not to love?"

"Indeed." Blane's lips twitched at this. He was learning more about Kathleen every moment. She apparently thought rocky road ice cream an irresistible treat. He filed that information away for later as he took a seat opposite her at the table. She was still eating and Blane knew he was a little too interested in watching her lick the ice cream from the spoon, though she seemed unaware of his fascination.

"You have a really beautiful home," she said. "Do you live alone?"

Blane could detect no avarice in her tone, just the curiosity of polite conversation. "Thank you," he said. "And yes, I live alone." He wondered if she thought he had a live-in girlfriend or something. As if he could tolerate a woman living with him.

"Your brother?" she asked.

Blane shook his head. He was certain he and Kade would kill each other if forced to live together for an extended period of time.

"Your . . . parents?"

"They're no longer with me." And that's all he wanted to say about that. Blane changed the subject. "Do you know why anyone would have done that to your apartment?" He wanted to know how much Kathleen knew of how deep she was in this mess. It was too much to hope for that this had been a random thing and not tied to Sheila's murder.

"No, I don't," she said. "I don't really have any enemies here and I don't own anything of any real value."

"Maybe someone with a vendetta," Blane persisted. "A jilted lover?" That he would kill with his bare hands.

She blushed, clearing her throat before answering. "Um . . . no, that couldn't be, I mean, there's not . . . just . . . . no."

Blane would have bet his next paycheck that she was a virgin, though the idea that she was untouched at her age was a bit of a stretch. If she wasn't a virgin, then she was still decidedly inexperienced. Though the way she was licking the spoon for every last smear of chocolate had him imagining her tongue doing other things.

Kathleen finished the ice cream and seemed to cement Blane's assessment of her sexual experience, or lack thereof, by simply dismissing him with a "Well, good night."

Nice try. Blane's hand circled her arm. "I'll walk you back upstairs," he said. "It's dark and I don't want you to trip and fall." Right. And there was absolutely no chance he'd have her naked and making those little panting noises again inside of ten minutes.

But she seemed to buy it, following him trustingly up the stairs, which oddly made Blane feel a twinge of guilt at the direction of his thoughts.

"I'm sorry I fell asleep and missed dinner," Kathleen said. "That was rude of me."

Now the guilt was more than a twinge, which just irritated Blane. Kathleen's innocent trust made him want to grind his teeth in frustration. Surely she knew where this was going. He'd been fantasizing about seducing Kathleen for weeks and now his conscience was going to fuck it up.

"You were tired," he said, the internal war waging inside his head making the words more curt than he'd intended. She didn't respond and a moment later they stood in front of her door. Blane knew with a sinking feeling in his gut that he wasn't going to follow through on his plans to seduce her.

Damn it to hell.

"Mona put some clothes for you in the bureau and closet," he said. "They should fit well enough until your apartment is back together." She didn't need to know that some of the clothing had been Kandi's.

To his dismay, Kathleen seemed to choke up at that, her eyes filling with tears.

"Thank you," she managed to say. A lone tear traced down her cheek.

Blane lifted his hand to wipe it away. "I'm sorry," he said. Sorry this had happened to her, sorry for the thoughts raging inside his head of what he wanted to do to her, sorry he'd ever laid eyes on her because she was going to be his eventually—she just didn't know it yet.

"It's all right," she said.

Her light dismissal of what had happened angered Blane, at the same time that her obvious vulnerability frustrated and worried him.

"It's not all right," he said. "You need someone to take care of you." And that someone was going to be him. But he knew immediately that he'd pushed too hard, too fast. Her eyes widened and she stepped back, beyond his reach.

"I don't need anyone to take care of me. I can take care of myself."

Blane's eyes narrowed at the obvious lie and she took another step back from him. "Because you're doing such a great job?" he bit out. Next time, they wouldn't just break into her apartment, they'd find her, take her, and God only knew what they'd do to her. It terrified him just thinking about it.

Kathleen didn't say anything else, the truth of his words seeming to sink in as the fire faded from her eyes. She slipped past him into the bedroom. It was only through sheer force of will that Blane didn't follow her inside.

Blane knew he couldn't sleep and didn't even try. He paced his room, thinking. The shower started in Kathleen's bedroom and he tried not to think of her naked and wet just a few yards from him. What was he going to do? He had to protect her, but couldn't if she kept pulling this whole "I can take care of myself" routine. She responded badly to an outright challenge, but there was something between them. Blane could use that to his advantage, tie her to him emotionally, then she wouldn't have any problems with him protecting her, taking care of her.

The shower stopped and Blane still paced, trying to come up with the best way forward. He needed to talk to her, that was all. Explain that he wanted to help her. She'd listen. She had to.

That decided, Blane set out down the hall to Kathleen's door. He raised his hand, preparing to knock, when he heard it.

Kathleen was crying.

Blane opened the door, the faint light from the window illuminating the huddled figure on the bed. She'd buried her face in the pillow, probably trying not to make any noise.

In seconds, Blane was at her side. Scooping her in his arms, he cradled her against his chest as he sat on the bed, much like he had the night of Sheila's death. Kathleen clung to him, her body wracked with sobs and her tears dampening his shirt.

Blane stroked her damp hair, crooning softly to her. "Shh, it's all right. Don't worry. I'll take care of you." It became a mantra and a pledge, a promise he made to her and himself. Nothing was going to happen to her, not while he was around.

Finally, she quieted, her sobs fading into silence. Blane lifted her chin so he could see her face. Long, wet lashes framed her eyes, the tears making the blue depths sparkle in the night. Her eyes were wide and innocent, her trust for him like a vine reaching out to bind Blane to her.

To Blane's utter surprise, Kathleen leaned forward and pressed her lips to his, her arms wrapping around his neck. For a moment, Blane was too shocked to respond, then the dormant heat in his blood surged and he kissed her back hungrily.

Kathleen's lips were as soft as he remembered, her taste just as sweet. He devoured her, holding her close against him. She moved to straddle him and his erection pressed against her softness. Blane groaned, his kiss deepening as his fingers threaded through her long hair. She kissed him back just as fervently, the heat between them spiraling out of control.

Kathleen unbuttoned his shirt, her soft hands tracing the lines of Blane's chest, her tentative touch more arousing than Blane would have thought possible. His hands gripped her hips underneath the T-shirt she wore. He could feel the tiny scrap of fabric covering the part of her body where he most ached to be, but the part of his brain still able to think coherently knew he shouldn't go there. And he was doing okay, just kissing her, right up until she tugged her shirt off.

He was only a man and the temptation of her breasts was too great to resist. Their heavy fullness in his hands made his dick almost painfully hard. Her nipples were silken tips against his rough palms and he was dying to know how they'd taste. Kathleen gasped at his touch, her head lolling back on her neck. The light shone on her hair, causing it to glow silvery gold in the night.

Blane could spend hours just watching her reactions as he touched her, but it seemed she had a different agenda. Her hands reached for his belt and clarity finally came to Blane through the fog of arousal.

Could he do this? Hadn't he just been dwelling on how young she was? Too innocent and trusting for her own good?

Blane caught her wrists with his hands, halting her attempt to undo his pants.

Kathleen looked up in surprise at him. Her mouth was swollen from his kisses, her cheeks flushed, her eyes bright with desire. She pressed herself more firmly against Blane's erection, making it clear what she wanted.

As if she was in any proper frame of mind to make a decision like this, and that thought decided it.

"Stop," Blane said through clenched teeth.

Kathleen frowned, as though she didn't understand. Leaning forward, she kissed his jaw, the tips of her breasts grazing his chest.

Blane's grip on her wrists tightened. If she kept doing that, no way was he going to be able to control himself. He couldn't remember ever wanting a woman as badly as he wanted her.

"I said stop," he repeated, pushing her backward until she lay flat on her back. Blane was above her now, pinning her arms over her head as he crouched between her spread thighs. Light from the window illuminated her body and Blane hesitated. She was every man's dream, ready and willing. His resolve wavered.

"Make love to me," she said, her voice pleading.

And Blane knew he couldn't do it. Every part of his body was clamoring for his head to shut up and just fuck her already, but that's not what she wanted, not really. Her words had just confirmed it. Blane could have sex with her, could fuck her until both of them were dripping with sweat and exhausted, but he could not make love to her.

"I . . . can't," he said finally. "I won't."

Her expression turned aghast. "What? Why?"

Blane released her wrists, his gaze devouring what he'd probably never see again, and his hands followed where his eyes touched. Moving slowly down her arms, his fingers brushed the skin of her shoulders, her sides, over her collarbone and down to cup her breasts, to her stomach that quaked under his touch, to the delicate swell of her hips.

"You're beautiful, Kat. Perfect," he said. "And I thought I could, but I can't. You're too young and innocent and I'm not going to do that to you."

"You're Blane Kirk," she spat. "Since when do you care?"

Blane expected the bitterness in her voice; after all, he was rejecting her in the most intimate way a man could reject a woman. But he had no choice, not if he wanted to be able to live with himself. And she was right. He'd made no secret of the revolving door of women he'd had sex with, but hearing Kathleen say it made shame creep over him.

"Usually, I don't," he said, his voice hard. Selfish anger made his fingers grasp the fragile fabric that still kept part of her from being bare to him. One quick pull and it'd be over. He'd be inside her, pushing his straining cock into her wet heat, making her cry out his name as she came. The fabric was soaked from her arousal, the evidence of Kathleen's desire for him nearly making Blane lose the careful grip he had on his control. Then another thought hit him.

"I doubt you're on any sort of birth control either, are you?" His cold question seemed to break through to Kathleen, her face paling. *Yes, darling, this is sex.* Two people using each other to get off, and the consequences of that wasn't a white wedding and a happily-ever-after. Not with him.

Blane let out a vicious curse at the shattered look on Kathleen's face, hating that he was responsible for it. But he knew she'd hurt even worse in the morning if they did this tonight. He didn't do relationships, even with a woman as lovely as her.

Grabbing his shirt, he covered her torso with it so he could at least make it out of the room. Blane kissed her one more time, and knew he was being much too rough, but couldn't seem to help taking his frustration out on her. A moment later, he left, slamming the door behind him.

~

Seventeen Years Ago

After Blane brought him back, Kade gradually settled in to living with his brother. Blane spent time with him every day, trying to get to know him, which was harder than he thought it'd be for a kid Kade's age.

Kade was suspicious, cynical, and always guarded. He was also funny, his dry sense of humor very similar to Blane's. He acted much older than his age, and Blane tried not to dwell on why that was the case. When they talked, it was of inconsequential things, just building a relationship. Blane didn't push for Kade to spill his guts. It was a learning curve for Blane, too, learning how to deal with Kade as both a brother and a father figure.

Mona and Gerard were a godsend. Kade took to Mona immediately, and she was soon cooking as many of his favorites as she could discover. Kade put on weight, which eased Blane's mind. He also stopped sneaking food into his backpack as time passed, which Blane took to be a good sign.

It was late in August when Blane thought maybe Kade would want to play catch with him. Grabbing a baseball and two gloves, he went to search for Kade, finally finding him in the kitchen. Unsurprisingly, he was eating a snack Mona had made for him, though dinner was only a couple of hours away. The kid was a bottomless pit, but then again, Blane remembered he'd been a bottomless pit at that age, too.

"Hey, want to go play catch?" he asked, handing Kade a glove.

Kade took it, looking at it like he'd just been given a manure-crusted shoe. "Why?" he asked.

Blane shrugged, hiding a smile. "It's nice out and I haven't played in a while. You'll like it. C'mon."

Kade followed him outside, wearing jeans and a short-sleeved black T-shirt. Blane had tried to buy him some shorts, but Kade had refused. He only wore jeans. And it had been a concession just to get him to wear short sleeves. His wardrobe was mostly black, though Blane had snuck in a few items that were navy and a couple of white shirts as well.

It was obvious right away that Kade had never done this before. Without drawing too much attention to that fact, Blane helped him with the glove and showed him the basics. It was enough and soon they were tossing the ball back and forth underneath the shade of the oak trees out back.

"A friend of mine is coming over tonight," Blane said, catching Kade's toss. He threw it back.

"Who?" Kade asked, catching the ball with only a little awkwardness.

"A girl. I've known her since we were little. Her name is Kandi."

"Is she your girlfriend?"

Blane hesitated. "Sort of. She's a junior and we've been seeing each other on and off for a while. Been friends for a long time, though. I'm anxious for her to meet you."

Kade considered this. No one had been by to visit since he'd been here, and until today, he hadn't thought much of it. Now he wondered if Blane was embarrassed by him. Absently, he caught the ball, the leather glove smacking with the impact, and threw it back. This was kind of fun. He'd never done it before.

"Tomorrow we need to go enroll you in school," Blane said. "They'll want to give you tests, that kind of thing, to place you properly."

Kade shrugged. Tests were easy. The less he cared, the better he did.

The girl, Kandi, came by for dinner. She was beautiful. She had long, blonde hair that hung in a straight, gleaming curtain down her back, blue eyes, a golden tan, and legs that seemed to go on forever. She smiled when Blane introduced her to Kade, but Kade quickly saw that though she said all the right things, her eyes were calculating, measuring him. A nearly imperceptible disdain curled her lip and tinged her voice when she spoke.

Kade wasn't a bit surprised that perfect-golden-boy Blane had a perfect-Barbie-doll-girlfriend. What did surprise him was how Blane didn't seem to see her for what she was, a spoiled, selfish brat who thought she was better than Kade, and probably everyone else, for that matter.

Kade excused himself to go to the bathroom. When he returned, he caught his name and stopped in the hallway to eavesdrop.

" . . . worried about you," Kandi was saying to Blane. "You barely even know this kid. And you're telling me he grew up on the streets? You have to be careful, Blane. For all you know, he could steal from you, or get his friends to come rob you one night. You could get hurt."

"That's enough," Blane said, his voice stiff. "Kade's not like that. He's my brother, and he's here to stay."

"I'm just trying to warn you—" Kandi continued, but Blane cut her off.

"I don't need a warning," he said. "And if that's how you're going to view Kade, treating him like a criminal, then maybe we shouldn't hang out anymore."

Kade's eyebrows climbed. He was defending Kade to the Barbie doll?

"Blane, listen to me—"

"It's time for you to go, Kandi. We'll talk some other time."

Kade waited where he was and in a moment, Kandi came stomping out of the den. When she spotted Kade, she marched over to him.

"You may think you've really pulled one off," she hissed, "but Blane isn't stupid. He'll see you for the conniving piece of trash you really are."

Kade's eyes narrowed. She didn't seem so pretty anymore. "Ditto," he said.

Kandi flounced past him to the door, slamming it on her way out. When Kade turned back around, Blane had emerged from the den.

"Sorry about that," he said with a smile that didn't reach his eyes. "Kandi had to leave suddenly. She said to say bye to you."

"Sure she did," Kade replied, his gaze steady on Blane's.

Blane sighed and pushed his fingers through his hair. "She'll come around," he said. "She's just a little protective . . . "

Possessive, Kade thought.

" . . . but it'll be fine," Blane continued. "And if it's not . . . " He shrugged. "Hey, I'm hungry. You want ice cream?"

The worry that had churned in Kade's stomach all day, the anxiety he hadn't even acknowledged, eased. Blane had stood up for him, taken his side. Emotion clawed at his throat and he couldn't speak, so just nodded.

"Awesome," Blane said, flashing another blinding smile. This time, his eyes smiled, too. "Let's go."

CHAPTER SIX

Blane was up before the sun, carefully knotting his tie and checking his cuff links before heading downstairs. Mona was waiting with fresh coffee and a bagel for him.

"Do you have that spare quilt that matches the one in the Garden Room?" he asked.

"Of course," she said, her brow furrowing. "Why?"

"I thought Kathleen would like it." He took a sip of the scalding coffee. "I'll drop it by her apartment. Did you get those things I asked for?"

"I did," Mona said. "Poor thing. She hardly had anything in that refrigerator of hers."

"Thanks for doing that," Blane said. Gerard was sitting at the kitchen table finishing his breakfast and reading the sports section of the newspaper. Blane grabbed the front page from his discarded stack and skimmed it while he ate.

"Gerard, could you ride with me to work?" he said once the older man had finished the last of his bacon. "I need you to bring Kathleen's car back to her this morning. I don't want her to feel like she's a prisoner here." Though Blane would have very much liked her to be, at least until he knew for certain she was safe.

Gerard readily agreed. "Let me get my jacket," he said. He pushed himself back from the table and headed down the hallway.

"Kathleen will be so excited to see all you did for her apartment, Blane," Mona said, picking up Gerard's empty plate. "You're a good man."

Blane felt a twinge of guilt that must have shown on his face. Or maybe it didn't and it was just a testament to how well Mona knew him that her smile faded.

"She does know, doesn't she?" Mona asked.

Blane glanced at his watch. "I've got to go. I have court this morning." He tossed down the paper and stood.

"Blane Kirk, what are you doing?" Mona's no-nonsense voice made Blane wince, but he just gave her a tight smile and she sighed. He didn't want a lecture from Mona. Not today. What was he supposed to do? Just send Kathleen back to her trashed apartment? He knew she didn't have the money to replace what had been damaged and the thought of her having to live with broken things and ripped furniture was untenable.

"Make sure Kathleen wears a coat when she leaves today," he said. "It's going to be cold out there."

Mona nodded, her expression still disgruntled as Blane gave her a swift kiss on the cheek. He followed Gerard down the hallway and out to his car. Soon they were on their way to the firm, the early morning gray and misty as the sun's rays peeked over the horizon.

Blane had swiped Kat's keys from her purse and handed them over to Gerard so he could drive her car back to his place.

"This girl," Gerard said as he was getting out of Blane's car. "I've never seen you quite so worked up before." His eyes held a question.

"She's in trouble," Blane explained. "And she has no one else."

Gerard nodded, seeming to take Blane at his word. He shut the door behind him and Blane headed to Kathleen's apartment. He hadn't been completely honest with Gerard. Yes, Kathleen was alone with seemingly no one to notice or care what became of her. But Blane wasn't just being a Good Samaritan, and he knew it. It had occurred to him this morning that perhaps Kathleen hadn't told him everything. Maybe whoever had searched her apartment knew something he didn't.

It was an unsettling thought. Was he wrong about her? Was the innocence an act?

Blane reached Kathleen's apartment at the same time the furniture guys arrived. He let them in and they began clearing out all the damaged furniture. Heading for Kathleen's bedroom, he spread the quilt Mona had given him over the crisp sheets. It suited Kathleen and was a silent message from him to her. He wasn't going anywhere and if she was hiding something from him, he'd find out what it was. A subtle warning wrapped in flowers and cotton.

Once he was finished, Blane called a locksmith who agreed to come and replace her locks as well as drop him a copy of the key. A quick glance at the furniture the men were moving in to make sure it was what he'd ordered, and Blane had to leave. The sun was shining brightly as he got in his car and headed downtown.

Blane had two hearings and it wasn't until late morning that he got back to the firm. Immediately upon entering, he knew something was up. A cluster of three women stood by a desk, their heads close together as they talked. A twinge of curiosity stirred, but having been the topic of gossip often enough, Blane didn't pay much heed. Until he heard Kathleen's name.

Freezing in place, Blane turned from his path toward the elevators and headed directly for the women. One of them saw him, her eyes widening to saucers as she nudged those with her. They all fell silent as Blane stepped up to them.

"What's going on?" His expression was carefully blank, his tone one that demanded an immediate answer.

They all looked like the proverbial deer in headlights and no one answered. He fixed one of them with a look and raised an eyebrow expectantly. That seemed to nudge her tongue loose.

"Um, yeah, Diane fired someone," she said.

Blane frowned. People were occasionally let go, this was a business after all, but it usually wasn't cause for watercooler gossip.

"Who?" he asked.

"The runner," another girl answered. "Kathleen."

"Diane called her white trash," the third said in a scandalized whisper.

Fury consumed Blane so fast, he thought his head might explode. His anger must have shown because all three women seemed to cringe.

"Take this upstairs," he ordered, handing his briefcase to one of them. He didn't wait to see if she obeyed—she would—before turning and heading directly for Diane's office.

Diane Greene was an efficient office manager. Personally, Blane didn't care for her, but she'd been at the firm for a long time and things seemed to run relatively smoothly under her. This was the first time he'd ever heard of Diane making such a vitriolic and inflammatory remark to an employee.

And she'd said it to Kathleen.

Blane didn't knock before entering Diane's office, though she was talking to someone who sat in the chair opposite her desk. Blane didn't spare a glance for that person, merely fixing his gaze on Diane.

"Out," he barked. Whoever it was scrambled up and hurried out, closing the door behind him.

Diane looked too shocked at his abrupt arrival to say anything.

"Am I to understand that you fired Kathleen Turner this morning?" Blane asked, his voice deceptively calm. "And that you proceeded to call her, and I quote, 'white trash'?"

Diane's face grew mottled as she stammered a reply. "Yes, Mr. Kirk, but she's been on my warning list for a while now. She was over two hours late this morning, with no word or anything. And she left early yesterday, again without permission or warning."

"Both instances were because she was assisting me," Blane retorted. "Am I to check with you first before availing myself of our employees?"

"Of course not—"

"And then you made it personal by calling her a name," Blane continued, "thereby subjecting this firm to the possibility of a discrimination lawsuit."

Diane looked stunned at that.

Blane leaned over her desk, planting his palms flat on the surface. "Do you have any idea what it would look like?" he said softly. "Miss Turner on one side of the courtroom, you on the other? We'd have to settle in a heartbeat. I don't think I need to tell you what the status of your job here would be if those circumstances came about."

"N-no, sir."

Blane stood upright and adjusted his cuff links. "You'll reinstate Miss Turner to her former position," he said, "starting Monday morning."

"But, sir, James Gage was the one who told me to fire her!"

Blane's gaze jerked back to Diane's. His lips pressed in a thin line and when he spoke, leashed anger coated his words. "James is not a senior partner of this firm. Therefore, my decision overrules his. Is that clear?"

Diane nodded.

"Excellent. Let's not have this problem again, shall we?" His dry statement was greeted with a faint "No, sir" that Blane barely heard since he was already out the door and striding down the hall.

When he reached his office, he still hadn't calmed down.

"Get James Gage down here," he called out to Clarice. He heard her on the phone, then she hurried into his office.

"What happened?" she asked. Clarice was tuned to his moods, though right now it wouldn't have taken a psychic to see he was royally pissed.

"James had Diane fire Kathleen," he said.

Clarice's eyes widened. "Why?"

"Because he's a jealous fuck," Blane bit out. The ding of the elevator distracted him and Clarice left just as James walked into his office.

"You wanted to see me?" James asked, irritation evident in his tone. Although he was William Gage's son, he was still beholden to the partners and he knew it.

"Since when did you decide that firing the office runner was under your discretion?" Blane asked.

"She was shitty at her job and since when do you care?" James's insolent tone sent Blane's fury to a new level.

"You're a lying prick," Blane spat. "Let me guess, you went out with her the other night and when you couldn't fuck her, you decided to fire her."

James blanched, unable to conceal his surprise that Blane knew about his date with Kathleen, but he recovered quickly.

"You're getting awfully worked up over a bitch in heels," James sneered. "Did you have your eye on her already? Or were you afraid you'd get my leftovers for once?"

Blane had James by the throat and shoved against the wall before the man could take another breath.

"Listen, you sonofabitch," Blane hissed. "Even on my worst day, I'm a thousand times better than you in every way. You know it. I know it. Fuck, everybody knows it. And you may think because you're daddy's little boy that you have some pull around here, but you don't. So keep your tiny dick in your pants and keep far away from Kathleen, or so help me God, you'll regret it."

James was clawing at Blane's hand around his throat, his eyes bulging, and Blane shook him one more time, just to make sure he got the message before he let him go.

James retched, gasping for air. "You're fucking insane," he rasped, hurriedly backing toward the door.

"And don't you forget it."

James rushed out of the office and past Clarice's desk. She stared wide-eyed after him as he pushed open the stairwell door and disappeared. She turned to Blane, who stood at the edge of her desk.

"Wow."

He raised an eyebrow. "Happy Halloween."

~

To make Blane's day just about fucking perfect, Kandi called.

"Kandi, we broke up," Blane said, striving for patience. "No, I don't want to go to a party tonight with you."

"It's a friend of my father's," Kandi persisted. "He's quite well connected in Washington, knows all the names to contact for donors. You should come. It would be beneficial to your career."

And hazardous to his mental health, Blane thought. Kandi and he went way back. He didn't want to hurt her, but neither did he want to encourage her. Their most recent breakup might very well be their last. At one point, he'd thought he'd marry her when the time was right. It would be advantageous and she'd make a good politician's wife.

But perhaps not a good wife for *him*.

"I can't," he said, trying a different tack. "I have plans."

"Oh? What kind of plans?"

Kandi's tone was different now, not pleading but edged with jealousy. Blane rubbed his tired eyes. He thought he felt another headache coming on.

"Just going with some buddies to a bar," Blane said. It wasn't a lie. He was going to a bar and with a couple of phone calls, he was sure he could have a few buddies who'd love to come along.

"I bought a special costume," Kandi pouted.

"Listen, I have to go," Blane said. "I'll call you." He hung up before she could say anything else. To his relief, she didn't call back.

Meetings sucked up his afternoon and lasted into the evening. He told Clarice to go ahead and leave early. There was no sense in her sticking around when she had kids who probably wanted to go trick-or-treating.

Blane went to work out first before going to The Drop. He needed to vent his frustration on something, and a punching bag took the brunt of it for a while. Alone in the steaming shower, he thought of Kathleen and wondered if she'd even speak to him when he saw her. After last night, she was probably pissed. Not that he blamed her. Then she'd been fired this morning. He hoped she'd just chilled out in her apartment today and enjoyed her new things.

Was she glad he'd done what he had? Did she like it? Maybe it would salve the hurt feelings from last night. Blane hadn't met a woman yet who couldn't be soothed with a few new, preferably expensive, possessions.

Speaking of last night . . .

It wasn't hard to conjure the memory of Kathleen, her naked body pinned beneath him. Blane's eyes slipped shut and his hand skated down his stomach to curl around his dick. He was already hard just thinking about the way she'd looked, her breasts full and ripe, the rosy tips puckered and beckoning him. He imagined what it would have been like, the taste and texture of her nipples on his tongue, the noises she would have made when he sucked.

Blane could pretend the hot water sluicing over his chest was her hands, touching him, exploring. His hand tightened on himself, stroking as he played out in his mind what he hadn't allowed himself to do last night.

The fabric of her panties would have been so easy to tear, revealing her dripping pussy that just begged for his tongue, his cock, sliding inside her wet heat, stretching her, filling her. She would be tight, her body gripping his as he pumped inside her. He'd make her moan and gasp as he brought her to the edge. Her cries would echo in his ears as he made her come and she'd say his name in that breathy way . . .

His balls tightened, his hips thrusting his cock in his fist as Blane's orgasm crashed over him. Warm semen coated his hand before it was washed away by the water and Blane had to brace a hand against the wall to remain standing.

If he thought fantasizing about her would ease his craving, he'd been mistaken. After dressing in jeans and a shirt, he still wanted Kathleen with the same intensity as before, perhaps more. And he honestly didn't know what he'd do when he saw her again. He felt out of control when it came to her and it scared the shit out of him.

The Drop was wall-to-wall people, many in costumes. Blane spotted Kathleen immediately and froze.

He knew she'd look good in that costume, but damn. He hadn't counted on *how* good.

Kathleen's midriff was left exposed by the shirt she wore, or rather, barely wore. Tied between her breasts, the fabric exposed more than it hid, despite the black sports bra she had on underneath. A miniskirt that barely covered her ass, socks that came to the tops of her knees and showed too many inches of naked thigh, and braided pigtails made her every schoolboy's wicked fantasy in the flesh.

And judging by the crowd of men surrounding the bar in front of her, Blane wasn't the only one who thought so.

"I thought you'd show up tonight."

Blane's attention was forced from Kathleen as another woman stepped in front of him. She was dressed as a glittering fairy, her sleek blonde hair falling in a straight waterfall down her back. Her arms, dusted with a shimmering powder, twined around his neck.

"Kandi," Blane said, though his greeting was perfunctory at best. "You look lovely, as always." How the hell had she known he'd be here?

"Aren't you going to wish me a happy Halloween?" she asked, pressing against him. Blane could smell alcohol on her and frowned. Kandi wasn't nice at the best of times. Drunk, she could turn into a total bitch.

"What are you doing here?" Blane asked instead. "This isn't your crowd. Why aren't you at the party?" His hands settled on her arms, but removing them from around his neck was easier said than done.

Kandi stood on her toes and Blane obediently leaned down so she could speak into his ear.

"Don't make me beg, Blane," she hissed. "Stop playing hard to get and take me home. You know you want to fuck me."

Annoyance flashed through Blane, along with disgust followed by guilt. He'd toyed with Kandi for too long, their relationship on and off again too many times, for her to realize that this time he'd really meant it.

His cell phone buzzed and this time Blane was able to pry Kandi off him enough to reach it. The caller ID said it was Kade.

"I'll be right back," he said to Kandi. "Stay here." She was drunk and he felt responsible for her safety. He'd take the call, then stick Kandi in a cab home.

Blane answered while he was still making his way to the door.

"Where the fuck are you?" Kade asked.

Blane finally got outside where it was blessedly quiet, the sounds of the bar and bad karaoke muffled now.

"Don't worry about it," he said. "What do you have?"

"Yeah, so bad news and good news, brother," Kade replied. "The bad news is, Mark's house burned to the ground today, courtesy of Jimmy."

Blane closed his eyes with a sigh and pressed his fingers to the bridge of his nose. "Please tell me you're joking."

"Wish I were, but now for the good news. There's a good chance whatever he had on TecSol made it out. Some chick has it, but I figure I'll have it by tonight or tomorrow night at the latest."

Blane's eyes shot open at this. Some "chick" had it? Surely that couldn't be . . . no. "How are you going to get it?" he asked.

"I have my ways."

"Don't hurt anybody," Blane reminded him. "And for God's sake, don't kill anyone either."

"You take all the fun out of this, you know?"

Blane rolled his eyes. "Just do it my way, okay?"

"Fine," Kade groused. "But no promises when this is over. That Jimmy asshole is really starting to piss me off."

Blane couldn't disagree with him there. He pocketed the phone and returned to the bar, just in time to see the second bartender placing a shot glass full of tequila between Kathleen's breasts.

The crowd cheered and Kathleen reached up to the guy's mirrored shades, taking them off and smiling at him. His arms slid around her waist as he whispered something in her ear. Blane's hands curled into fists at the sight of his hands on her. He wanted to break each and every one of the bastard's fingers.

But there wasn't a damn thing he could do as the guy licked Kathleen's neck, sprinkling salt before licking her again. His face was too deep in her cleavage for too long before he tossed back the shot glass. Kathleen seemed to be having a good time, putting the lime in her mouth for the guy to take. Their lips met briefly and a wave of possessive fury like Blane had never known swept over him. Kathleen and the guy hugged and she laughed, but all Blane could see was the hands on her, his mind replaying the other man's tongue against her skin.

It was almost as if she could sense Blane, feel the burning heat of his gaze as she suddenly looked up and their eyes met.

Her face paled and for a moment, everything around them seemed to disappear, leaving just him and Kathleen. Lust, fury, jealousy, desire—they consumed him. Kathleen held his gaze for a long moment, then her chin lifted, as if in challenge, before she broke their staring contest and went to the far end of the bar, away from him.

Blane would have to be a bumbling idiot not to get that "Fuck off" message.

Uncomfortably close to losing his cool, Blane found Kandi and hauled her outside and put her into a cab, his ears deaf to her protests. After she'd gone, he headed for his car. Kathleen had to come home sometime, and when she did, he'd be there.

~

Mark's last words, "Think like a smuggler, Kathleen," echoed in the apartment as Blane hit the button on the television, shutting it off.

So much for hoping it was just a coincidence, a "chick" having what Mark had been hiding.

She'd lied to him. Blane had asked Kathleen specifically if she knew of any reason why someone would break into her apartment and she'd denied knowing anything. She wasn't stupid. She had to have realized that the only thing that had changed was the backpack Mark must have given her. Though the fact that she'd given Kade the slip, twice, was something Blane would have to give Kade shit about later.

Blane paced while he waited, glancing at his watch too often. The bar should've closed nearly an hour ago. Where the hell was she? Maybe he should have waited. Did they know where she worked? Blane didn't even have a cell number for her. That was going to have to change.

Just when he'd about worked himself up into a frenzy and was debating going back to the bar to search for her, the door to the apartment opened and Kathleen stepped inside.

Overwhelming relief was followed quickly by anger and Blane was in front of her in two strides, his hands closing on her upper arms.

"Where the hell have you been?"

Kathleen's eyes flew open and she jumped. She hadn't even seen him and now Blane regretted scaring her, but not enough to curb his anger. The sight of her in that bartender's arms still burned in his mind's eye and when he spoke, he couldn't stop jealous accusations from pouring out.

"You should have been home an hour ago. Where were you? With that pretty-boy bartender who had his hands all over you?"

"What is it to you?" Kathleen retorted, recovering quickly. "Shouldn't you be fucking your fairy about now?"

She'd been watching him, seen him with Kandi. It surprised him, as did the profanity. Hearing it come out of her mouth made it sound even more vulgar. "Don't talk like that," he said. "I didn't know Kandi was going to be there tonight."

"That didn't stop her from telling me exactly what she thought of me," Kathleen shot back. "As if I haven't had enough of that today."

Yes, Blane could imagine what Kandi had said to her. Obviously, she'd seen Blane staring at Kathleen and had jumped to conclusions. Kandi would have made her contempt clear, adding to the "white trash" Kathleen had already been called today by someone under his employ. Abruptly, his anger drained away.

"So I heard," Blane said, loosening what he now realized was a too-tight grip on her. "You shouldn't have lost your job. I've taken care of things. You can come back to work on Monday."

"Why?"

Blane stared at her, his hands running a path up and down her arms now.

"Why?" she repeated, stepping away from him. "Why are you doing this? Why the apartment makeover? The new clothes? New furniture? Why are you even here?"

Blane stiffened. Her questions were more like accusations, angry and suspicious.

"Am I some sort of project?" she continued. "A charity case for you? Just tell me, because I don't know what you want from me."

Blane instinctively denied that. She was anything but charity. "I don't want anything from you. I told you last night that I would take care of you and that's what I'm doing." No matter how insane it must seem to her. And surely it must. She'd been on her own for years now and suddenly a man, her boss, had insinuated himself into her life.

"But why?" Her exasperation was obvious. "It doesn't make any sense. I'm nothing, no one to you, so why would you care what happens to me?"

Obviously "Because I want to" wasn't going to fly. How to put into words the way he felt, was feeling, for her when he couldn't even put a name to it? Blane reached for a kernel of truth in the morass of confused emotions inside him.

"Because I like you," he said. "And because you needed help and I'm in a position to offer it."

"And you want nothing in return?"

"Nothing." Which wasn't precisely true and they both knew it.

"Right. Because life really works like that."

It suddenly struck Blane how much she reminded him of Kade, when he'd first come to live with Blane. Distrustful of everyone, he hadn't been able to understand why Blane would do something for him just because he wanted to, without expecting anything back, not even thanks. Blane sensed that Kathleen was as disbelieving as Kade had been, neither believing they deserved something for nothing.

Kathleen turned her back and stumbled, her arm flailing to grab the wall so she wouldn't fall. Blane rushed forward, sliding an arm around her to keep her steady. He caught the whiff of alcohol and realization struck.

"You're drunk," he said. Had she driven home like this? He was going to kill her.

"I've had a really bad day," she groused. "I thought I deserved a drink."

Perhaps she had a point there. Blane would have hugged her, but didn't think she'd appreciate that. Instead, he gave her shoulder a little squeeze, then abruptly let go when she yelped in pain.

"What? What's wrong?" He hadn't squeezed that hard. But she just shook her head.

"It's nothing. Just a bruise."

Blane flipped the switch on the kitchen light, scrutinizing Kathleen who squinted in the sudden brightness. But Blane didn't notice that. What he did notice was the livid bruise on Kathleen's cheek. He could swear she hadn't had that earlier at the bar. If this was evidence of Kade's methods, then Blane was going to kick his ass.

"What happened to you?" he bit out.

"It looks worse than it feels," Kathleen said, shrugging off his concern. She moved past him to the sink and started peeling Band-Aids from her hands.

Blane followed, stepping up behind her. Reaching around, he grasped her hands, turning them palm up. Angry red cuts marked the fair skin of her palms. What had she done? Then it hit him. Mark's message, Kade saying his house had burned to the ground. Somehow, Kathleen had gotten caught up in whatever had happened there—and gotten hurt in the process. Exactly how close a call had she had today?

"You went to Mark's," he said.

"How did you . . . "

"I saw his message to you on the DVD," Blane answered the unfinished question.

Kathleen turned around to face him, her expression angry and hurt. "That was a private message. You have no right to go through my things!"

Blane was sick of pretending. He didn't know how it had happened or why, but he was drawn to Kathleen, tied to her in a way he couldn't understand. But it was a fact, whether they liked it or not, and he was willing to bet she knew it, too.

"Don't I?" he said. His fingers brushed the bruise on her cheek. "Tell me what happened today." Blane needed to know not only who had dared to strike her, but wanted her to come clean with whatever she was hiding from him. To his relief, she started talking.

"Well, you know Diane fired me," she said.

Blane nodded, his hands dropping down to settle on her waist. He noticed with satisfaction that though they stood so close, she made no move to back away, but just accepted his proximity. That was a good sign.

"She said James told her to fire me," Kathleen continued. "So I came home, and that's when James showed up."

Blane stiffened, but kept his face as impassive as possible. He didn't want her to stop talking, so he held his tongue and just listened, which became nearly impossible when she told him how James had hit her, attacked her. The only thing that enabled him to hold on to his control was planning exactly what he was going to do to James.

When she kept talking, explaining the fire at Mark's, how Jimmy had been there and killed another man and how she'd hidden in the bathroom before escaping out the window, Blane thought he couldn't have been further from the truth this morning when he'd hoped she'd just chill out at home today.

Finally, she finished recounting her harrowing escape. The thought of how easily she could have been more seriously hurt today, or killed, was enough to have Blane barely hanging by a thread. He couldn't think about it or he'd go crazy, so he focused on something else she'd said.

"What did you do with the drive?" he asked. If he could get that from her, that should alleviate some of her immediate danger.

"I hid it somewhere safe," she said, glancing away from him.

She didn't trust him. That stung more than it should have.

"You should give it to me," Blane pressed.

"You'll have to get in line," she answered. "Kade's already said I have to give it to him tomorrow."

"Kade?" She was on a first-name basis with him and Kade hadn't said a word? "Kade Dennon?"

"Yeah. You know him?"

"We've met." Blane told no one about Kade being his brother. Not because he didn't want to acknowledge the relation, but because of a promise he'd made to Kade a long time ago.

Blane turned Kathleen around again and washed the cuts on her hands. None were that deep, thankfully. As he toweled her hands dry, he asked, "Were your hands all that got cut?" He wouldn't put it past her to be hurt somewhere else and just refuse to tell him.

She nodded, but Blane could tell by the way she wouldn't look at him that she was lying. When would she learn?

"Where else?"

"My . . . legs," she sighed tiredly. "But it's fine, not a big deal. I'll just take a shower and they'll be fine."

"You're not showering in this condition," Blane retorted. At least, not without him.

"And what condition is that?" she blustered.

"Drunk. You're liable to fall and break your neck. Go sit down." He aimed her in the direction of a kitchen chair.

"I'll be fine," she protested. He shot her a look that said he'd put her ass in that chair if she didn't, and luckily she wasn't too drunk to not understand. She sat.

Blane filled a bowl with warm water and grabbed a towel, crouching down in front of her. He took off her shoes and socks, inspecting the smooth skin of her legs, and finding nothing.

"Where?" he asked.

"Hmm?"

Blane glanced up. Kathleen was staring at him with desire in her eyes. Her gaze was a little unfocused, but he knew what she was thinking. Damn it. As if there was anything he could do while she was drunk.

"Where are the other cuts?" he asked, speaking slowly and clearly.

"Um . . . higher," she mumbled, looking away from him again.

Shit.

It was a real hardship to push Kathleen's skirt up and spread her knees. Blane's mind was busy trying to go places it shouldn't when he finally saw the bandages on her inner thighs. They were reddened with blood. As he carefully removed them, he said, "Do you have any idea how close you came to cutting your femoral artery?" Good God, the woman was a walking death magnet.

Kathleen sighed, rubbing her eyes like a small child. "Biology wasn't really my strongest subject," she muttered.

Blane cleaned and bandaged the cuts, which had stopped bleeding, as quickly and gently as he could. When he was done, he helped Kathleen to her feet. The alcohol was really starting to take effect now, her eyes drooping and her body limp.

"Let's get you to bed," he said. Talking to a sober Kathleen would likely produce better results than talking to her now.

"Only if you're joining me," she said with a teasing grin. She hooked her fingers into Blane's belt and tugged.

That was not going to happen and it seemed Kathleen must have figured that out from the look on Blane's face because she scowled and let go.

"Fine," she retorted, before flouncing away into her bedroom.

Blane followed her. The last thing he needed was her passing out and hurting herself. But she ignored him, stripping off her sweater and shirt as she walked.

A sinking feeling in his stomach told Blane what was going to happen next, and that not only would he be powerless to stop her, he was wholly incapable of turning away.

Sure enough, she tossed him a saucy grin over her shoulder before proceeding to remove every stitch of clothing right in front of him. As she removed her skirt and panties, she bent over, giving Blane a mouthwatering view of paradise. His hands clenched into fists, his dick at full attention, as she casually walked to her bureau and found a set of silk pajamas.

Blane would have preferred a long-sleeved flannel nightgown that came to her chin, but she chose a shorts-and-camisole set that barely covered her. A moan climbed up his throat but he swallowed it back down as she dressed. When she was finished, she grabbed a brush and walked over to Blane, not stopping until she had to tip her head back to look him in the eye.

"Will you help me with my hair?" she asked, handing him the brush.

Considering at the moment Blane would have gladly cut off a limb if she asked, what else could he do but nod and follow her to the bed? She sat in the middle and Blane knelt behind her. Tentatively, he reached for the braids, carefully undoing them and sliding the bristles of the brush through the long, wavy strands.

It was something Blane had never done before, had never thought to do. It was innocently erotic, brushing her hair. Kathleen sighed as he brushed and he was careful to not pull too hard, he didn't want to hurt her. The scent of her shampoo and perfume drifted toward him as he worked.

"I remembered there's a case pending with the firm regarding Tec-Sol," Kathleen suddenly said out of the blue. "I need to know what it's about."

"Why do you need to know?" Blane asked, still brushing her hair.

"Mark worked for them," she said. "He was afraid of them. Afraid they were after him. That Sheila was killed because of him."

"What else did he say?" What all did Kathleen know and why hadn't she told him sooner?

"He said it might have something to do with Eve. Is there someone named Eve involved with the case?"

"No," Blane said, deciding to explain before she did anything else rash. "EVE's not a person, EVE's a thing. They call it Electronic Voting Evaluation. TecSol wrote the software that the city is using for the first election where all voting will be done online."

"The case with TecSol—wasn't it about election fraud?" she asked.

"Yes," Blane said, impressed at her memory. "Six months ago, someone came forward from TecSol claiming to be a whistleblower, saying that the software had security flaws. They were terminated and sued for disclosure of proprietary information. They countersued for wrongful termination under the Whistleblower Protection Act."

"What do the Santini brothers have to do with any of this?"

"They own TecSol through a front company," Blane answered.

"What's the status of the case now?"

"The case is no longer pending, as the plaintiff is dead," he said. Conveniently dead, unfortunately.

Kathleen turned around to face him. "The whistleblower is dead?"

Blane nodded. "Car wreck." With a little help from Jimmy, he was sure.

"You know they were killed," she said and Blane nodded. "But they can't do that. They just can't go around killing people!"

"I know," he said, "and I'm working on it. But you need to stay out of it. It doesn't concern you."

"It concerns me now," she retorted. "Mark said he knew about the problems with EVE, and that he'd come forward. He said someone at the firm betrayed him and now Mark's dead. But he gave that information to me. I can't just ignore that. And you!" Her eyes narrowed at him and she quickly pushed backward on the bed, away from him. "You work for them! Whose side are you on? Did you betray him?"

Blane's hand flashed out and snagged her waist, dragging Kathleen back toward him. She fought briefly, but Blane quickly pinned her down. He needed her to listen to him, not be afraid of him. Her life could depend on it.

"I didn't betray him, Kathleen, I'm on your side," he said, "but you're not helping me protect you. I don't want them to know about you or what Mark told you. You could very well end up dead."

It seemed like Blane had finally gotten through to her because she paled. "I think they might already know," she said weakly, "or will soon."

"What do you mean?" he asked.

"Kade," she said. "He threatened to tell them if I didn't bring him the drive."

Growling a curse, Blane sat up, releasing her, thinking quickly. Perhaps he could play good cop to Kade's bad cop.

"I was going to give it to him," she said, sitting up. "He said to meet him tomorrow night at Monument Circle."

Perfect.

"Good," Blane said. "He'll leave you out of it so long as he gets what he wants. Kade's number one priority is himself." He glanced at the bruise that stood in stark relief on her cheek. "And I'll take care of James." That part he was very much looking forward to.

Blane went to stand, but Kathleen grabbed his arm. "No! You can't!" she said, trying to tug him back down.

Blane paused. "Don't tell me you have feelings for him," he said. "Not after what he did to you?"

"Of course not! He's a bully and a jerk!"

"Then why are you stopping me?"

"Because he's crazy!" she said. "Really crazy. And he has this weird competition thing with you and I don't want you to get hurt!"

It was the first time she'd admitted feeling anything for him except sexual attraction or gratitude. Their eyes caught, held.

"I couldn't handle . . . " she began, then stopped and took a deep breath. "Please. Just . . . stay. With me. Please stay."

Blane's gaze raked Kathleen's body, his memory filling in what was currently covered up. "This isn't a good idea," he said, almost to himself. But it was pointless to pretend he wasn't going to do exactly as she asked. The challenge would be to stay and not have sex with her. Her inebriation might make her less inhibited, as proven by her striptease, but it would be up to Blane to keep his hands to himself.

Blane turned off the light and kicked off his shoes. As he went to climb into the too-small bed, he was stopped by Kathleen. She'd risen to her knees and now was proceeding to undo the buttons of his shirt. The prospect of her touching him again kept Blane from interfering and he was gratified by the pleased sigh that left Kathleen once his shirt was off and tossed to the floor.

"You're still drunk," Blane said, a reminder to himself more than to her, but she only shrugged, scooting back to make room for him under the covers. She wasn't shy, cuddling right up next to him and laying her head on Blane's chest as he held her.

"I'm not a virgin, you know," she said.

Blane stilled. *Talking About Sex With Kathleen* was up there on his Don't Do list right beneath *Have Sex With Kathleen*, yet he found himself too curious for his own good.

"Tell me about your lovers," he coaxed. Just how experienced was she? Enough to assuage any guilt he might feel if he were to add himself to her list?

"Not lovers, plural," she said. "Lover, singular. Men are always thinking women are as promiscuous as they are." Her disgruntlement made Blane's lips twitch.

"I stand corrected," he said. "Tell me about your lover." Only one? Probably a long-term thing. Maybe she was on the rebound? Blane wouldn't mind being her rebound guy.

"That's really too romantic a title for him," she continued, oblivious to the direction of Blane's thoughts. "I was sixteen. It was homecoming and his father had a big sedan. End of story."

Blane squeezed his eyes shut. This wasn't as bad as if she'd been a virgin, but damn close. "How was it?"

Her answer took longer in coming and was preceded by a long yawn. "Quick. Painful. Embarrassing." She said nothing else and Blane could tell that she'd fallen asleep.

This was bad. This was very bad. At least, that's what Blane kept telling himself even though the side of him that was growing increasingly possessive of her seemed to stretch its claws, like a lion scenting prey, and anticipation oozed through his veins. He could show her what sex could be, what it should be. Blane would worship her body with his until every bad memory of her first time was wiped away.

Blane's last thought before he drifted to sleep was *So much for chivalry and not wanting to hurt Kathleen.* It seemed he was willing to risk the possibility if it meant he could have her.

Dreams of Kat merged with a warm reality when Blane woke in the morning. She lay on her back beside him, the covers tossed aside. The pajamas she wore were twisted and askew, her breasts nearly falling from their silken confines. The shirt had ridden up, exposing her smooth abdomen. Sunshine fell on her hair, making it shine like molten gold against the pillow.

Being a SEAL had conditioned Blane to being fully aware immediately upon waking, so there was no grogginess in his thoughts as he looked at her. Turning on his side, Blane rested a hand on the bare skin of her stomach. Depending on whether she woke with a hangover, a Saturday spent in bed with Kathleen seemed an excellent idea. And if he wasn't overestimating his talents, Blane would lay odds he could persuade her to acquiesce in less than sixty seconds.

His thumb brushed her ribs and she stirred, like a kitty cat purring. Her eyes fluttered open, their depths a clear blue. When she saw Blane, a small smile curved her lips and her eyes slipped closed again.

"I knew this was a bad idea," Blane whispered in her ear. "I can't seem to keep my hands off you." His hand skated down inside her shorts, insinuating itself between her thighs. She was warm and slick and it was almost too easy to slip a finger inside her.

Kathleen gasped, a sound that went straight to Blane's dick, and he covered her mouth with his. She kissed him back eagerly, her tongue sliding against his as Blane stroked in and out. Her arms went around his neck and he added a second finger to the first, her tight passage growing wetter as he pumped his hand.

She tore her mouth away, her breath in quick little pants. Her hips pushed up against his hand and Blane moved his thumb to press against the little bud of engorged flesh hidden between her dripping folds. She jerked in his arms and he did it again.

"God, I want you, Kat," he groaned. She was so responsive. Another few seconds and she'd come with just his fingers fucking her.

A pounding at the door made Blane freeze. His first thought was maybe they could both ignore it and pick up where they left off. His second thought, as the pounding came again, was that perhaps it was James.

That was enough to propel him up and out of the bed. If James was out there, Blane was going to kick his ass, and if it was someone else here to hurt or intimidate Kat . . . Well, he would have a surprise for them. Blane grabbed his gun off the coffee table, racking the slide before he pulled open the door.

The girl from next door stood there, hand raised to knock again. Her gaze swung from Blane to somewhere behind him. Kathleen must have followed from the bedroom.

"Er, sorry to interrupt," she said.

"Not a problem," Kathleen said before introducing her to Blane. Her name was CJ.

"I was just wondering if you saw this." CJ handed Kathleen a newspaper.

Kathleen gasped and Blane leaned over her shoulder. "What is it?"

"It's James," Kathleen said. "He's entered the race for district attorney. It says here the previous candidate pulled out of the race citing the need to spend more time with his family. He's endorsed James in his place."

Blane took the paper from Kathleen, skimming the article. James had given no indication that he was contemplating running for DA. Considering what was going on with TecSol and the Santinis' union, James's move looked highly suspicious to Blane.

CJ was saying something to Kathleen, but Blane didn't pay attention as he read and when he put down the paper, he belatedly realized she'd left. Dropping the paper on the couch, Blane turned back to Kat, just now noticing that she wore his shirt over her pajamas.

It looked much better on her than it did on him.

She was blushing, her cheeks turning rosier by the second. Blane would have liked nothing more than to take her right back to the bedroom, but he had to talk to Kade, figure out what this meant with James.

"I'd better get going," Blane said, tucking the Glock in the back of his jeans. He grabbed his keys, cell and wallet before approaching Kat. She was watching him, her eyes drinking in every move he made.

"I'm going to need that," he said, peeling his shirt slowly from her body. His hands brushed down her arms and he heard her breath catch. Blane pulled on the shirt and did up a couple of buttons, his eyes still locked with hers. Her tongue darted out to wet her lips as she watched him. The tension between them hadn't abated. If anything, the interruption had served to fuel the fire. Sometimes anticipation was foreplay in and of itself.

Blane's gaze fell on the bruise on Kathleen's cheek. Raising his hand, he brushed the damaged skin. James would pay for that. It would be an excellent way for Blane to relieve some of the sexual frustration he was currently feeling.

Pulling her into him, Blane kissed her, wanting to leave with her taste on his tongue. He would have preferred the more intimate flavor between her legs, but that would have to wait. When he pulled back, she was breathless.

"I'll see you tonight," he said. She just nodded, her lips wet and swollen.

And if he didn't leave now, he wouldn't leave at all.

The chill in the air was a stark contrast to the heat in his blood as Blane jogged down the stairs to his car. He was on the phone with Kade before he'd even left the parking lot.

～

Seventeen Years Ago

The first real snag they ran into after Kade came back was when Blane wanted to take Kade to the doctor for a physical before school began.

"I'm not going," Kade declared, plopping down on the couch in the den and flipping on the television.

"You have to go," Blane said. "It's required for school that you have a physical."

"I'm fine," Kade said. "I don't need a physical."

Blane knew better than to attempt to physically force Kade to the doctor. He hadn't touched Kade since that first time outside the orphanage.

Bribery had worked before. Maybe it'd work again.

"I need to hit the electronics store," Blane said. "Want to come with?"

Kade cocked an eyebrow at him. "What are you going there for?"

"I could use a new computer," Blane said. "Or, maybe you could." Blane had caught Kade a few times messing with his computer. He'd said he didn't do anything to it and Blane believed him, but thought he might as well get him one of his own.

"Really?" Kade asked.

Blane nodded. "Sure. We could stop by . . . after we go to the doctor."

Kade heaved a sigh. "Bribing me for my cooperation? That's not what the parenting books say to do."

"Lucky for you I'm your brother, not your dad," Blane tossed back. "Do we have a deal?"

And that was how Blane got Kade to go to the doctor. He'd had the foresight to call ahead and inform them of Kade's . . . unique circumstances, so there were no surprises when they arrived.

The doctor was a nice man who was friendly despite Kade's sullen demeanor. He didn't say a word about the scars on Kade's back as he listened to his lungs. Blane didn't turn away this time, making himself once again view the scars.

Kade's eyes met his, but neither spoke as the doctor finished his exam.

"Clean bill of health," the doctor said with a smile. "I'll send the nurse in with the necessary vaccines, then you should be good to go."

Blane thanked the man as he left, leaving him and Kade alone. Kade quickly threw on his shirt.

"Chicken pox scars," he said curtly.

Blane nodded as if he believed him. "And the one on your chest?"

Kade shrugged and glanced away. "Got in a fight."

Blane let it slide, knowing he'd get nothing further out of him. Mona had been trying to convince Blane it hadn't been his fault, what Kade had gone through. There was nothing he could've done. But it didn't ease the guilt that gnawed constantly at his gut. At times like this, it became a sharp stab.

"I don't want the vaccines," Kade said abruptly. "I got the clean bill of health. Let's go."

"You have to get the vaccines," Blane explained. "They won't let you in school otherwise."

"I don't give a shit. I don't do needles." He headed for the door but Blane blocked his path.

"Kade, I understand if you don't like needles, but you have to get the vaccines. It's not optional."

The nurse came in then and Kade's face went stark white when he saw the needles in the tray she carried. Beads of sweat broke out on his forehead and Blane realized Kade hadn't been exaggerating when he said he disliked needles. He looked terrified and inches from passing out.

"Ah, listen," Blane said to the nurse, who seemed utterly oblivious to Kade's anxiety as she readied her supplies, "can we just take a minute? He doesn't really care for needles."

The nurse looked up in surprise, finally realizing the state Kade was in. "Oh! Of course," she said quickly, stepping back to give Kade some space.

Blane stepped in front of Kade, blocking his view of the needles. "Look at me," he said quietly. Kade didn't move, didn't even blink from where his gaze had been fixed. "Look at me," Blane repeated more urgently.

Kade's eyes finally lifted to meet Blane's. His breathing was fast and shallow, every muscle in his body tight and stiff.

"It's going to be fine," Blane said. "Just keep your eyes on mine, okay? Don't think about it. Just breathe."

Kade's blue gaze didn't waver and he didn't blink as he stared into Blane's eyes. Blane motioned with his hand and the nurse moved quickly and efficiently. When she wiped Kade's arm with the alcohol swab, he flinched. Instinctively, Blane reached for Kade's hand. To his surprise, Kade let him touch him, gripping his hand tightly in return. His palm was cold and clammy with sweat.

It was the first time Kade had shown any fear to Blane, and the first time he'd let Blane touch him, help him. They stood there, eyes and hands locked, while the nurse injected the vaccines. She was quick and Kade didn't so much as twitch again as she gave him the shots, though Blane knew they stung.

Finally, it was over and the nurse left without another word.

Kade blew out a breath, his body sagging, and Blane guided him to a chair, giving him a little push so he sat. Blane crouched down in front of him.

He forgot sometimes that Kade was only ten, just a child. He acted so much older, spoke with the wit and cynicism of a person twice his age. Kade hadn't yet let go of Blane's hand and neither did Blane.

"When my mom died," Kade said, his voice a hoarse rasp, "they sent me to this place with other orphans. But they didn't separate us by age, so the young kids were mixed in with the teenagers. A lot of the older guys were into drugs, turned tricks to score a hit. One night a group of them, three or four, were high. They wanted me to try it and I wouldn't. So they tied me down, stuck a needle in me, and shot me full of meth."

Kade was staring over Blane's shoulder at nothing. Blane listened in horror as his brother described the effects of crystal meth, how he'd nearly died by the time they found him the next morning, how even with just the one dose, he'd had to go through detox. Finally, he stopped speaking. His eyes refocused on Blane.

"And that's why I don't like needles."

It seemed he just then realized he still held Blane's hand and abruptly let go, getting to his feet and moving past where Blane still crouched, unable to move. His mind reeled, trying to cope with what had just happened. What to do? What to say? Not only did Blane feel woefully inadequate to know how best to help Kade, the guilt was crippling.

Kade was waiting, so Blane forced himself to stand. His gaze fell on Kade, who seemed to read what was inside his head.

"I don't want your pity," Kade said, his face darkening. "It is what it is. I just thought you deserved an explanation for my freak-out."

"I don't deserve anything," Blane said baldly. "But I'm glad you told me. I'm sorry I made you get the shots. I won't do that to you again."

Kade nodded stiffly.

They left the doctor's office in silence and Blane drove to the electronics store. He could understand now, the compulsion divorced parents had to try to assuage the hurts of their children with material goods. He would have bought the whole damn store if it could've taken away even an instant of the pain Kade had suffered.

The computer Kade chose wasn't the high-end one Blane would have thought he'd pick, but just your average PC. They took it home and Blane helped him set it up in his room. After firing it up, Kade sat down in front of it, looking utterly captivated. Considering the tests for school had put Kade at two grade levels above where he should be, Blane hoped the computer would grab his interest and challenge him.

Blane had no idea that his "bribe" would forever alter Kade's life.

CHAPTER SEVEN

This is early, even for you," Kade said as he answered the phone, and indeed it sounded like Blane had woken him.

"I've got some bad news," Blane replied, grabbing his sunglasses and sliding them on while he drove. "James is running for DA."

"Just a sec," Kade said.

Blane heard the rustle of cloth and the sound of a feminine voice. Finally, Kade came back. "Okay, sorry about that. What were you saying?"

"Where are you?"

"Leaving. So what's this about James?"

"He's running for district attorney," Blane repeated. "It's in today's paper."

"Well, that'll certainly come in handy if he wins. No one will prosecute TecSol if he's in on it."

"That's what I was thinking."

"Have to be some pretty deep pockets behind him, though, to enter the race this late in the game."

"We need to know where the money's coming from," Blane said.

"I got a lead on that," Kade said, and Blane heard the slam of a car door. "That escort service takes in some pretty serious cash."

"You think they're funneling it to TecSol?"

"They'd have to launder it first, but yeah. We need to find out more about the escort service."

"Then we're in luck," Blane said. "Frank Santini invited me to some party tomorrow night. I think it's for the service. He sent me directions, a code name, password, and get this—you have to wear a mask."

"Sounds like my kind of party," Kade joked.

"You can be my plus one," Blane said.

"All right, but I'm not putting out. Not without dinner first."

"By the way," Blane said, "the thing of Mark's? That the chick has? It's a hard drive."

"Perfect," Kade said. "But how do you know?"

"Because the chick is a bartender at The Drop."

"You know her?"

"You could say that," Blane said evasively. He was pulling up to James's house now. "I tried to get her to give it to me, but she said she was supposed to give it to you tonight. Let's play good cop, bad cop and you get it from her."

"Will do."

"And don't hurt her," Blane forcefully added. "I gotta go. Call me when you know what's on the drive." He ended the call and got out of the car. He'd briefly considered telling Kade the whole story of Kathleen, but had stopped at the last second. Blane couldn't explain his obsession with her to himself; how was he supposed to tell his brother? Who would no doubt laugh himself silly if Blane started waxing poetic about a woman.

Blane rang the doorbell, buttoning his shirt the rest of the way while he waited. He'd opted to leave his gun in the car. No sense testing his self-control.

To his irritation, no one answered the door. Knowing James, he was probably at his country club playing golf this morning. An expensive and very exclusive club, members had to be nominated for entry and the entry fee was upward of twenty grand. If James was looking for some campaign cash, it was an excellent place to start.

Unfortunately for him, Blane had a membership there, too.

Blane went home to quickly shower and change. A short while later, he was pulling up to an elaborate two-story brick building situated on an expansive golf course. A teenager clad in white ran to greet him as Blane opened the car door.

"Good morning, sir," the boy said, eyeing the Jag with excitement in his eyes. "Shall I park your car for you?"

"Sure, kid." Blane said with a small smile as he handed him the keys and a tip before heading inside. "Go easy on her."

As luck would have it, Blane spotted James right away. He was heading out the back with two other men whom Blane recognized as business owners with deep pockets. No doubt James was courting them for their money and the influence they wielded.

"James," Blane said as he casually stepped into their path. "I didn't know you were playing this morning." Blane's practiced smile fell easily into place as he eyed the younger man. "And with Andrew and Jake, too. Good to see you guys."

"Kirk, it's been a while," Jake said with a smile as they shook hands. "How've you been?"

"Great, thanks for asking. Hey, how's Alice doing?" Alice was Jake's wife and they were expecting their second child. Blane memorized information like that for situations just like this.

"She's doing well, only six weeks to go," Jake said, obviously pleased.

"Don't you owe me a Colts game?" Andrew said good-naturedly as Blane turned to shake his hand.

"I keep waiting for them to get back into the Super Bowl," Blane responded, noticing that James was looking increasingly irritated.

"You playing this morning, Kirk?" Jake asked.

Blane shook his head. "Too last-minute to get a buddy to come with me," he lied. "Thought I'd hit the driving range for a while."

"We could use a fourth," Andrew suggested.

"Yeah, get your clubs," Jake added. "We'd love for you to join us."

Blane pretended to hesitate. "You're sure?" he asked. "I don't want to intrude on your game."

"You're not intruding," Andrew scoffed. "James won't mind, right?" He looked expectantly at James, who wasn't nearly as good as Blane at faking a smile.

"Yeah, sure. We'd love you to join us," James said, his voice flat.

"See?" Jake said, slapping James on the back. "Get your clubs, Kirk. We'll meet you out back."

The next four hours were spent with Blane, Jake, and Andrew having a good time while James proceeded to sulk. Blane carefully kept the conversation light, steering it away from anything James brought up. A refreshment cart came by offering them beer. Though they all took one the first time, Blane noticed that James kept getting more each time the cart came by.

"So, Kirk," Andrew said as they pulled up to the tenth hole. "Rumor has it you might be throwing your hat in the ring for governor."

It was a question even though it was framed as a statement.

Blane adjusted his sunglasses and flashed him a shit-eating grin. "If I do, you can bet your ass I'll be calling you for a donation." He grabbed his driver from his bag as Jake and Andrew both laughed.

By the seventeenth hole, James had stopped playing, electing to sit in the cart and drink. Jake and Andrew didn't seem to care, though, as Blane kept them entertained with stories from when he was deployed in Afghanistan.

"You're shitting me," Jake said. "The kid had a grenade?"

"Yep," Blane said. "Couldn't have been more than nine or ten."

"What'd you do?" Andrew asked.

Golf was forgotten. Their attention was fixed on Blane.

"I did the only thing I could," Blane said with a shrug. "I jumped out the window. Luckily, there was a steaming heap of garbage for me to land in. I took some shit for that one, let me tell you. For a while I thought I was going to be permanently nicknamed Dumpster Dive."

Jake and Andrew looked in disbelief at Blane before they burst out laughing.

"Holy shit, I can't believe you jumped out a friggin' window!" Jake said before heading to the tee.

"Gotta say, you've got balls, Kirk," Andrew added, shaking his head.

Back at the clubhouse, Jake and Andrew gave a friendly farewell to Blane and polite nods to James before leaving together. Blane smiled and watched them go, but when he turned to face James, the smile was gone.

"You're an asshole," James spat at him. "You know I wanted those guys to pony up some cash for my campaign."

"Of course I did," Blane said, his disdain obvious. "You're an amateur at this game, James." Moving close, with contempt coating each word, he said, "I doubt they even remember your name."

James face turned mottled red and he swung at Blane, who could have stepped aside, but didn't. The hit landed on his jaw without much force, but now Blane had the perfect opening and he took advantage of it, landing several punishing blows to James's face and ribs before James collapsed, groaning on the floor.

They'd attracted an audience by now, most of whom had seen James throw the first punch. No one intervened. The men gathered took note of what happened and who was on the floor before quietly melting away, their voices a low hum. Blane knew the story would spread quickly of how James had started a fight and gotten his ass handed to him.

Crouching down, Blane grabbed James by the collar and hoisted him upward a few inches.

"That's for what you did to Kathleen," he hissed in James's ear. "Next time I give you a warning, I suggest you heed it. Touch Kathleen again, and I won't go so easy on you." Giving him a rough shove, Blane rose and headed for the door. A man intercepted him on his way out.

"Mr. Kirk," he said, hurrying to keep up with Blane. "I'm Randall Jennings, the manager here, and I must extend our apologies for Mr. Gage's behavior today. I hope you realize that we don't tolerate violence in our club and Mr. Gage's membership will be revoked forthwith."

"I would hope so," Blane said as the valet pulled up with his car. "I came here today for a relaxing round of golf, not a fistfight."

"Yes, sir, I completely agree," Jennings said. "I guarantee this won't happen again."

"See to it," Blane said before climbing into his Jag and driving away.

Looking in the rearview mirror, he saw Jennings hurrying back into the club and a satisfied smile curved Blane's lips.

~

When Blane walked into The Drop that night, he didn't like the scene that met his eyes.

The bartender from the other night was working with Kathleen again, only now he had her cornered and was standing much too close. Blane stood in the shadows, watching. After a moment, Kathleen smiled and reached up, brushing her fingers through the guy's hair.

Jealousy reared its head, its claws digging in deep, and Blane clenched his fists and took a breath. Beating the shit out of that guy wasn't going to earn him any favors with Kathleen.

She turned then and spotted him. A huge smile spread across her face, easing the strangling possessiveness Blane was feeling. He slid onto a barstool just as Kathleen set a Dewar's and water in front of him. Her gaze seemed caught on his hands and Blane wondered what she was thinking, if she was remembering this morning. Seeming to catch herself staring, she glanced up at him, her cheeks rosy.

"Who is he?" Blane asked, nodding toward the guy.

"Scott," she answered. "We work together a lot."

So he'd noticed.

"You're here early," she continued.

"I wanted to see you," Blane said. No sense lying to the girl. Reaching forward, he lightly grasped her chin, turning her cheek toward the light. She'd skillfully applied a thick layer of makeup to cover the bruise, but Blane could still see its shadow under the surface.

Kathleen moved back slightly, enough so that Blane had to drop his hand.

"James won't be bothering you anymore," he said.

"Why? What happened?"

"I spoke with him and was able to convey how . . . displeased . . . I would be if there was a repeat of his behavior yesterday."

Kathleen seemed to take a moment to digest this and Blane really hoped she wasn't going to be all anti-violence and shit, not after what James had done to her. To his relieved surprise, her next question was all about him.

"Won't that make things difficult for you at work?" she asked.

"No. I'm a partner. Since I'm an owner, I actually have more of a say in that business than James does, regardless of his family connection."

"You warned me about him," Kathleen said. "How did you know?"

It didn't take a rocket scientist to know James was a piece of shit. A misogynist at heart, it was a wonder any woman went out with James. Plus, Blane had heard rumors occasionally of James's proclivities in the bedroom, something Kathleen, in her innocence, most likely hadn't heard and perhaps wouldn't know what to make of if she had.

"I've heard things," Blane said evasively.

Someone called her name then and Kathleen had to get back to work. Blane watched her as she talked to customers and filled orders. Too many men eyed her in a way Blane didn't like, not that he could blame them. Her hair was pulled back in a jaunty ponytail that bounced when she walked. The deep blue of her shirt matched her eyes and was snug enough to cling to her curves. Add to that her innate friendliness and kind smile and you had a sweet, desirable package that caught and held Blane's attention.

Blane's phone buzzed and he dug it out of his pocket. The screen showed a text from Kandi: *I need to see you.*

Shit. Kandi was the last thing he wanted to deal with tonight, but he had no choice. He couldn't ignore her, there'd be hell to pay if he did. It was easier to just go by and see what she wanted.

Blane finished his drink just as Kathleen came back over to him.

"Did you want another?" she asked, but Blane shook his head. Pulling out his wallet, he tossed a twenty onto the bar to pay his tab.

"I've got something to do first and then I'll be back," he said. Blane felt a twinge of guilt knowing what was coming when she left the bar tonight, that she was going to be scared. But Kade wouldn't hurt her. Probably. Most likely. No, he wouldn't. Hell, maybe he should rethink this whole thing . . .

Kathleen was staring at him as he stood, her eyes undressing him from his shoulders to his thighs. It didn't take much to imagine what she was thinking and Blane's dick was hard in seconds. He cursed, leaning across the bar to grab that damn ponytail that had been taunting him for the past hour. Blane tugged on it, making Kathleen lean toward him.

"Keep looking at me like that and I won't be held responsible for my actions," he said. She wet her lips and Blane obliged the silent request. The kiss was brief, but intimate, his tongue lightly stroking hers before he pulled away.

"I'll be back," he said.

Kathleen looked a little dazed and Blane hid a smile as he left the bar.

The streets were moderately busy for a Saturday night. The air had the wet, crisp chill of November in it. Blane dug in his pocket for his keys as he approached his car.

A tingling on the back of his neck, a sixth sense he'd learned to never, ever dismiss, gave him a split second's warning.

Blane spun around, throwing himself to the side just as a knife came whizzing by his shoulder. It crashed against the brick wall behind him and Jimmy Quicksilver stepped out of the shadows.

Blane reached for his gun, but froze when he heard the scuff of a shoe behind him and felt the cold press of metal to his back. Glancing over his shoulder, he saw a man he didn't recognize.

"I wouldn't so much as blink, if I were you," the guy rasped.

"I wouldn't dream of it" was Blane's dry reply before glancing back to Jimmy, who'd approached and now stood quite close. "Jimmy," Blane said. "Do your bosses know what you're getting up to? Or is this freelance?"

"I was sent to give you a message," Jimmy said. "You still haven't recovered what that guy said he had."

"And neither have you," Blane said.

Jimmy shrugged. "My ass isn't on the line. Yours is."

Blane didn't reply as Jimmy sauntered closer, playing with another blade he'd pulled.

"You know, I don't think you hanging out in a bar and making out with the hot bartender is really doing us a lotta good, ya know?"

Blane stiffened and his eyes turned cold. Threatening him was one thing. Bringing Kathleen into it was quite another. That protective impulse that jumped into hyper-mode where Kathleen was concerned blazed to life. "You should mind your own business, Jimmy," he hissed, ignoring the guy with a gun to his back as he got in Jimmy's face. "And tell Frank to keep you on a tighter leash lest he find his attack dog's been neutered."

They stared daggers at one another and Blane spoke again. "Now tell your buddy here to point the gun somewhere else before somebody gets hurt," he ordered.

Jimmy looked at him for a long moment, then gave a curt nod to the other guy, who stepped away.

"Frank wants to talk to you," Jimmy said. "Pronto."

"I'll be sure to give him a call," Blane said. Turning his back, he walked to his car and got in. He glanced out the window before he pulled away, but Jimmy and the guy had already melted back into the shadows.

It took twenty minutes to drive to Kandi's home, a grand two-story affair that oozed old money. Her parents lived nearby in an even bigger home, but Kandi had insisted on her own place a few years ago and daddy had obliged.

Blane knocked on the door and waited. After a minute or two, the door opened to reveal Kandi. As he'd expected, she was dressed in expensive lingerie. The champagne silk nightgown had tiny straps over her shoulders with a lace bodice, the deep V neckline revealing a lot of cleavage. The fabric floated around her ankles as she backed up, beckoning him in with a smile.

"Glad you could make it," she said.

"Your text said you needed to see me," Blane said, careful to keep some distance between them once he'd shut the door.

"I do," Kandi said, walking down the hall to her parlor. She went to the sideboard and poured two drinks, offering one to Blane. "I hear you've been slumming lately."

Blane took the drink, frowning at her. "What are you talking about?"

Kandi took a healthy swallow before answering. "I know about the bartender. The redhead that looks like she graduated high school yesterday. A little young, don't you think?" Bitterness laced her voice. "I mean, I know men like women younger and younger now, I just didn't expect you to be like other men."

Blane sighed. "I didn't break up with you because of your age," he said. "You're a beautiful woman." Which was true. Kandi was in her early thirties but looked like a woman in her twenties.

"Then why?" Her plaintive tone made guilt twist in Blane's gut. "It's supposed to be you, us. We've planned it forever. Why are you doing this to me?"

Blane shoved a hand through his hair in frustration. God, this was so fucking hard. It was easier when she was pissed and mad, but when she was like this, it just killed him to hurt her. Setting his glass on a nearby table, he walked over to her, resting his hands lightly on her upper arms. She tipped her head back to look at him and tears made her eyes bright.

"Please, Kandi-cane," he said, calling her the nickname he hadn't used in years, "please listen to me. I love you, you know that. And you love me. But we're not *in* love with each other."

Tears spilled down her cheeks and Blane brushed them away. "We've become a habit, you and me. You don't deserve that and neither do I."

"You're my best friend," Kandi whispered. "I can't lose you."

"Shh, you won't lose me," Blane said, pulling her close and hugging her. "We just need to step back. We tried to make it work, but we're meant to be friends, and that's all."

Blane leaned back so he could see her again. Her face was pale, but she'd stopped crying. "Soon you'll meet someone that makes you feel like you've never felt before," he said. "And you'll fall in love and you'll be glad we called things off. I promise."

Kandi pushed against him and Blane let her go. "You have no idea, do you?" she accused with a bitter laugh. "You are such an arrogant bastard, Blane." She was crying again as she seethed at him.

Well, so much for consoling her. It didn't seem to matter what he said. Short of getting back together, she was going to be pissed no matter what.

"I'll see myself out," he said flatly.

"When you're done screwing little girls, don't think you can come crawling back to me, because I may not be there," Kandi called after him. "You'll have to beg me to take you back."

But Blane was already out the door. It had been pointless to come here, pointless to try to assuage Kandi's wounded pride. He wondered what she'd do now, if she'd give up and move on like he'd told her to do. Kandi wasn't the type to let things go. *Hell hath no fury* and all that.

Glancing at his watch as he drove, Blane realized the bar should be closed by now, which meant Kade should have gotten the drive from Kathleen. He headed back to the bar, parking nearby and making his way through the back alleys.

There they were. Blane drew his gun and pointed it just as Kade spun around to face him. How he'd even heard him, Blane had no idea. Sometimes he thought Kade had a sixth sense, too.

"What are you doing here, Kade?" he called.

"Blane! I'm here," Kathleen yelled back.

Kade grabbed her arm and they said something Blane couldn't hear, but in a moment, Kathleen was walking toward him. When she was close enough, Blane grabbed her around the waist.

"What are you doing out here with him?" he asked. Hopefully, she'd given the hard drive to Kade.

"I thought it was you," she said. "He . . . surprised me."

Blane glanced down, realizing she was wearing Kade's shirt. What the hell? "What happened?" he asked.

"I got shot. Sort of. Just a graze, I guess."

Fury filled Blane. Couldn't Kade have just done what Blane said one fucking time? "You shot her?" he bit out. Kade didn't answer, which just pissed Blane off more.

"No, no!" Kathleen said, tugging on Blane's shirt. "Someone else was following us. Kade didn't shoot me. He helped me."

Blane stared at Kade. He'd better pray Kat was telling the truth or Blane was going to kick his ass.

"Please, let's just go," Kathleen begged, pulling on his arm.

Acquiescing, Blane backed up until they rounded the corner before lowering his gun. He led Kathleen to his car and she relaxed into the seat with a sigh.

"Tell me what happened," Blane said.

"Kade was waiting out back for me," she said. "I wouldn't have gone except I thought it was you. We were supposed to meet in Monument

Circle. I guess he didn't think I'd show. Anyway, he had a gun so I didn't really have much choice but to give him the drive."

"And that's when you got shot?"

"Someone started shooting at us," Kathleen said. "We ran and he shot back, but one of the bullets hit me."

"Do you need to go to the hospital?" Blane asked.

"No, it's not that bad."

It could only have been Jimmy shooting at them. But why? A message to Blane? Or did Jimmy know Kathleen had found something? Blane had mistakenly assumed Jimmy would leave once he'd delivered the message. That assumption had nearly cost Kathleen her life. Was Jimmy waiting for her at her apartment, ready to ambush her? If so, he'd be waiting a long time.

It wasn't until they were pulling up to Blane's house that Kathleen spoke again.

"Why are we here?" she asked. "You should have taken me back to my apartment."

"I'll feel better with you here," Blane replied. No need to scare her by telling her his suspicions about Jimmy. She didn't argue as they went inside. "Can you make it to your room by yourself?" he asked. "I have a phone call to make."

Kat nodded and headed upstairs while Blane went to the den. A few moments later he was on the phone with Frank.

"Kirk, glad you could call," Frank said.

"Well, Jimmy made it quite clear that you expected to hear from me." Blane cut to the chase. "I thought you were going to let me handle this," he said. "Instead, you've got Dennon and Jimmy both on the hunt for Mark's evidence."

"I saw no reason not to put all my best people on it," Frank replied.

"If more people die, it'll only draw suspicion," Blane said. "You need to call off Jimmy."

"The election is in a few days, Kirk. We can't afford anything to go wrong at this point."

"I understand that. Just trust me."

Frank was silent for a moment. Finally, he said, "All right. You've got twenty-four hours. Then we'll take matters in our own hands." He hung up.

Shit. Blane leaned back in his chair with a sigh. He could really use a cigarette about now. Hopefully, Kade could get the information off the drive and it'd be enough to not only thwart Frank's and TecSol's plans, but also put them behind bars. And Kathleen should be safe. For now.

Speaking of which . . .

Blane got up and took the stairs two at a time, anxious to check on her. After grabbing some ointment and bandages, he went to her room. When a knock at her door produced nothing, he stepped inside.

The bathroom door was ajar a few inches and he slowly pushed it open. Kathleen appeared to be in the bathtub.

His day was definitely looking up.

Crossing to the sink, Blane leaned against it, openly taking in the view the spot afforded. Thank God he didn't have bubble bath. The water was clear, giving him an unobstructed look at Kat's naked body. She appeared to have fallen asleep, her head resting on the back of the tub.

The water lapped lightly at her breasts like a lover's caress, her chest rising and falling with each breath. Her knees were pressed together and bent, modestly hiding the most feminine part of her.

The curve of her neck held his gaze, the delicate pulse that beat just under her skin, and Blane abruptly realized there was nothing he wouldn't do to protect this woman. So trusting of him, perhaps naively so. Her innocence and purity were something to be cherished, it was so rare.

Kat deserved to be made love to, deserved to experience what sex could really be. And Blane would be more than willing to show her.

Just then she woke with a start, jerking upright when she saw him. Blane appreciated the view until she slid back down in the water, a rosy flush creeping into her face and neck.

Blane grabbed a nearby towel. "I want to see your injury," he said, *among other things*, "and how your cuts are healing."

Kat didn't argue. She just pulled the plug and stood, allowing Blane to wrap the towel around her. His gaze dropped to the curves of her breasts above the fabric.

"I wonder how far down the blush goes," he teased, which made her skin turn even redder. He laughed, her modesty charming, and lifted her in his arms. Carrying her to the bed, he rested her on it and sat beside her.

"Let's take a look," he said, but she grabbed his hands, stopping him from removing the towel. "Shy tonight, Kat? I don't recall you being shy last night."

At the reminder, she groaned and covered her face. "A gentleman doesn't remind a lady of her embarrassing behavior," she mumbled behind her fingers.

"Ah yes," Blane said, sliding his hands up her thighs and under the towel, "but I'm not a gentleman, am I?"

Removing the towel was very much akin to unwrapping a present, though she wasn't exactly something Santa would bring. The perfection of her skin was marred by a livid scrape on her side. Blane frowned and moved her arm above her head, turning her slightly, so he could get a better look.

Lips thinning, he grabbed the ointment he'd brought and rubbed some onto her skin as gently as he could. Even so, a breath hissed between her teeth. Carefully, Blane placed a bandage over the wound.

It was barely the width of his hand, the expanse of skin between the wound at her side and the area over her heart. None of this would have happened if he hadn't led Jimmy right to her. Then he'd left her, alone and unprotected, save for Kade.

"What is it?" Kat whispered. "What's wrong?"

Blane's gaze lifted to hers and he made himself tell her the bald truth that she probably hadn't even thought about yet.

"Four inches," he said. "The difference between life and death for you tonight was four inches."

She said nothing to this, the rosy tint of her cheeks fading somewhat.

Blane tore his thoughts away from the morbid path they were traveling. This hadn't been what he'd intended tonight. If he begged her forgiveness, she wouldn't understand. She'd want to know why he was guilty, and he couldn't tell her that.

What he could do was take care of her, in every sense of the phrase.

"May I see how the cuts are doing?" he asked, sliding his hand down to her hip.

Her blue eyes widened and Blane could practically feel her body tense under his hands.

She shook her head. "They're fine," she squeaked.

Nerves. Kat wasn't playing the shy virgin, as so many women were wont to do, but actually was one, in any practical sense. A quickie in the back of a car was a shitty way to introduce a woman to the art of lovemaking. No wonder she was tense. She'd never been seduced, much less by someone who knew how.

Blane reached up to her hair, grasping the band holding the ponytail that had teased him earlier tonight and sliding it down until her hair was free. His fingers slowly combed through the silken strands until the heavy mass rested over the curve of her shoulder, just brushing the side of her breast.

Kat's gaze was rapt on his, her pupils dilating and her breath coming faster. Blane moved slowly, deliberately, letting her absorb his movements. This was a seduction, not an ambush, and the ending was a foregone conclusion. She just needed to trust him.

Sliding his hand under her knee, he bent her leg, exposing the soft ivory skin of her inner thigh. He moved so he was situated between her thighs, then did the same thing with her other leg. It wasn't until he'd positioned her the way he wanted her that he dropped his gaze.

The cuts from yesterday were better and Blane lightly traced them with his fingers. For what he had planned, they were healed enough to not cause Kat pain.

Her spread thighs were a temptation Blane couldn't resist, lust making his heart pound as anticipation heightened his senses. His dick was stiff with desire, but he knew it wasn't time yet. She wasn't ready, instead eyeing him with trepidation.

Blane bent and moved farther down the bed before pressing a kiss on the inside of her knee. His lips brushed the satin skin of her inner thigh, his tongue tracing the length of a long cut. Her legs trembled under his hands and he tried to soothe her. He wanted to pleasure her, not scare her. And nothing made a woman quite as warm and willing as an orgasm.

"I want to kiss you, Kat," Blane said. It wasn't really a request, more of a warning, because he was quite sure this hadn't been one of the activities she'd experienced in the back of that sedan.

The moment Blane moved his head between her legs, she balked, letting out a squeak and trying to scoot away.

As if it would be that easy for her to escape him at this point.

Her attempt to get away set fire to his blood. Easily holding her in place, Blane nuzzled the triangle between her thighs, inhaling the sweet scent of her arousal. She stilled and Blane took that as consent, his hands moving to part her folds, eager to taste her, a flavor no one but he would know.

She was fire under his tongue, a sweet crackling of electricity that shot straight to his groin. Blane's hips reflexively pressed against the bed as he lapped at her. He pushed her thighs farther apart, exposing more of her to his eyes and mouth. Kat was whimpering now, completely at his mercy. Her warm, wet folds were silk against his tongue, the engorged tissue of her clit begging for him to take it in his mouth.

He teased the bit of flesh, flicking it again and again before dipping his tongue inside her, bringing Kat to the edge and keeping her there.

A litany of sounds fell from her lips mixed with his name, spoken in broken whimpers and gasps. Lust rode him hard, but Blane held tight to his control. His cock begged to be where his tongue was. Taking her clit in his mouth, he sucked hard and she shattered, crying out his name as she came.

Blane crawled up Kat's body, stopping along the way when he couldn't pass up the chance to kiss a spot, or two, or three. He nuzzled her neck, licking the pulse pounding under her jaw.

"You're beautiful," he whispered against her lips before kissing her, letting her taste herself on his tongue. Her hands tangled in his hair, her leg curling around the back of his thigh.

Reluctantly, Blane pulled away and she made a sound of protest. Scooping her in his arms, Blane carried her to the open door.

"What are you doing?" she asked, her voice a throaty purr. She sucked at his neck and Blane smiled to himself. She was warm and willing, her nerves forgotten.

"Taking you to bed," he said, carrying her down the hall.

"We were just in bed." The warm brush of her lips against his skin sent a shiver through him.

"Not my bed."

Blane set her down in the center of his bed, aware in the back of his mind that this was the first woman he'd allowed in this position. He couldn't explain the sudden need to bring her in here, nor did he want to dwell on it.

He stood, but didn't get far, Kat reaching for his shirt, tugging him back toward her so she could undo the buttons. Her hair lay in waves down her back and Blane buried his fingers in the silken mass as his mouth found hers again, their tongues tangling in a heated kiss. She managed to push his shirt down and off his arms, then her nimble fingers moved to his belt.

Blane pushed her onto her back, climbing on top of her, his hips cradled between her thighs. She persisted at his belt until Blane brushed aside her hands so he could pay homage to her amazing breasts. The little noises she made started again as Blane licked and sucked. He quite literally could spend hours just doing this.

Reaching down between her legs, he pushed two fingers inside, testing her readiness. Kat cried out and Blane went still.

"Am I hurting you?" he asked.

She shook her head, gasping, "More."

Blane was only too happy to oblige, her slick heat coating his fingers as he stroked her, slow but relentless, until she was begging for him.

Turning away, Blane quickly shed his remaining clothes and put on a condom before returning to Kat.

"Tell me if anything hurts you," he said, conscious of the need to be gentle. Kat nodded, the trust in her eyes as she gazed at him further prodding his protective instincts.

Pushing inside her was a master's class in self-control. Blane gritted his teeth to keep from thrusting into her, going slow to allow her body time to accommodate him.

"God, Kat," he said on a rough exhale, "you feel incredible. So tight." The words were a desperately inadequate description, but all he could come up with at the moment. She seemed to understand his heartfelt appreciation, though, wrapping her legs around his waist and arching her hips, pulling him the rest of the way in. Blane groaned at the sensation, his eyes slamming shut.

"Make love to me," she whispered against his lips, and it was like dangling prey in the path of a hunter. Blane kissed her, his tongue mimicking his cock, thrusting inside the welcome heat of her body. His control now gone, Blane distantly hoped he wasn't hurting her, but judging by the way she was kissing him back and the scratch of her nails on his back, he wasn't.

Tearing her mouth from his, she gasped for air, panting and moaning as Blane pounded into her. He couldn't think, couldn't have moved out of her arms if a gun had been pointed at his back. She fit him perfectly, and when she came again, crying out his name, Blane couldn't withstand the intimate grip of her body tugging on his cock. His orgasm crashed over him and he kissed her, wanting to feel her tongue against his as her passage milked him until he was spent.

Blane took a moment to catch his breath, but realized he was probably crushing her and rolled away. As he went to dispose of the condom, he noticed pale streaks of blood on his hip. Shit. He must've been wrong about those cuts on her thighs.

A strange sensation went through him. Maybe it was too many years spent as a SEAL in the brutal day-to-day grind of war. Blood was life and death. He'd had the blood of his friends and his enemies on his hands, literally and figuratively. Blood was sacred, the shedding of it not to be taken lightly. The mark of Kathleen's blood on him, blood she'd shed while giving herself to him, spoke to the warrior still inside Blane and something shifted. He didn't question it. It just was.

Turning back to her, Blane gathered her in his arms, lightly kissing her brow, her cheeks, her lips. Brushing Kat's hair back from her face, Blane searched her eyes. Leaning slowly down, he kissed her as tenderly as he knew how. When he rose again to look at her, he smiled a bit, rewarded with a shy smile in return. Words seemed unnecessary.

It felt like the most natural thing in the world to tuck her against him, her bottom cradled by his hips, and drape his arm in the curve of her waist. In a few moments, she was fast asleep.

Blane lay next to her for a while, unable to sleep. The problem of Kathleen and what to do with her, how to keep her safe, weighed on his mind, as did the foreign emotions she'd stirred inside him.

After a while, he heard his phone buzzing. Still in the pocket of his pants, its vibration was muffled by the fabric.

Carefully easing back from Kat so as not to wake her, he got up. Digging his phone out, he saw it was Kade texting him: *Need to talk. I'm downstairs.*

Blane pulled on his pants and didn't bother with a shirt. Kat lay in his bed, still sound asleep. Going to her room, he got her purse and placed it on the bureau in his room. She wouldn't be needing a separate place to sleep any longer. Silently closing the door behind him, he padded downstairs to the den, pushing his fingers through his hair to arrange it properly. Just-fucked hair on a woman was sexy. On a man, it was just tacky.

Kade was sitting on the leather sofa, drink in hand and staring into the burning embers of the fireplace. He glanced up as Blane entered.

"Sorry to disturb, brother," he said, not sounding overly sorry. "Thought you'd like an update."

Blane poured himself a drink and took the seat opposite Kade. A small hard drive sat on the table.

"It couldn't wait 'til morning?" he asked.

"If it could, do you think I'd be over here?" Kade said. "And what's with the girl? She said you were her *boyfriend*." Kade's contempt was clear, the look he shot Blane one of sardonic amusement. "Really? Are you going to give her your letter jacket to wear?"

A thread of pleasure twined through Blane. Kat had called him her boyfriend?

"She works for the firm and bartends," Blane said. "I didn't realize she was the same one you were talking about the other day. I've been trying to protect her, keep her out of it. But her neighbor—friend—was Mark's girlfriend."

"The one Jimmy killed?"

Blane nodded. "I was hoping she'd tell me what she knew, give me the drive, but then you found her, so . . . " Blane shrugged, taking a healthy swallow of the scotch.

Kade frowned, glancing away from Blane to the fireplace as he took another drink.

"I'm pretty sure I told you not to come here," Blane continued. "It's too dangerous if you're seen. No one can know we're working together." Regardless of how invincible Kade seemed to think himself, worry gnawed constantly at Blane that his little brother would get hurt.

"You have so little faith in me that you'd think I'd let someone see me?" Kade scoffed. "Please."

Blane sighed, gulping the rest of his scotch in one swallow. "Did you find it?" he asked.

"No," Kade said, still staring into the dancing flames. "It wasn't on there. And I think your pretty little girlfriend is hiding something from you."

"What? Why?"

Kade finally looked at him. "Because all that was on that drive was gay porn. More than I ever wanted or needed to see."

"Are you fucking kidding me?" Blane said. It couldn't have been for nothing, the danger Kat was in, the danger he and Kade still faced.

"Would I kid about this?" Kade shot back. "Maybe you don't know her as well as you think. And why the hell didn't you tell me you were involved with her? I could have shot you in that alley."

"Because it wasn't any of your business," Blane said automatically. He was thinking of what could have happened to that code, the only evidence Mark had, the thing he'd died for. "She doesn't even own a computer, Kade, and I doubt she'd know what to do with it if she did. You probably just missed something."

"I didn't miss anything," Kade said. "And we need that code or we're screwed."

"I'm well aware of that," Blane said. "Has Frank contacted you about it yet?" He left out the part where Frank had threatened him and given him only a twenty-four-hour window. Kade didn't need to know. It was enough to keep himself alive, he didn't need to be worrying about Blane.

"Yes. He said he's getting impatient. There's too much riding on this election. You and I both know that."

They were both silent, thinking.

"So let's go see your girlfriend," Kade said, "and make her tell us what she knows. You know where she lives, right?"

"She's not there," Blane said, wishing he'd poured a bigger shot of scotch in his glass.

"Then where is she?"

Blane shifted his gaze to meet Kade's. "In my bed."

Kade looked surprised for a moment, then barked a laugh devoid of humor. "I swear, you're more ruthless than I am sometimes, Blane," he said, shaking his head. "I guess those scratches on your shoulders must be from her. I trust now she'll tell you anything you want to know?"

Before Blane could answer, a crash sounded outside the room. Kade was up and moving to the door, gun in hand, before Blane. He threw open the door, staring into the hallway beyond. Blane stepped up behind him in time to see Kathleen turn tail and run.

Shit.

Kade took off after her, as did Blane, but she was quick, beating them to the back door and flinging herself outside.

"Kat! Wait!" Blane called, but she ignored him. He couldn't let her escape. He didn't know what she'd heard or what she believed, but she was safer here than on her own, if she didn't break an ankle first.

They were gaining on her, thank God. Where was she going anyway? She didn't have her purse or car keys.

Kathleen turned suddenly, and Blane abruptly realized she had a gun in her hand, and it was pointed right at them.

Blane shoved Kade to the ground just as shots rang out, the bullets flying over their heads, then Kat turned and ran. Blane scrambled to his feet, sprinting after her, only to see a car idling at the street. Kade was right behind him and they were nearly on her when she dove into the car and it took off. Kade raised his gun and Blane shoved his arm down.

"Don't shoot her!" he barked.

Standing in the street, his chest heaving, Blane stared after the car as it disappeared into the night, taking Kat away from him.

≈

Seventeen Years Ago

Blane vowed Christmas would be different now that Kade was here. He went all out, taking Kade with him to cut down a tree before decorating it. They shopped for new decorations since the ones Blane had weren't meant for a kid to handle. Blane practically bought out the toy store, getting anything he thought Kade might like in the slightest. Electronics and games, sporting equipment and a BB gun were all gaily wrapped and stuffed under the tree until it looked as though there were ten kids in the house instead of just one.

But Kade seemed only halfheartedly interested no matter what Blane did. He got that Kade probably hadn't had anything close to a normal Christmas in years, but damned if he knew what else he could do. Mona made cookies, dragging Kade into the kitchen to help her despite his protests. He'd emerge, hours later, with flour on his shirt and a small smile on his face.

On Christmas morning, it took hours for Kade to open all the presents. When he was finished, he was dumbfounded at the pile of new belongings in front of him.

"Why'd you get all this?" Kade asked, bewildered. He couldn't imagine how much it had all cost. A small fortune, he guessed.

"Because I wanted to," Blane said with a shrug. He reached for something electronic and started prying it out of the box. "This looks cool, right?"

Kade just looked at him. Blane had already given Kade a place to live. He didn't need to buy him shit. But he looked as happy as could be, setting aside the toy he'd opened and working on another, a remote-controlled helicopter.

"If you use this inside, make sure Mona isn't around," Blane said, using his switchblade to open the box. "She'll kick your ass."

Kade glanced at the boxes Blane had opened that contained his gifts. Mona had taken Kade shopping, buying some things for Blane. A new wallet, a couple of ties, a new baseball glove. All of it seemed desperately inadequate to show Blane how he felt, how glad he was to be here, despite his terror that Blane would one day change his mind.

Kade was watching Blane, who pretended he didn't notice. Finally, he looked away, picking up the remote for the helicopter and putting the batteries inside it.

Blane dug in his pocket for the small box he'd stuffed there. He handed it to Kade, who looked questioningly at him.

"I got this for you, too," he said.

He fidgeted as Kade opened it, anxious that it was dumb, that Kade was too young to understand. The fireplace crackled, filling the silence as Kade lifted the lid on the small box and gazed inside. He didn't speak.

"It's a key," Blane said.

Kade's eyes lifted to his. "I see that."

"I mean, it's a key for here. To the house. I realized you didn't have one, and . . . " Blane hesitated. "I just wanted you to know that you're always welcome here, no matter what."

Kade's expression didn't change, not that Blane was surprised by that. Emotions weren't something Kade willingly expressed. But his eyes, the eyes that were older than his years, looked at Blane and saw what he was really saying with the gift.

"Thanks," Kade said, his voice a little rougher than usual.

"Merry Christmas," Blane replied. He would have liked to give Kade a hug, but he refrained. After the disastrous doctor visit, he hadn't tried to touch Kade again. Now Kade sat on the couch opposite Blane in his pajamas. He looked good, healthy. Mona's cooking had put meat on his bones and Blane had taken him to get his hair cut. He was a good-looking kid.

They sat in comfortable silence together, examining their loot, the lit tree in the corner festive while the fire danced in its grate. It was the happiest Blane could remember being in a long, long time.

"It wasn't always bad, you know," Kade said out of the blue.

Blane glanced over at him, a question hovering on his lips, but something made him keep quiet.

"There was this one family," Kade continued. "A guy and his wife. They were young, but couldn't have kids. They both thought they should do something for older orphans, so they didn't go for the usual baby or toddler. I caught their eye. No clue why. And they took me home with them. I was eight, maybe, I guess. They were nice and sweet and I couldn't believe my luck."

He stopped talking then. Blane both wanted and didn't want to know what had happened. Since Kade hadn't stayed, there was obviously not a good ending to the story and he didn't know if he could take hearing another tale of the abuse and neglect his brother had endured. The thought shamed him. Kade had gone through it, not him. The least Blane could do was listen.

"What happened?" he forced himself to ask.

Kade looked over and shrugged. "The guy lost his job before the adoption went through. The state then declared they were unfit because he was unemployed and took me back. I didn't see them again after that."

Again, his tone and expression were so bland that he could be discussing the weather, whereas Blane had to swallow, twice, to keep his voice even.

"I'm sorry to hear that," Blane said.

"Shit happens," Kade replied. "But it was nice while I was with them. They did the whole Christmas thing—Santa Claus, filled the stockings, the works. I just wanted you to know." His gaze found Blane's and held it. "It wasn't all bad. Some was okay. Some was good."

Blane had to clear his throat and looked back at the fireplace, blinking rapidly. Kade was too perceptive. He knew Blane was blaming himself, buying all these things to try and make up for how very much he'd failed Kade. Now he was trying to comfort Blane, make him feel better with this story. The irony wasn't lost on him.

"Thanks for telling me," Blane said. "I'm sorry—"

"Don't apologize," Kade interrupted. "This is new for you. I get it. But listen to me when I say this."

Blane glanced over.

"Man, it's not your fault."

And Blane realized this was Kade's gift to him. A ten-year-old boy was providing absolution and forgiveness for things that never should have happened to him. He didn't know what to say, how to react to this child, his brother. He just knew he'd do anything to protect Kade, the fierceness of his love a revelation.

Blane forced a smile. "You're a good man," he said. "A better one than me, that's for damn sure."

Kade grinned. "Does that mean I can drink with you now?"

Blane laughed. "No. But we can go sneak some of those cookies Mona has set aside. I won't tell if you won't."

It was late that night and Kade couldn't sleep. The scene earlier today with Blane still weighed on his mind. He hoped Blane had understood why he'd told him that story. It wasn't to make him feel worse. Kade just couldn't stand to see the guilt in Blane's eyes when he looked at him. Yeah, some bad shit had happened to him, but things were looking up now, thanks to Blane.

Restless, Kade got out of bed and headed downstairs. Another couple of cookies sounded good. Mona might have a fit, but puppy-dog eyes and a smile went a long way toward forgiveness with her.

Kade was munching on the cookies when he stepped into the library. To his surprise, Blane was still up. He opened his mouth to speak, but a second glance had him keeping his silence.

Blane was sitting on the couch looking at something he held. He didn't seem to be aware as Kade eased closer.

Blane sniffed and swiped a hand across his face, then seemed to notice Kade for the first time.

"Hey," he said. "Is everything all right? Did you need something?"

"What's that?" Kade asked, motioning to the framed photo Blane was holding.

Blane glanced down. "It's my mother," he said, handing the picture to Kade.

"Did she die?"

"Yeah."

"When?"

"A few months ago," Blane said, sniffing again and clearing his throat. He got up and went to the sideboard, pouring himself a drink.

Kade studied the photograph. The woman was pretty. Long blonde hair, blinding smile. She looked delicate somehow, and not just because she was petite.

"She was pretty," Kade said.

"That she was," Blane sighed, taking the frame from him and setting it gently on the table.

It struck Kade then that he and Blane had something in common. They'd both lost their mothers. He remembered with vivid clarity the morning he'd woken to find his mother cold in her bed, her eyes open and staring at the ceiling. He'd sat beside her for hours. Until he'd been forced to answer the phone, its ringing incessant as his mother's boss called asking why she wasn't at work.

The pain, old but still remembered, struck him now and sympathy made him reach out and rest his hand on Blane's shoulder. Blane was a big guy and Kade's hand looked awfully inadequate, but he left it there despite the fear of rejection that clawed at his stomach. What if Blane laughed at him? Pushed him away?

Blane looked up in surprise when he felt Kade's touch. Kade hadn't ever touched Blane of his own volition, had only allowed the one touch in the doctor's office, when he'd been so terrified he'd barely known what was happening.

But Kade had lost a mother, too. The sadness in his eyes as he looked at Blane spoke of a grief they both shared.

Blane managed a small smile, reaching up to squeeze Kade's hand resting on his shoulder.

"You have me," Kade said simply.

The words, so honestly given, made Blane's chest constrict.

"No," he corrected him. "We have each other."

CHAPTER EIGHT

Now what?" Kade said.

"She'll probably go to her apartment. She has nowhere else to go. We can pick her up there," Blane replied. Though how easy that was going to be, he didn't know. Kat had looked terrified, running as if her life depended on it. This wasn't exactly how Blane had planned on the rest of the night going.

He went upstairs and finished dressing, meeting Kade back in the den. "I'll drive," he said. A few minutes later, they were on their way to Kathleen's apartment.

"So who is this girl and why are we treating her with kid gloves?" Kade asked.

"She got pulled into this by accident," Blane answered. "She doesn't deserve to be hurt or killed because she was in the wrong place at the wrong time."

Kade sighed. "You and your weakness for women. Some girl bats her baby-blues and suddenly you'll bend over backward for her. You don't know anything about this girl. She could be a plant, for all you know."

"She's not a plant, for chrissake," Blane retorted, stung.

"How do you know?"

"Because I know."

Kade snorted. "So if she was supposed to be asleep in your bed, awash in post-orgasmic bliss, why was she hiding in the hall spying on you and how'd she have someone outside waiting for her?"

Blane didn't have an answer for either of those questions. His lips thinned and they didn't speak again until they reached Kat's apartment.

"That looks like the car in the street," Blane said, nodding toward a black four-door compact. "I bet it belongs to her neighbor."

"I thought you said her neighbor was dead?"

"New neighbor."

"And they're BFFs already?" Kade asked. "No, that's not suspicious at all."

Blane shot him a look, but Kade was already getting out of the car. Doubt crept in. Had Blane been taken in by Kathleen? Had it all been a setup? A damsel in distress perfectly placed for him to rescue and protect? The very thought produced a sick feeling in his stomach.

No. It couldn't be. Blane made his living off reading people and he hadn't read Kat wrong. She was not a plant. She was the real deal. She had to be.

"I think we found our getaway car," Kade said, his palms flat on the hood. "Engine's still warm."

Blane took the stairs two at a time, pulling his gun from its holster before unlocking Kathleen's door. Kade covered his six, weapon in hand as well. While Blane didn't believe that Kat was involved in any of this, beyond the fact of being dragged in, he also knew she was scared. And people did crazy things when they were scared.

But she wasn't there.

Standing in the living room, Blane holstered his gun, thinking. Where could she have gone?

"I can take a crack at the neighbor," Kade said.

"No, I'll go," Blane replied. The last thing he needed was Kade hurting the girl. "You go wait in the car." He watched as Kade retreated down the stairs.

CJ had said she worked nights, so Blane knew she was up before he knocked. Sure enough, it only took her a moment to answer the door. Unfortunately, she also had a gun pointed at him.

Blane slowly raised his hands, palms out. "I'm not here to hurt you, CJ," he said, keeping his voice calm and level.

"Then why are you here?" she asked.

"I know you took Kathleen," he said. "Is she here?"

"Why should I tell you?"

Suddenly, Kade came into Blane's field of vision behind her and pressed the barrel of his gun to the back of her head. "Because if you don't, I'm going to decorate your apartment with skull fragments. Coincidentally, they'll be yours."

CJ froze, glaring at Blane as Kade took the gun from her hand. "I thought you weren't here to hurt me," she mocked.

"I told you to wait in the car," Blane snapped at Kade, lowering his arms.

"I vaguely remember you saying that," Kade replied with a shrug. "I assumed you were talking to somebody else."

Blane huffed in irritation. "Is anyone else in the apartment?" he asked Kade.

"Nope."

"Where is she?" Blane directed his question back to CJ.

"You think I'm going to tell you anything with a gun pointed at my head?" she snapped.

"You're lucky I didn't shoot first and ask questions later," Kade hissed. "I don't like it when people point guns at him. It pisses me off."

"Who's this? Your bodyguard?" she asked Blane. "This is breaking and entering, you know."

"So call the cops," Kade said with a shrug. "And I'm sure you have a permit for that gun, right?"

CJ didn't answer that, her jaw clenched tightly closed.

"Listen," Blane said. "We're not going to hurt you." He shot a look at Kade, who reluctantly lowered his weapon. "And we're not going to hurt Kathleen. But we need to find her. Where is she?"

CJ hesitated, then said, "I dropped her off at a friend's house. She said you guys would come for her, so she couldn't come back here."

"What friend?" Kade asked.

She glared at him. "I don't know. I stayed in the car."

"What's the address?" Blane asked.

"I don't remember," CJ said.

"I can help you remember," Kade threatened, taking a step forward.

"Kade," Blane barked, giving him a minute shake of his head. "Don't stonewall us, CJ," he warned. "Kathleen's in danger. I want to help her."

CJ seemed to weigh the truth of his words, then finally muttered an address. Blane quickly memorized it.

"Thank you," he said sincerely. He jerked his chin at Kade, who followed him down the stairs.

The friend's apartment was in a nicer complex and it looked like everyone was asleep. No lights burned in the windows.

"I can go check, make sure she's there," Kade offered.

Blane thought about it. He really needed to know she was okay. He didn't wonder at why he needed to know so much, he just did.

"Can you do it without getting caught?" Blane asked.

"Please." Kade rolled his eyes. "If she's there, you want me to grab her?"

Blane shook his head. Kat had been through enough tonight. Now that he knew where she was, he'd come back later.

"No. Leave her be."

Kade got out of the car and disappeared into the darkness. Blane waited, nerves on edge. Finally, after what felt like forever, Kade returned.

"She's there and she's fine," Kade said, sliding into the passenger seat and shutting the door.

Relief filled Blane. "You saw her?"

"Sleeping like a baby."

"Who's the friend? Guy or girl?" Maybe the bartender? Blane knew he hadn't kept the jealousy out of his voice, but he didn't care.

Kade sighed, rolling his eyes at Blane as he answered. "Girl. And I don't know who she is, but I'll find out."

∼

Blane's cell phone rang and he answered it blindly, his eyes on the file in his hand.

"Kirk."

"So the friend is Gracelyn Howard, goes by Gracie," Kade said.

Blane dropped the file onto the surface of his desk, giving his full attention to Kade.

"She's enrolled in her second year at IU's School of Medicine," Kade continued. "Moved to Indy three years ago from Fort Wayne. Worked as a waitress for six months, then quit. However, she didn't take another job, at least not one that's on the books. She moved out of an apartment she shared with two other girls and into a more expensive place with no obvious source of income. She's lived there ever since."

"Maybe her parents?" Blane speculated.

"Dad works the assembly line for GM. Mom's a nurse. Their income level isn't such that they could afford it, nor could they afford her med school tuition. Gracie also has no outstanding student loans. The one she had for her undergrad degree was paid off, in full, nine months ago."

Blane rubbed his eyes with a sigh. "You thinking what I'm thinking?" he asked.

"That you should listen to your little brother more?" Kade said dryly. "She works for the escort service, and if your girlfriend is staying with her, chances are she does, too. She was a trap, Blane."

Everything inside Blane rebelled at the thought. "I just can't believe that," he said.

"What else is it going to take for you?" Kade retorted. "A tattoo on her ass?"

"You don't know her," Blane said.

"Neither do you," Kade shot back.

"No one could be that good an actress."

Kade heaved a sigh. "Fine. Have it your way. But I'll bet she's going to be at that party tonight."

"She won't be."

"Fifty bucks."

"Done."

" . . . *and* you have to admit I'm a better shot than you," Kade continued.

"That's bullshit," Blane said. "I taught you, remember?"

"And the student has surpassed the teacher . . . "

"In your dreams," Blane scoffed.

"We could put an end to this if you'd let me go get her," Kade reminded him.

"Forget it. It'd take too long and at this point, she'd just be collateral damage we don't need."

"Well, since we don't have the code from the drive, and you're unwilling to let me rattle the girl, I'm going to have to do it the hard way and break into TecSol's network," Kade said.

"Should be a piece of cake, right?" Blane taunted him. "Or are you all talk?"

"Don't try that reverse psychology shit on me, brother," Kade said. "I'll hack their network. Just give me time."

"We have precious little of that," Blane reminded him.

"Don't I know it."

"Be here tonight by nine."

"It's a date."

Blane ended the call and pushed the phone into his pocket. There was no possibility that Kat would be at that party tonight. She didn't work as an escort. If she had, it would have shown. No one could fake that kind of naive innocence.

Not unless that someone was very, very good.

Blane cursed, fighting back the urge to fling something at the wall. It didn't matter. The seed of doubt had been planted. Kade had a point. Why had she been spying on them last night? How had CJ known to come for her? Kathleen would've had to call her, told her to come.

Questions with answers Blane didn't want to think about drifted through his mind all day. His sheets still smelled of Kathleen's perfume and he found long strands of her hair on his pillow. Scrutinizing his reflection as he tied the bowtie for his tux, he tried not to remember the feel of her, the taste of her. After automatically adding his silver and onyx cuff links, he headed downstairs.

Kade had arrived and was having his usual drink in the den, studying one of the masks that had been lying on Blane's desk.

"At least there aren't feathers," he joked as Blane walked in.

Blane had sent Mona out today to find an additional mask for Kade that was like the one he'd been given. Elaborately made, they were both black with tiny designs woven in silver thread, the ties made of silk ribbon. When worn they would cover more than half their faces.

Pouring himself a drink, Blane asked, "So did you have any luck?"

"TecSol's network is behind three firewalls," Kade said. "The last one is proving to be a slightly tougher nut to crack."

"But you can do it, right?"

"Have I ever let you down?"

Blane swallowed the liquor. "No."

"Then let's go and don't worry about TecSol," Kade said.

"Oh, don't you boys look nice!" Mona stepped into the den, a wide smile on her face. "My, my! So what's the occasion? A post-Halloween party?"

"A rather . . . eccentric client," Blane replied.

"Well, you both look quite dashing. I daresay you'll catch quite a few ladies' eyes," she teased. "Speaking of which," she said to Blane, "what happened to that sweet girl you brought home the other night? Kathleen?" Mona looked expectantly at him.

"I . . . think she got a new job somewhere else," Blane said, glancing away from her. He never could lie to Mona and he disliked doing it now.

After a moment, she said, "Well. That's too bad. I liked her." There was a world of meaning in that sentence and it wasn't lost on Blane.

"Me, too," he said quietly.

"You need to return Tigger at some point," Mona continued. "Though I have grown attached to him. He's been staying with us, so just let me know."

Blane's gaze met Mona's. An excuse to see her again. As if she could read his mind, Mona smiled a little, her eyes twinkling, before she turned to Kade.

"Now be good," she admonished him, straightening his tie.

"You never tell Blane to be good," he groused.

"There's a reason for that," she said archly, giving him a knowing look.

Kade's lips twisted in something close to a real smile. He lightly kissed Mona's cheek and her face softened. To say Mona had a soft spot for Kade and he for her was a massive understatement. Not that Blane minded. On the contrary, Kade had been the best thing to ever happen to this family . . . or to Blane.

"Don't wait up," Blane said, grabbing his keys and wallet. His Glock was already in the holster under his jacket.

"Good night, boys," Mona called after them as they left. "Have fun!"

"I'm driving," Kade said, heading toward his Mercedes. "You drove last time."

"Or I could drive your car," Blane suggested, just to irritate Kade. Kade never let anyone drive his precious Mercedes, not even Blane.

"Like that'll happen."

Blane hid a smile as he slid into the passenger seat.

The address Blane had been given led them to a house that resembled a Victorian mansion. Kade parked, and after they'd donned their masks, they walked to the wrought iron gate. Blane spoke the password he'd been given to the man guarding the entry and they were allowed through.

"Yeah, this isn't creepy or anything," Kade muttered as they headed down the long sidewalk to the front door. "What's your name again?"

"Enigma," Blane said in an undertone. No one was around, but the stillness of the scene made him want to speak as quietly as possible so his voice wouldn't carry to anyone who might be listening.

"And what's mine?"

"I don't know," Blane said, thinking. "How about . . . Omen."

Kade seemed to think this over. "Hmm. Omen. Yeah, I like that. Omen it is."

"Well, I'm glad *that's* settled," Blane said.

A woman wearing a long silver gown and matching mask met them at the door.

"Good evening," she said to Blane. "You must be Enigma." She held out her hand, palm down.

"I am," Blane replied. He grasped her hand, bending to lightly brush the back of it with his lips.

Her attention shifted to Kade. "And your friend?"

"Omen."

"Lovely to meet you both," she said. "Please. This way."

They followed her down a long hallway, lit only by a few candelabras. Shadows danced along the walls as they passed. Kade walked a couple of steps behind and to the left of Blane. At the end of the hallway, there was a set of imposing double doors nearly twelve feet tall.

Two men guarded these doors as well, one of them moving quickly to open the entry.

Stepping inside the room, Blane realized they were in a converted ballroom. Tapestries and curtains covered the walls while the room itself most closely resembled a luxury outdoor lounge, complete with expensive furniture, potted trees, private alcoves, and candles scattered everywhere.

The woman led them to a bar set up in one corner before turning to them. "Let me inform you of the rules," she said.

"The rules?" Blane echoed.

"It's very simple," she continued. "Do not press anyone for their true identity, neither should you give them yours. If you find a lady who captures your interest and she is agreeable, you are welcome to enjoy her here. Further interactions can be arranged for the usual fee."

"Which is?"

She smiled. "Five hundred an hour."

Well.

"Enjoy yourselves, gentlemen." With that, she left them, heading back the way they'd come.

Kade approached Blane. Speaking low so only he could hear, he said, "Five hundred an hour? That's a lot of money just to get screwed."

"And they don't even have a law degree," Blane muttered back.

Kade snorted at the joke, moving away to get a couple of drinks from the bartender and handing one to Blane.

"At those prices and with the number of people here," he said, "that's a lot of money funneled through their fingers."

"Agreed," Blane said. "A little laundering and it could be what's funding TecSol."

"Why would Frank invite you here?" Kade asked.

"To have dirt on me, I'd imagine," Blane said. "Blackmail."

"Then don't give him any opportunities."

"Wasn't planning on it." Not to mention that paying for sex wasn't really Blane's thing.

"Let's split up," Kade suggested. "See what we can find out."

"Don't go far and we'll meet back here," Blane said. "I want to be able to leave in a hurry if necessary."

"Roger that."

Blane meandered through the paths laid out in the room. He ran across a few men who were willing to look him in the eye and give him a nod, but most continued past without acknowledgment. The women he saw were dressed impeccably and all beautiful, though they too wore masks.

Appearing like colorful birds of paradise, the women were artfully arranged on chaises and couches. It seemed a few had already been engaged for their services, judging by the couples in passionate clinches, hidden in the cozy alcoves.

Pausing behind a group of trees, Blane listened to a couple seated on the couch on the other side. He knew the man's voice and was just trying to place it.

"I do believe you're new," the man said.

"Is it that obvious?" the woman replied, her voice nearly too soft for Blane to decipher.

"A bit," he answered. "But don't worry. We're really all quite harmless. Well, most of us are harmless," he paused. "I'm called Mercury."

And Blane realized who it was. James Gage. Now why wasn't he surprised that James would be here?

Moving slightly so he could peer through the leaves, Blane couldn't see James. But what he did see made his blood go ice-cold.

Only one woman he'd ever known had hair that color.

"I would like very much to get to know you better," James was saying to her. "Would you like that?"

"I just need to get something to drink," Kathleen said, getting to her feet. "I'll be right back."

Blane stepped back into the shadows as she hurriedly brushed past him.

He couldn't believe it. Kade had been right. Had Santini hired her? Blane wouldn't have thought Frank was that smart. Guess he was wrong.

Furious, Blane followed her, though he had no idea what he was going to say. Though *Will I get a bill for last night or was that a free sample?* might be a good place to start.

She headed unerringly for the bar, glancing to the side now and then. When she spotted a couple screwing in a chair, she sped up.

Kade was loitering by the bar and Blane made eye contact, moving to stand a few yards away by a fireplace. He tipped his head toward Kathleen as she stepped up to the bar. Kade glanced over, and to his credit, no shit-eating grin crossed his face that he'd been right. He just gave a curt nod to Blane and closed in behind her.

Blane couldn't hear what Kade said, but she jerked around when he spoke and Blane got his first good look at her, which promptly robbed him of breath.

She was gorgeous. The dress she wore tightly fitted the curve of her waist and hips while accentuating her cleavage with a dipping neckline. It was strapless, leaving her ivory shoulders and the tempting swell of her breasts bare. The color was an iridescent aqua that shimmered in the light. Her hair was pulled back on the sides with jeweled combs that sparkled when she turned her head. The heavy mass of her hair lay in perfectly crafted waves down her back, smooth and begging for a man's hands to sift through it.

After a moment, Kade sidled closer to her. He whispered something in her ear and Kat's gaze lifted, meeting Blane's. Her hand visibly shook when she saw him, her lips parting slightly in shock. It looked like the mask was no more a deterrent to her knowing his identity than it was to him knowing hers.

Setting the glass of champagne down on the bar, Kat turned and hurried away from him. Blane started after her, but was intercepted by Kade.

"I found out Gage is here," Kade said.

"Yeah, I saw James, too," Blane said, watching as Kathleen turned a corner out of sight.

"Not Junior," Kade corrected. "Daddy."

Blane jerked his attention back to Kade. "William Gage?"

"One and the same. Code name is The Patron."

Blane stared for a moment. "No shit," he muttered. "Looks like we may have found our launderer."

"What do you mean?"

"Gage's specialty is finance," Blane explained. "He's the best. Laundering money would be child's play for him."

"And if he knew of a company who could deliver a specific election result—"

"—you could get your son elected as district attorney and even if there were suspicions, there'd be no one to prosecute—"

"—and you could sell any election to the highest bidder," Kade finished.

"You know that software TecSol wrote isn't just running the Indy election," Blane said. "I dug through their books this morning. They've sold that software to hundreds of municipalities all over the country. All set to go live on Election Day."

"We need that code," Kade said.

Blane glanced down the path where Kathleen had disappeared. He needed to know the truth. Had she played him? He made to push past Kade.

"What are you doing?" Kade said, grabbing his arm. "Forget the girl."

"I want to know why she's here," Blane insisted.

Kade sighed. "Fine, but she knows your name. She knows you're Enigma. Said she was Lorelei and that she was looking for you."

"Then why'd she run off?"

"How the fuck should I know?" Kade hissed, glancing around them. "Maybe she didn't recognize you."

A thought struck Blane. "Or maybe someone told her that Enigma killed her friend and when she saw it was me, she panicked."

Kade's look was one of disbelief. "Yeah, that's not a reach or anything," he scoffed. "C'mon, Blane. Think with your head and not your dick."

Blane pulled his arm loose. "Give me a few minutes, then we'll leave." He heard Kade snort in disgust but ignored him, intent on following Kathleen.

It took him a few minutes to find her, and when he did, the anger he'd felt earlier was a pale shadow of the raging jealousy that consumed him now.

Kathleen and James were seated on a couch in a private alcove, James's head buried in her neck, his arm around her shoulders.

"Mercury," Blane barked, his hands clenching into fists. James didn't react, but Kathleen did, jerking back, her gaze flying to his. "Mercury," Blane repeated more harshly. James finally looked up.

"What do you want?" he asked. "Can't you see I'm busy?" He attempted to pull Kathleen closer for a kiss, but she turned her head and tried to push him away.

The sight of Kat struggling against James's advances broke the fragile grip Blane had on his control. Snarling in anger, Blane grabbed the collar of James's tux and hauled his ass off the couch.

"The Patron wants to speak with you," he said, giving James a hard shove out of the alcove. James looked pissed and Blane would have liked nothing more than to kick his ass again, but he just walked away, leaving Blane alone with Kat.

"Lorelei, I believe?" he asked, approaching her. Kat just nodded and he wondered if she really thought he hadn't recognized her. "I was told you were looking for me." Blane took the seat James had vacated, draping his arm on the couch behind her and sitting close enough that she was forced to tip her head back to look at him.

"Yes, I was," she said. Her voice oozed Southern elegance, the words

196

lilting in a soft cadence that was utterly charming. "I was told you might be looking for someone with whom you could spend some . . . quality . . . time."

Was this a game? Or was she really a prostitute that had been sent to trap him? Blane studied her. Under the facade of Southern belle, she was nervous. Her hands were restlessly gripping the fabric of her dress, her eyes darting to his and away.

"Are you offering?" he asked, wanting to see how far she'd take this.

"Perhaps," she breathed, managing a fake smile.

"I can be quite demanding," he said, his gaze falling to her lips. "And I don't share." He couldn't deny the urge to kiss her any longer, his body hungering to again feel hers beneath him.

Kat responded immediately, her mouth opening beneath his while her arms lifted to circle his neck, her fingers pushing into his hair.

Blane wrapped his arms around her waist, pulling her closer, as logical thought fled in the face of the fire burning through his veins. At the moment, he didn't care who she was or if she had played him. He just wanted her.

His mouth trailed down her neck to the tops of her breasts. Blane didn't hesitate to pull her dress down, exposing her plump breasts to his hungry gaze. He groaned, fitting his lips over a nipple and covering the other with his palm. Kat's hands clutched him to her and Blane could feel the racing of her heart inside her chest.

It was the matter of a moment to slide a hand up her skirt, her thighs parting eagerly for him. The lace covering her was no barrier as Blane moved it aside to push a finger inside her wet heat. Kat whimpered as he stroked her dripping folds, finding her clit and teasing it. She was so wet, her tight passage gripping his finger and making him wild to have her, consequences be damned.

"God, Kat, what you do to me," he murmured, pressing his lips to hers again.

At the sound of her name, she began struggling. "Let me go, Blane," she hissed, pushing at his shoulders. So she'd really thought he hadn't recognized her.

"Did you think I wouldn't know it was you?" he whispered in her ear. His hand still moved, his fingers coated with her arousal. Her hips lifted to meet his thrusting fingers. "Did you think I wouldn't recognize this body? The way your skin tastes, the softness of you against my fingers, the sounds you make when I touch you?"

Blane bent his head to suckle her breasts, his teeth gently tugging her nipple before he soothed it with his tongue. Kat gasped and Blane smiled as she stopped struggling. He stroked her clit, intent on her falling apart in his arms, eager to hear her make those sounds again. She was close, he could tell—

A blinding pain struck the back of his head and everything went dark.

∾

Blane woke to Kade shaking him and the pain of a dull headache that promised to be worse later. Blane groaned as he sat up, clutching his head.

"What the hell happened?" Kade asked, standing up from where he'd been crouched next to Blane.

Blane's eyes fell on a heavy brass candlestick lying on the floor. "She must've hit me with that," he said.

"She *hit* you?" Kade said furiously. "That could've killed you."

"Relax," Blane said. "It was my own fault." He'd pushed her, giving her no option but to do something drastic. He was willing to bet Kat had no idea what she was involved in, which side he was on, or how dangerous this was.

"We need to leave," he said to Kade. "Did you see where she went?"

"Fuck no. I was a little busy checking to see if you were alive or dead."

"Get the car. Meet me out front," Blane ordered, getting to his feet. Kade gave a curt nod and left. Now to find Kat.

Blane took a quick trip around the room, but didn't see Kat anywhere. Had she gone? She'd been scared, he knew that much, and he'd been responsible for part of her fear. Someone had tipped the scales against him, setting it up so she'd think he'd killed Sheila.

Emerging from the room into the hallway, Blane headed for the front door, only to spy Jimmy dragging someone in the same direction. Blane stepped up his pace as they turned a corner and he recognized the dress.

Jimmy had Kathleen.

~

Seventeen Years Ago

When your world falls apart, it seldom gives any warning. It just . . . happens. Kade should've known that better than anyone. And yet, it still took him by surprise.

It happened when he was walking home from the bus stop. It was the beginning of March so it was cold, but spring was a scent in the air.

A car pulled up beside him, its speed matching Kade's pace. He glanced over and his blood went cold.

"Hey, Kade. Where you been?"

The guy talking to him sat in the passenger seat of the rundown Buick, the window rolled down so he could stick his head out. It was Willie.

Willie was twenty and had been living on the streets since he was eight. He'd survived, even thrived, making himself the leader of a gang of thieves and prostitutes, and even sold drugs on the side. Kade had met him the first time he'd run away from the orphanage.

"What do you want?" Kade asked, still walking. Willie'd had Kade steal before, when it was either do that or starve. Small, quick, and quiet,

Kade had broken into a few houses, handing over the stolen items in return for food and a bed for the night. Willie had wanted Kade to turn tricks, too, said he'd make good money at it, but Kade hadn't been able to bring himself to do it.

"Heard you done got yourself a Daddy Warbucks," Willie said. "A rich dude who took a shine to your skinny, white ass. That true?"

"Nah, man. Just another foster home," Kade lied, his step quickening. The car picked up its pace as well. He could see Blane's house up ahead. Part of him wanted to run to it, to the safety it represented. But the part of him that would always be a part of the streets knew that safety was an illusion. And he'd lead them right to Blane.

Kade stopped. "I ain't got nothin' for you," he told Willie.

Willie got out of the car just as Kade saw Blane emerge from the house and head his way. Sometimes he met Kade walking home.

"Listen up," Willie said. "I don't give a shit what you think you got or don't got. You're livin in a fuckin' mansion now and you owe me."

"I don't owe you shit," Kade retorted, praying this would be over soon. He didn't want Blane to see.

Willie grabbed Kade by the collar, hauling him up to his face as he bent down.

"Don't be mouthin' me, boy," he hissed. "I'll cut out your fuckin' tongue and feed it to the dogs." A knife flashed in his hand.

Kade stared him down though he was quaking inside. He refused to show fear to this motherfucker.

"Kade?"

Kade heard Blane's call and glanced behind Willie to see that Blane had spotted them. In a second, he was running flat out toward them.

"Aw, that's so sweet," Willie sneered. "Looks like he likes you a helluva lot." He shook Kade until his teeth rattled. "You better bring me somethin' good tomorrow, or maybe we'll hafta pay your sugar daddy a visit. Tell him all the shit you done. He'll have you in juvie so fast, it'll make your head spin."

Willie gave Kade a shove, knocking him to the ground before jumping back in the car. It sped away in a squeal of smoke and tires just as Blane got to him.

"Kade!" He reached down, helping Kade to his feet. "Are you okay? Who was that?"

"Nobody," Kade said, brushing off his jeans. Blane picked up his backpack from where it had fallen.

"Don't give me that," Blane said. "That asshole touched you, knocked you down. If you know who it was, then by God you'd better tell me."

There was no way in hell Kade was telling Blane about Willie. How could he possibly explain that he'd broken into people's homes and stolen from them? He'd see Kade as a thief, or worse.

"It was just some creepy dude who stopped to harass me," Kade lied. He could tell Blane was angry, but knew it wasn't directed at him.

Blane studied him and Kade held his gaze. He knew if he looked away or faltered, Blane would know he was lying. After a moment, Blane relented.

"All right, but I don't want you walking home alone from the bus stop anymore. I'll pick you up from now on."

Kade nodded, trying not to show the relief he felt that Blane had dropped it. As they walked back to the house, he half listened to Blane talk as he tried to figure out what he was going to do. Willie wouldn't just go away, and now he knew where Kade, and subsequently Blane, lived. He wanted money, wanted Kade to steal from Blane, and that was something Kade refused to do.

His only real option was staring him in the face, but he didn't want to think about it. Not yet.

They reached the house and Kade headed upstairs, which was unusual since his first destination upon getting home from school was invariably the kitchen.

Blane stood frowning at the foot of the stairs as Kade disappeared inside his room. Kade had lied to him about that guy, he was sure of it. Luckily, Blane's memory was such that he'd gotten the plate off the car. He headed to the den to call a buddy whose dad was a cop. With any luck, Blane would know by morning who the asshole was who'd roughed up Kade.

Kade stood upstairs, staring at his room. His room. It had been the first time since his mom died that he had a place to call his own. He should have known it wouldn't last. Life just wasn't like that, not for him. For Blane maybe, but he deserved it. He was a good guy, honest and loyal, with all those big words grownups liked—character, integrity, honor. None of those traits described Kade.

He was an orphan with too much street dirt coated on his skin to ever be clean. The things he'd done—the things that had been done to him . . . if Blane knew even half of it, he'd never look at him the same. And Kade couldn't stand to see the disgust in Blane's eyes, or worse, pity. Kade should've known it wouldn't be so easy to escape who he really was, though it had been nice pretending for a while.

At dinner, Kade tried to memorize the feeling of being part of a family. Mona teased Gerard about his inability to capture the two chipmunks tearing up the flower beds out back while Blane chuckled. Gerard threatened to make Blane help him but Blane held his hands up in surrender.

"I won't be party to the capture and possible maiming of Chip and Dale," he said with a grin. "Next thing you know, all the woodland creatures will be ganging up on you. They talk, you know." He winked at Kade.

Kade tried to smile, but his chest hurt. His stomach churned as he ate, but he forced the food down anyway. God only knew when he'd get another meal, much less one like this.

He caught Blane looking at him a few times, his gaze thoughtful, but he didn't say anything.

Kade waited until the house was quiet and still. It was late, nearly two a.m., before he shrugged on his coat and backpack. He didn't take any of the new possessions Blane had given him. What use did he have on the streets for a remote-control helicopter? The only thing he did take, the thing he couldn't leave behind, was the key. Finding a string, he tied it around his neck, the cold metal pressing against his chest underneath his shirt.

Kade crept down the stairs, skipping over the one step he knew squeaked. He was almost to the front door when the hallway light came on.

"Where you going, Kade?"

Kade turned around to see Blane standing a few feet away in front of the open door to the den. Shit. There wasn't anything he could say, so he remained silent.

"Why would you do this to me?" Blane asked. "Again? I thought we had a deal, that you liked it here."

The hurt and betrayal on Blane's face made Kade's gut clench even tighter and he was sure he was going to lose the dinner he'd made himself eat. He forced his face to be blank before he replied.

"Yeah, it's not working out, man. I didn't want to deal with any sloppy goodbyes, so thought I'd just leave quiet-like." He waited, barely breathing. If he didn't get out of this house, Willie would be back, and if Kade didn't have something for him, he'd come get it himself. Blane, or Mona, or Gerard, could get hurt, even killed.

Blane crossed his arms over his chest and moved closer until he stood within arm's reach. "Now why don't I believe that," he said quietly.

Kade shrugged. Unable to hold Blane's penetrating gaze any longer, he looked away.

"Look," he said, "this brother bonding shit, it was a real good try. But it's pointless. I'm not staying. You can't make me. You may stop me tonight, but I'll just leave another time."

"So why don't you tell me the real reason you're leaving," Blane said. "And no more shit about not liking it here. The truth."

"What do you want from me?" Kade exploded, panicking now. "Just because we're related doesn't mean I give a shit! You think I want to stay here and play house forever? You're not my dad and no matter how much you try, this isn't going to work." He was breathing hard now, his hands clenched into fists.

The words stung, hitting Blane where he was most vulnerable, but he refused to give up. He didn't know what had happened today with that guy, but that was why Kade was trying to leave, not because he wanted to go.

It had been patently obvious something was wrong all evening, Kade uncharacteristically quiet during dinner. Kade rarely let an evening go by without a cynical, snarky remark or two that made Blane laugh. He'd looked like he was eating the proverbial last meal before an execution.

Determined not to be taken by surprise this time, Blane had sat in wait, hoping he was wrong, hoping Kade wasn't going to try to run away again. His heart had dropped when he'd recognized Kade's light step on the stairs.

"This is about that guy, Willie, isn't it?" Blane said. He could tell by the flicker of surprise in Kade's eyes that he was right.

"I told you, it was just some guy. I don't know who it was," Kade protested.

"Bullshit. I know who he is, that he runs a gang of kids on the street." Thanks to a late phone call from his buddy on that license plate. "What did he want? Did he threaten you?"

Kade just shook his head, glancing away and shifting his weight from one foot to another.

"I can help you," Blane persisted. "Give me a chance."

"What can you possibly do?" Kade blurted, exasperated. "You don't know anything about these people, what they're capable of. This isn't a game."

"I know that," Blane said, relieved. "You just need to trust me. Can you do that?" He needed to prove to Kade that he was serious, that this was real, what he felt for Kade was real. It wasn't going away and it wasn't conditional. He just prayed Kade would give him that chance.

Kade hesitated. He wanted to, but he'd taken care of himself for so long, it went against every survival instinct he had to nod his head.

Blane breathed a sigh and reached for him, catching himself as Kade stiffened. He drew back again and took Kade's backpack.

"Let's get you to bed," he said.

Kade followed him back upstairs, wondering if he was making a mistake, and if so, how much he was going to regret it.

~

The next day, Blane was standing at the bus stop waiting for Kade. Kade had warned him that Willie was going to be looking for him today. Blane hoped so. There were a few things he'd like to say to Willie.

They were only a block from the bus stop when the Buick pulled alongside. Blane moved Kade behind him.

"You must be Willie," Blane said, bending down to the window.

"Aw, Kade, you bring your sugar daddy today?" Willie sneered. "You know this ain't how it's s'posed to go down."

"Let me tell you how it's gonna go down," Blane said, his voice like ice. "I know who you are, and so do the cops. You leave now and don't come back? We're square. You come around Kade again? Try to threaten him again? Touch him again? Then you're going to have a big problem. I hear you're legally an adult now. You know they don't throw you in juvie as an adult, they put you in with the murderers and rapists. Guess which group will be looking for you."

Blane stood up as Willie stared daggers at him, then the car took off down the street.

Kade stared after them in surprise. He didn't know what he'd expected, but it hadn't been for Willie to back down, at least not so quickly.

He glanced up at Blane, who smiled at him. "I think Mona made a fresh batch of cookies for you," he said. "Let's go see."

They headed for the house while inwardly Kade reeled. He'd never heard Blane sound like that before. He'd sounded like somebody you didn't want to fuck with. And he'd done it on Kade's behalf. No one had ever taken Kade's side before, tried to protect him. It gave Kade that odd sensation again in the middle of his chest, a tightness that made his throat close. He wanted to say thanks, but the word wouldn't come.

Blane chatted like nothing big had happened, telling him how Gerard had finally caught the chipmunks, but then couldn't kill them. Instead, he'd taken them across the street to the Clarks' house and let them loose in their backyard.

Kade dared to hope, as they entered the house to the aroma of fresh-baked chocolate chip cookies, that maybe things would be okay. Which just goes to show how little he knew.

CHAPTER NINE

Blane pulled his gun, running flat out now until he drew near the exit. Hugging the wall, he could hear Jimmy talking.

"If you're really good, I may even keep you alive for a day or two."

Any doubt Blane had regarding whether or not Kat had been hired to trap him evaporated. She was a threat to them, as he'd thought from the start, and now they were going to eliminate that threat.

Jimmy yelped suddenly, and Blane eased around the corner in time to see him punch Kathleen in the stomach. She doubled over and would have collapsed if Jimmy hadn't still had his fist in her gut. Cold fury filled Blane, but he shoved it aside. Emotion had no place in a fight.

Blane pressed the barrel of his gun against Jimmy's temple. "Let the girl go," he said.

Jimmy froze, but didn't release Kathleen, who struggled upright. She was bound and gagged, her eyes wide with fear.

"I said, let her go," Blane said again.

"Kirk, you're messing with stuff you should leave alone," Jimmy said. "Walk away and I'll forget we had this little conversation."

"Not gonna happen, Jimmy," Blane countered. "Let her go or you die." And he'd be more than happy to do the honors.

Jimmy spun around, knocking the gun from Blane's hand. He leaped for Blane, a glittering knife in his hand. Blane jumped back, dodging Jimmy's strikes. At one point, he miscalculated and the burning slice of the blade struck his arm. Dodging to one side, Blane saw an opening and grabbed Jimmy's wrist. A quick twist and the bone cracked. Jimmy cried out, the knife dropping to the ground, and Blane smashed his fist into Jimmy's face. Blood spurted from his nose and Blane pressed his advantage, unleashing his fury and replaying the image in his head of Jimmy hitting Kat.

Only when Jimmy collapsed did Blane stop, his chest heaving from exertion. He swiped his sleeve across his mouth, wiping away the blood there from a punch Jimmy had landed. Blane had barely felt it, his rage burning away the pain.

Blane grabbed his gun from the ground and hurried to Kathleen, who'd sidled away from where he and Jimmy had been fighting.

"Time to go," he said.

Kat's eyes suddenly widened, her gaze fixed behind Blane, and she screamed, the sound muffled by the gag.

Blane reacted on instinct, throwing himself into her so they both hit the ground. He heard Kat's head hit the concrete hard as a knife whizzed by over their heads. Blane rolled onto his back, pulled the trigger, and Jimmy fell, dead.

"You all right?" Blane asked anxiously, helping Kathleen to her feet. He wanted to get the bindings off her, but they needed to get out of here first, before the sound of the gunshot brought people out to investigate.

Taking her arm, he hurried them down the path to the street just as Kade pulled up with the car. Kathleen put on the brakes, stumbling to a halt and resisting Blane.

"That's our ride," he reassured her, tugging her with him. Throwing open the back door, he pushed Kathleen inside, quickly following her into the backseat.

"Go," he barked to Kade, who stepped on the gas.

"It's about fucking time," Kade said. "Thought you were going to need help."

"Not likely," Blane retorted. Killing Jimmy had been deeply satisfying.

It was time to free Kat from the ties around her wrists and the gag. Digging in his pocket, Blane pulled out his switchblade, flicking it open and leaning toward her. She flinched, scooting away from him, her eyes wildly rolling from him, to the knife, to Kade sitting in the front seat.

She was terrified.

Blane froze in place, his gut churning with guilt. Kathleen was caught up in all this, had been inches from being killed, and had no one she could trust. God knows he'd given her no reason to trust him.

"I'm not going to hurt you, Kat," he said, keeping his voice calm and quiet with an effort. "I just want to get the gag off. Will you let me do that?" Too bad he hadn't asked her permission before putting his hands on her earlier. She might trust him now if he had.

Her eyes filled with tears, which burned him more than the slice of Jimmy's blade. She nodded and Blane wasted no time slicing through the fabric, which he belatedly realized was a black tie.

"Turn around," he said, and she obeyed, moving so her back was to him. Another quick slice and she was free. She sat back in the seat, flexing her fingers and keeping her gaze on her lap. Blane watched her, worrying. Was she okay? Blood seeped from a cut on her lip, its garish red accusing Blane. If he hadn't doubted her, he could have gotten her out of there a lot sooner. She wouldn't have been hurt.

Pulling the square of white linen from the breast pocket of his tux, Blane reached over, gently blotting the blood from her lip. Kat didn't respond, which only heightened his concern. Had Jimmy done something else to her? Something Blane couldn't see?

Tipping her chin up, he gently turned her face toward him until her gaze lifted to his. "Are you all right?" he asked. "Did he hurt you?"

Tears spilled from her eyes, pouring in crystal rivulets down her cheeks, and Blane felt as though a hot knife had sliced into his gut.

She let him pull her onto his lap, his arms wrapping around her trembling body to hold her close, while she cried into his neck. Sobs shook her, each one notching up the guilt he felt that much higher. She seemed so tiny in his arms, her fragility mocking him.

After a few minutes, she seemed to get hold of herself, her sobs tapering off, but Blane made no move to release her. He couldn't. Not yet.

"Is she done yet?" Kade asked, irritation lacing his voice.

"Shut the fuck up, Kade," Blane said.

"Blane, you're such a bleeding heart," Kade accused. "Remember, this is the same chick that coldcocked you less than an hour ago."

Kathleen's voice whispered weakly in his ear. "I'm really sorry about that," she said. As if she was the one who needed to apologize.

Blane lightly kissed her lips, mindful of the cut. "It did take me by surprise," he said, "and hurt like a son of a bitch."

Her smile was tentative as she curved her hand around his neck, pulling his mouth down to meet hers. The heat between them exploded instantly, her lips parting and their tongues entwining. The taste of her was an intoxicant and he was an addict. The adrenaline rush of fighting Jimmy, the fear of nearly losing her, all of it built into a frenzy of passion. A feminine moan reached his ears, and if they hadn't had an audience, nothing would have stopped Blane from parting her legs and burying himself inside her.

"Not in my backseat, please," Kade interrupted from the front. "I just had it cleaned."

Kat pulled back, her face flushing red in embarrassment. Blane ignored Kade, lightly tracing his fingers over her brow, her eyes, brushing the tender skin of her cheek and lips. She was beautiful, pure. Innocence shone in her eyes as she looked at him. She was mesmerizing.

"So, what were you doing there tonight, if I may ask?" Kade continued.

"I was trying to find out who killed Sheila," Kat said, answering to Blane rather than Kade.

"By becoming a prostitute?" Kade shot back. This time, he must've irritated her, because she turned toward the front and leaned forward as she answered.

"I wasn't a prostitute," she retorted. "I wasn't going to have sex with anyone."

Innocent and naive, Blane thought with a sigh.

Kade just laughed. "Your innocence is charming," he said, "and also incredibly stupid. You were almost killed tonight, and nearly got Blane killed as well."

"Well, I could ask you the same question," Kat said. "Why were you two there? I know Mr. Gage had Sheila killed because of her involvement with Mark. Were you the one he sent to murder her?"

Looked like money laundering wasn't the only thing Gage had been up to. Jimmy had been working for him. But Kat hadn't put two and two together yet.

"Kat," Blane said, pulling her back onto his lap, "Kade didn't kill her."

"I know he's a gun-for-hire," she hissed at him, as if Kade couldn't hear her in the front seat. "And he works for the Santini brothers. Mr. Gage is obviously in cahoots with them. It only makes sense that Kade is the one who killed her."

Did she just say "cahoots"? Blane pushed the errant thought aside. "It may make sense to you," he said, "but he didn't kill her. I'm sure they sent Jimmy to take care of Sheila."

Kathleen crossed her arms over her chest, her eyes narrowing at him. "How do you know?" she said stubbornly. "Kade's a liar. You can't trust what he says." She glanced toward Kade. "You see? He doesn't even deny it."

There was no help for it. He had to tell her.

"I know he didn't kill Sheila," Blane said, "because he's my brother."

Those words had an immediate effect. Her eyes widened and her mouth fell open, her head jerking around to look at Kade again, then she was sliding off his lap.

"Why didn't you tell me?" she asked. Her voice held anger and betrayal.

Kade answered before Blane could.

"You didn't give us much of a chance, did you? Dramatically running off in the middle of the night. And firing a gun at us."

"I ran off, as you put it, because I heard you two talking," she sneered at Kade, her dislike obvious. "You both wanted that code and neither of you seemed to care how you got it." Ouch. "God knows what you planned to do to me, Kade, whereas you"—she turned to Blane— "apparently your idea was to fuck me for it."

So much for their short-lived reunion.

Kade let out a low whistle. "And the kitty has claws."

Blane thought her reaction was probably for the best. He was too wrapped up in her to be emotionally detached. Her anger put some desperately needed space between them. Kade was right. He needed to think with his head, not his dick—or any other organ, for that matter.

"Do you have the code?" he asked.

Kathleen swallowed, her eyes briefly betraying her hurt before she concealed it.

"Not on me, no," she sneered, every inch a brat and lying to him on top of it. "You know, you should really see someone about that whole jaw-clenching thing. That can't be good for your teeth."

Kade laughed at that and Blane automatically clenched his jaw even tighter, before realizing what he was doing. Damn it.

"I need that code," he said, his voice harder. Blane really didn't want to try to threaten her or scare her. His threats would be empty ones and he was sure she'd see right through him.

"Why?"

Before Blane could answer, Kade stopped the car in Blane's driveway. Kade was out and opening her door in seconds.

"Let's go," Blane heard Kade say.

"Take me home," Kathleen demanded, not moving from her seat.

Blane stuffed his hand in the seat-back pocket, pulling out the pack of cigarettes and lighter he knew Kade kept there. Grabbing a cigarette, he got out on his side, knowing Kade would get Kathleen out of the car, one way or another. He lit the cigarette and waited, taking a deep drag. Sure enough, a few moments later she was hurrying up the sidewalk ahead of them. Blane fell into step beside Kade.

"At least this one is more entertaining than the others," Kade said. "It's like Hooker Barbie masquerading as Nancy Drew."

There was a nearly imperceptible hitch in Kathleen's step at Kade's remark.

"Enough," Blane said, shooting Kade a look. Kade glanced at the cigarette in Blane's hand and shut up. Blane took one more deep drag before dropping the cigarette to the ground and grinding it out with his shoe.

Blane stepped up next to Kat, who stood waiting at the door, and unlocked it. Unthinkingly, his hand settled on the small of her back as he guided her. She jerked away from his touch as though burned. Blane's hand dropped to his side.

Walking into the den, Blane discarded the tuxedo jacket and untied his bowtie while Kat and Kade took seats in two identical chairs. Blane moved to lean against his desk as he faced them, crossing his arms over his chest, and tried to figure out his next move.

"You're hurt!" Kathleen suddenly exclaimed.

Blane glanced down to where Jimmy's knife had sliced through his jacket and shirt down to the skin. Damn. Now he'd have to get a new tuxedo made.

"Just a scratch," he dismissed, settling on a plan of attack. If he answered her questions, chances were she'd feel better about cooperating. Getting her to lower her defenses and stop being so combative was key. "Now what do you want to know?"

Kathleen nervously licked her lips, then asked, "Who do you really work for?"

"No one," Blane answered. "You could say this situation happened by accident."

"How could it be by accident?"

"Kade and I don't usually work together," Blane said. Though he had to admit, he'd enjoyed knowing his brother had his back on this one, someone he could trust implicitly.

Kathleen glanced at Kade in disbelief, then back to Blane.

"Kade used to be FBI," he explained.

"Used to be?"

"They had a lot of rules that got in the way," Kade said with a careless shrug.

"Those are called laws, Kade," Blane chastised him.

"Whatever they are, I decided I would enjoy myself more as a . . . freelancer."

"Vigilante, you mean," Blane corrected. Kade wasn't exactly doing his part to inspire trust from Kathleen.

"You say tomato . . . " Kade sighed.

Blane looked back at Kat. "People hire him to find lawbreakers and be judge and jury."

"And executioner," Kade interjected, smirking at Kathleen, who eyed him with trepidation. "You'd be surprised how good business is."

"Last year," Blane said, pulling her attention back to him, "I realized something was amiss with the firm and its relationship with TecSol. I needed someone on the inside with the Santini family, so I asked Kade to move back to town and help me."

"And I'm not even charging him," Kade added.

"And why do you need the code?" Kathleen asked.

"Because of this." Blane walked behind his desk and brought up the election map, adding the new jurisdictions he'd discovered earlier today with a few clicks. When he hit a button, the image was projected onto the wall.

Kathleen got up and walked over to it. Kade rose as well.

"What's this?" she asked.

"It's all the elections that will be encrypted using that code in two days."

She looked stunned. "But . . . that's not possible," she stammered. "It's only supposed to be used in Indy."

"That's what you think, princess," Kade said.

That gave Blane pause. Princess? Where the hell had *that* come from?

"What you don't know," Kade continued, "is that TecSol is just one front company. There are dozens more, all using the same software to encrypt the returns. All going live on Tuesday."

"The Santini brothers—" she began.

"They're little fish," Kade interrupted. "This is much bigger. The problem is we haven't found the ones who are really behind this yet. The code would help us track this to them."

"How will that help you?" she asked. "What do you know about computers, codes, and encryption?" Her tone indicated a decided disdain for Kade's intellectual capabilities. Kade just smiled.

Blane sighed. "Quite a bit, actually," he said. "Kade's job in the FBI was in the cyber crime division." He left out the part where Kade had been hacking and writing code since before puberty.

Kathleen said nothing to that, still staring at Kade, who merely cocked an insolent eyebrow at her. Turning on her heel, she approached Blane.

"Will you give us the code?" Unlike Kade, he believed that sometimes you really could get what you wanted if you just asked nicely.

"Do I have a choice?" she asked.

Inwardly, Blane flinched. Whether she thought he would hurt her or that Kade would, she believed she wouldn't be allowed to leave this room unless she gave them what they wanted. And quite honestly, he didn't have a clue what he'd do if she didn't. Hurting her was out of the question.

"You always have a choice," he replied.

"Though you may not like the consequences," Kade added, making Kathleen spin around.

"Is that a threat?" she hissed at him.

Blane rubbed his forehead tiredly. He wouldn't let Kade hurt her, but maybe she didn't know that.

"It's a fact," Kade said, his voice like ice.

Blane stayed quiet, letting Kathleen assume what she would. A moment passed, then to Blane's relief, she capitulated.

"Fine," she spat. Turning to a chair, she set her heel-clad foot on it and began raising her skirt.

Blane's brows climbed with her hemline. He couldn't look away as the fabric rose to reveal her smooth leg, then higher to her thigh, and even higher, until he would have begged for just an inch more.

Kathleen pulled a thumb drive from her stocking, holding it up for him to see. "A precaution," she said. "Sorry your hands were too busy elsewhere to search me properly, Blane?"

Blane's gaze met hers. At the moment, she knew exactly what she was doing, knew she was affecting him. Another show like that and he'd haul her mouth-watering ass upstairs to his bed and show her just how thorough he could be.

As if reading his thoughts, she dropped her skirt and tossed the thumb drive onto his desk. "How are you going to trace it?" she asked.

"We need to get into their infrastructure, but I'm working on that," Kade said.

Kathleen didn't even look in Kade's direction, just raised an eyebrow at Blane.

"He hasn't been able to hack into their network yet," he clarified.

"*Yet* being the key word," Kade said.

"Your time is running out," she said. "Wouldn't it be better if you had someone on the inside?"

"That would make things a lot easier, yes," Blane answered. "But our last lead died with your friend Mark."

"Maybe I could help you," she offered.

Kade laughed outright, while Blane's immediate thought was that no way in hell was he letting her within a mile of those people. They'd already tried to kill her once. Who was to say they wouldn't try again?

"What are you going to do, princess?" Kade asked, stepping into her personal space. "Fuck the information out of Santini?"

Kathleen smacked Kade so hard, it echoed in the room. Kade looked as furious as Blane had ever seen him while Kathleen just stood her ground, staring him down. The hostility between the two of them was palpable.

So much for his brother and his erstwhile "girlfriend" getting along. It didn't look like they'd be catching a movie together anytime soon.

"Kade, take a walk," Blane ordered, before things could deteriorate even further.

For a moment, Blane thought he wasn't going to listen, but Kade finally turned and left the room. Kathleen blew out a breath, her hands clutching the chair next to her for support. Sometimes Blane forgot just how menacing Kade could be when he chose. Normally, he didn't like seeing his brother that way, but tonight it had worked in Blane's favor.

Blane moved closer to her. "I apologize for him," he said. "You didn't deserve that."

"Is he always such a charmer?" she asked dryly, her eyes avoiding Blane's.

"He's just . . . a bit of a cynic." With good reason, though Kathleen didn't know that, nor did she need to.

Kathleen was too tempting to resist and Blane had the passing thought that maybe he could persuade her to share his bed one last time. A princess, Kade had said? She certainly looked the part tonight and Blane was suddenly, fiercely glad that there was such antipathy between her and Kade.

He slid his arms around her waist, pulling her toward him. She came willingly, giving Blane hope that perhaps he wouldn't be sleeping alone tonight.

"Not that I'm going to complain that you two don't get along," he said. She looked up then, her blue eyes questioning. "I don't like competition."

Blane kissed her and this time she was ready for him, accustomed to the demands of his lips and tongue. Her hands clutched at his shoulders, her body pressed against his. His hands lowered to pull her closer while his mouth skated down the curve of her neck. She tipped her head to the side and gasped at the touch. Blane buried a hand in the soft waves cascading down her back.

"So beautiful," he murmured. And she was. Not just her looks, but her taste, the scent of her skin, the feel of her in his arms.

She said something, but Blane was too far gone to hear it, sucking her earlobe into his mouth. She shivered and Blane wondered if she'd agree to the couch instead. He didn't know if he could make it all the way to his bed.

"Blane, stop!"

This time, the words penetrated, as did the realization that she was pushing him away. Blane abruptly released her. She stumbled backward, looking dazed.

"What's the matter?" he asked, hoping whatever it was wouldn't take too long to fix. Desire was humming in his veins.

"I can't do this," she stammered. "I can't be your . . . flavor of the month."

"I never said you were," Blane replied.

"Then what am I?"

That was a good question. No, she wasn't a transient lay, in and out of his life—no pun intended. Neither was she someone he should seek to make permanent, though he realized that he didn't immediately shrink from the idea, at least, not with her.

But she was young, had never played this game before, and was a liability he didn't need. Even now he could see the hope in her eyes. The last thing either of them needed was her forming an attachment to him.

When Blane didn't answer, the light of hope in her eyes slowly faded. "Thought so," she said, grabbing her purse. She turned to go.

"Kathleen, wait," Blane said, grasping her elbow. He didn't want her to think it had meant nothing to him and it was on the tip of his tongue to tell her that, but what good would it do besides make her think there could be more than just casual sex between them? It was best to just let it go. Let her go.

Turning her hand palm up, Blane placed the spare set of keys to Kade's car in her hand. "To get home," he said.

She glanced down at the keys and when she said, "Thanks," it sounded as if she were fighting tears. Guilt hit him hard and Blane didn't try to stop her again as she walked to the door.

"Wait," she said, turning around. "Aren't these the keys to Kade's car?"

Blane grinned. "Yeah. It'll really piss him off." Kade deserved it for treating her like shit.

Kathleen laughed and Blane tried to memorize the sound.

"Blane, why were you there tonight?" she asked. "Are you a . . . customer?"

Good God. She was probably wondering if she needed to see a doctor after having sex with him. Worrying about STDs wasn't really the memory Blane wanted her to associate with their one and only time together.

"I know I haven't given you much reason to trust me," he said, "but believe me when I tell you that no, I'm not a customer."

She let out a small sigh of relief. "Then why did Gracie tell me that Enigma was the one Sheila was seeing?"

"She lied," Blane said. "She probably told you whatever they wanted her to say. I'd assume so you wouldn't trust me." Not that he'd needed any help getting her not to trust him. He'd done quite well at that on his own.

"Why were you even there?"

Blane decided she didn't need more information. She'd already proven to be too tenacious for her own health. "It's safer for you if you don't know that," he answered.

Kathleen looked disappointed, but thankfully didn't ask any more questions.

"Bye, Blane," she said.

"Bye, Kat."

She walked out without a backward glance. Blane felt a stab of regret as he watched her leave. He wouldn't ever see her again, wouldn't kiss her or make love to her again.

It was for the best, but he stared at that closed door for a long while.

~

Kade was pissed about his car, as Blane expected. He groused about having to ask Gerard to take him to pick it up, but Blane wasn't really listening. Kade said he'd be in touch when he got through TecSol's network and left, his irritation at Blane obvious.

It was late when Blane dropped onto the couch, staring into the dancing flames of the fireplace. He'd spent the last two hours poring through TecSol's finance records. He'd finally found the method Gage was using to launder the money through a half dozen shell companies. Gage was putting the firm at risk, so Blane had no qualms about leaving a voice mail for the current DA, an old law school buddy he'd kept in touch with over the years, detailing what was going on. It shouldn't take long for the cops to come knocking on Gage's door.

However, even with that part taken care of, Blane couldn't shake the bad feeling in his gut. Had he done the right thing with Kat? Sending her away? Logic told him yes, but that didn't stop thoughts of her from replaying in his mind. What if he'd said something different, told her he wanted to see her again? Would she have stayed? Is that what he wanted? Was it too late?

A slight sound in the hallway made Blane turn, his senses going on high alert. Silently, he got to his feet, moving behind his desk. He picked up the Glock that rested on the surface of the desk and tucked it in the back of his pants. Reaching under his desk, Blane hit the button on a tiny remote he'd glued there.

Frank Santini stepped into the room, followed by two men who looked like they didn't do much thinking for a living, their brutish faces cold, their eyes empty.

"Frank," Blane said, keeping it genial. "This is an odd time—and place—to see you. To what do I owe the pleasure?"

"It looks like you had a nice time at the party tonight," Frank said, moving forward to stand in front of Blane. He had a yellow manila folder in his hand from which he drew a sheaf of thick papers. One by one, he tossed them onto Blane's desk.

Images of himself and Kathleen making out on the couch at the party tonight stared up at Blane in stark black and white. Not that Blane was surprised. The only thing unexpected was that it had taken Santini this long to get over here.

"Are these for my collection?" he asked Frank. "Normally, I'm not into that, but with these"—he picked up one in particular that showed everything he'd bared of her during their encounter—"I might be persuaded to change my mind."

Frank laughed softly. "You're a man's man, Kirk," he said. "Nothing better than a glass of aged scotch and lying between a woman's spread thighs, am I right?" Frank walked over to the sideboard and helped himself to Blane's scotch, pouring an inch into a crystal highball glass.

"You haven't answered my question," Blane said, his voice turning steely. "Why are you here?"

Frank settled himself on the couch with a sigh, the cushions groaning in protest at his bulk. Blane stuffed the photos of him and Kathleen back into the envelope and tossed it onto his desk.

"I may understand something like those photos," Frank said, "but I doubt voters would. Everybody knows men pay for sex from women like that, but no one likes to talk about it, much less read about it in the Sunday paper over the breakfast table."

"I don't know about that," Blane scoffed, coming around the desk to face Frank. "I bet I could leak those to the paparazzi and I'd win in a landslide. There's no such thing as bad press, isn't that what they say?"

"That's an awfully big risk to take with your career," Frank warned.

Blane shrugged. "At the moment, we're the only ones who've seen those photos. So unless you're threatening me, I don't see the problem." He paused. "*Are* you threatening me, Frank?"

Frank smiled. "I'm your ally, Kirk. I want to see your career soar as much as you do. Those photos are just my insurance against my investment."

"So you're blackmailing me," Blane said. "What exactly do you want from me, Frank, that I'm not already providing?"

"You think I don't know you've been digging into TecSol?" Frank asked. His smile was gone now, anger creasing the worn lines of his face.

"They're your client," Blane said. "Your union people service their voting machines. If they're dirty, it's my duty as your lawyer to protect you."

"Bullshit," Frank spat. "We have a good thing going, Kirk, and I'm not about to let you fuck it up. Do you know how much money the right people will pay to ensure an election? Millions doesn't begin to cover it."

"Why are you telling me this?" Blane asked.

"I can tell you whatever I want," Frank said with a wave of his hand. "You can't repeat it. You think I don't know about attorney-client privilege?"

"That privilege doesn't extend to TecSol," Blane said. "They're not my client."

"Which is why I have the photographs, Kirk," Frank said. "Now be a good boy and don't make me use them." He rose laboriously to his feet, doing up the button on his strained jacket.

Furious, Blane got in Frank's face. "You think I give a fuck about those photographs?" he snarled. "Don't think for a moment that you can waltz in here and threaten me. You have no idea who you're dealing with."

Frank remained unmoved. "It's you who don't know who you're dealing with, Kirk," he said. "Like the girl. Did you think we wouldn't find out?"

Blane stilled, his expression going blank. "I don't know what you're talking about," he said. "The girl was just some whore."

Frank laughed. "Kathleen Turner, isn't that her name? Poor thing was just too curious for her own good."

A cold chill went up Blane's spine. "What do you mean?"

"We have her," Frank said. "You didn't think we'd leave it to chance, did you? I'd hoped the photographs could persuade you, but it's always a good idea to have a contingency plan."

Fuck. "What do you want?" Blane asked.

"You come with us until after the election, then you're free to go."

"And if I don't?"

"We'll kill her, of course," Frank said with a shrug, as though he were mentioning dinner plans for Friday. He smiled. "I believe Jimmy was tasked with that particular chore, but you already knew that, didn't you, Kirk? You wouldn't have bothered saving her and blowing your cover in the process if she was 'just some whore.'"

Blane had his gun in his hand before Frank even turned away. The men at the door pulled their weapons, pointing them at Blane, and nobody moved.

"If you die," Frank said, "so does the girl. And with two guns pointing at you, we both know you won't make it if you try to shoot your way out." He snapped his fingers and the men approached to flank him. "What'll it be, Kirk?"

Blane didn't see another way out, not if he wanted to rescue Kathleen. He released his hold on the gun, letting it dangle from his finger. One of the thugs took it from him.

"Let's go." One of the guys gave Blane a shove.

Blane followed Frank to the car waiting outside. He slid into the back, one of the guys sitting next to him while the other drove. Frank sat in the front with the driver. They drove for a while until they pulled up in front of a building.

"What's this?" Blane asked. "Where are we?" No one answered. The guy got out of the car and motioned for Blane to get out, too.

Stepping onto the pavement, Blane realized they were at TecSol. The parking lot behind the building was deserted. A few scattered lamp poles cast flickering fluorescent pools of light in the darkness. Their buzzing was a low thrum of sound in the otherwise silent lot. Blane looked over at Frank and gestured to the building, which looked forbidding at this hour, the glass circling the first floor opaque. "Is Kathleen in there?"

"The girl's dead, Kirk," Frank said. "Or at least, she will be by morning."

Shock went through Blane, followed quickly by rage. He flew at Frank, wrapping his hands around his thick neck.

"What the fuck are you talking about?" he snarled. "You told me she was alive!"

The two thugs grabbed Blane's arms, pulling him off Frank. A fist slammed into Blane's side and he grunted in pain before spinning around to take them on. One had a knife and Blane dove at him first. They grappled as they fought, the knife slicing through Blane's shirt to his chest. The other guy came at Blane from behind. Blane kicked out, nailing the guy in the knee, and he dropped.

A blinding pain in the back of his head made his legs give out. Blane fell to his knees, realizing Frank had hit him with the butt of his own gun.

Blackness edged his vision, but he fought it. The guy Blane had nailed in the knee hobbled over and grabbed Blane's arms, wrapping a long cord around his wrists to bind him. Then he hauled back and punched Blane in the face. Once, twice. By the third time, blood filled Blane's mouth and he spat it out, the concrete lot swimming in his vision.

"What a tough guy," Blane mocked. "Bet you gotta tie up your women first, too, so they don't get away, right? Oh wait, I bet girls aren't your thing."

Blane braced himself for the guy's retaliation, which came in the form of more punishing blows to his face and torso. Finally, blessedly, he couldn't remain conscious and slipped into oblivion.

~

Seventeen Years Ago

They came in the middle of the night, dragging Kade from his bed kicking and yelling. He fought them, biting and scratching, until one of them got pissed and slammed his fist into Kade's jaw. Kade went limp, unable to fight as pain ricocheted through his head.

"Grab the kid," one of them said, and Kade was picked up and tucked under someone's arm, his feet dragging on the carpeted hallway.

By the time they got to the bottom of the stairs, Kade had shaken off the pain and was fighting again.

"Let me go, you sonofabitch!" His yelling didn't seem to have an effect on the guy carrying him, though he finally dropped Kade to the ground. Kade scrambled to his feet and froze.

They had Blane.

He was on his knees and blood dripped onto his bare chest from his nose and mouth. One eyebrow was split, more blood streaking down the side of his face. Willie stood behind Blane, a gun pointed to the back of his head.

The sound of shattering wood and glass came from the den and Kade realized they were wrecking the house. A guy emerged from the den, baseball bat in hand. He grinned at Kade, then walked past him toward the kitchen. A moment later, a cacophony of ceramic and glass breaking filled the house.

"So you try to threaten me, sugar daddy, you see what I do?" Willie said. "I don't take shit from nobody." He nodded at one of the guys standing next to Blane, who hauled back and punched Blane again in the face.

Aghast, Kade ran forward, only to be hooked around the waist and stopped by the guy who'd carried him down the stairs.

"I don't think so," he said. He grabbed Kade's arm and twisted it behind his back until Kade bit the inside of his lip to keep from making a sound. "You're a tough little dude, aren't ya?"

Blane's face had been impassive before, even with the beating, but now Kade saw fear in his eyes.

"What do you want, Willie?" Blane asked, his eyes on Kade. "You want money? Is that what this is about?"

"Fuck that," Willie scoffed. "This is about respect, and me teaching you a lesson." He nodded again and the guy slammed another fist into Blane.

Kade felt like he couldn't breathe. Panic and terror for Blane clawed at him. Blane was still upright, though he swayed a little.

The guy holding Kade's arm twisted it higher until tears stung Kade's eyes and he tasted blood from biting his lip so hard.

"Stop!" Blane shouted. "C'mon, Willie, don't be a dick. Take the money. Leave the kid alone." The desperation in his eyes as he watched Kade belied the calm command in his voice.

"Fuck you," Willie said.

To Kade's horror, he hauled back and slammed the butt of his gun against the back of Blane's head. The sickening crack of metal against bone could be heard even over the sound of what they were doing to Blane's house. Blane slumped forward on the floor and didn't move.

Kade screamed in rage and anguish. Tears streamed down his cheeks but he didn't notice. Ignoring the pain, he fought against the man holding him until his arm was wrenched higher and a blinding pain went through his shoulder.

The guy let him go and Kade collapsed to the floor. His arm hung useless but he crawled forward to where Blane lay and laid a hand on his back.

"Blane, wake up," he croaked through his tears, pushing at Blane's body. Blane didn't respond. "Please, you've gotta wake up!" It was terrifyingly reminiscent of when he'd spent hours trying to wake his mother. "Wake up!" But Blane didn't move.

A moment later, they seized Kade's injured arm, dragging him to his feet. Kade screamed in pain, then everything went dark.

∾

Consciousness came slowly to Blane, and with it, pain. He groaned as he sat up. His nose wasn't broken, but a couple of teeth were loose and his left eye was matted with blood.

Kade.

Blane jerked around, praying he wouldn't see Kade dead on the floor. To his relief, the place was empty. They'd taken him, but at least he was alive. Hopefully.

Gritting his teeth, Blane pushed himself to his feet. Stepping carefully through the broken glass that littered the floor, Blane climbed the stairs. Several of the spindles in the banister had been damaged and broken. His bedroom had been trashed, too, but Blane didn't care. All he could think about was Kade.

Was he okay? No doubt he was scared. Were they hurting him?

Those thoughts and worse tormented Blane as he cleaned himself up, popped some pain medicine, and pulled on clothes. The fury he felt was ice-cold. That bastard had invaded his home, hurt him and his brother, then taken Kade.

Blane was going to find Kade and make Willie pay. And if something happened to Blane in the process, it didn't matter. He wouldn't stop until Kade was safe again, no matter what it took.

Unlocking the gun cabinet downstairs, Blane removed the 9mm Glock inside, checking its magazine was loaded and grabbing two more magazines that he put in his pockets. Throwing a jacket on to conceal the weapon lodged in the back of his jeans, he grabbed his keys and was out the door. The sun was just peeking over the horizon as he headed downtown.

~

It took Blane the better part of the day to track down the teenage boy he'd spoken to months ago when Kade had run away. Finally, Blane spotted a young kid and followed him to a back alley already cloaked in the gloomy darkness of nightfall.

Blane stuck to the shadows until he saw the teen that he sought.

"Kid," he said. "Remember me?"

The teenager looked wary as Blane approached, but he nodded.

"Whaddya want?" he asked.

"I'm looking for Willie," Blane said.

The kid was already shaking his head. "Can't help you."

"Bullshit." Blane grabbed the kid, shoving him up against the brick wall. "Tell me where I can find him."

"I don't want no trouble with him," the kid protested. "Ain't nobody that'll go up against Willie."

"I will," Blane said. "Now I don't want to hurt you, but I will if you don't help me. He has someone I'm looking for and I won't quit until I find him."

The kid's lips pressed together and Blane shoved him harder against the wall, desperation making Blane ignore his twinge of conscience.

"Alright, alright!" the kid said, caving. "I don't know where Willie is, but I know the kid you're looking for. Dark hair, blue eyes, about ten, right?"

Blane's eyes narrowed. "Yeah. Where is he?"

The kid looked a little sad as he said, "Willie's already got him workin'. They usually use the motel over off 16th."

Blane's stomach fell to his knees. "Motel?" he repeated, praying he'd misheard.

"Yeah, man," the kid shrugged. "There's good money in kids his age."

Blane thought he might vomit. Swallowing the bile that rose in his throat, he gave the kid a nod.

∾

Kade was hungry. Willie had refused to give him any food today, as "punishment" for what he'd done. His shoulder still ached, though it was back in its socket.

Now he sat in the cheap motel room, waiting. He knew what was coming, knew exactly what work Willie would have him do. He tried not to think about it.

The motel room smelled of mildew. The carpet was stained in several spots, the cover on the bed in the same condition. Police sirens screamed in the distance and a television could be heard through the paper-thin walls.

The door opened. Kade looked up, fear lapping at him despite his attempts to stay calm. Blane was dead, and even if he wasn't, he was never going to find Kade. Why would he want to? Look at what had happened to him because of Kade. He'd been beat up, his home nearly destroyed, and for what? Kade wasn't worth going through that shit.

A man walked in, maybe in his forties, Kade guessed. Oddly, he was wearing a suit. It was rumpled, the shirt and jacket straining over a soft belly. His face was bloated, his eyes shifty, and when they landed on Kade, they became greedy.

"Hey, kid," the guy said, closing the door.

Kade didn't respond. His hands were clenched into fists as he fought the urge to run. Running would do nothing but get him beaten. Willie said if he was good and behaved, he'd let him eat.

Afterward.

"You're a quiet one," the man continued when Kade was silent. He approached where Kade sat in a cheap wooden chair. "That's okay. You don't need to talk." He reached forward and Kade didn't stop him as he pulled Kade's too-large T-shirt over his head.

There was a place Kade liked to go inside his head when he didn't want to deal with the world around him. It was with his mom, a park they used to go to when she was alive. It was in the inner city and had been vandalized a lot, but there was usually a swing or two that still worked. She'd put him in one and push him, higher and higher, the wind in his hair and the sun shining. She'd laugh and call him her little prince.

The place was different this time. It was Blane's backyard. They were tossing the baseball back and forth, sunlight streaming through the leaves in the trees. Gerard was grilling, the smell drifting over the lawn to them. Birds sang and Blane laughed at something Kade said.

"Kade! Kade!"

Kade blinked once, twice, pulling himself with effort from the fantasy.

He was lying on the bed now, his pants around his ankles. The guy was on the floor, out cold, and Blane stood over him.

Shame washed over him and Kade scrambled away from Blane, yanking at his pants. Blane sat on the bed and reached for Kade, helping him pull his pants back up. When he was finally covered, he forced himself to look up at Blane.

"Thank God I found you," Blane choked out. His eyes were wet, bruises darkening his face from the abuse he'd taken last night.

Kade couldn't keep the sob in his chest bottled up. He threw himself at Blane, who wrapped him in his arms.

"Shhh, it's okay. I've got you," Blane murmured.

Kade's skin was ice-cold, his small chest heaving as he cried. Blane could feel the pockmarks on his back from the cigarette burns, reminding him of how much he'd already failed Kade in his young life.

It felt good to finally hold him, comfort him. As much as he'd been through, Kade was still a child and now, more than ever, Blane felt the nearly overwhelming responsibility to protect him, take care of him.

When Kade had calmed down, Blane grabbed the discarded T-shirt and slipped it over his head. He took off the jacket he wore and put that on Kade, too.

"Let's go home," he said.

Kade reached for Blane's hand, slipping his palm inside Blane's as they stepped over the guy on the floor. It had taken all Blane had not to kill the guy when he'd walked in the door and seen him touching Kade.

Two men were waiting in the parking lot. Willie was one of them.

Blane pulled his gun, pushing Kade behind him and out of the line of fire.

"Get out of the way, Willie," Blane said, then shrugged. "Or don't. I'll be glad to put a bullet in you."

Kade yelled, but it was too late. A third guy had approached from the back, slamming a pipe into Blane's side. The blow was enough to crack a rib and Blane fell, the gun dropping from his hand. The guy struck again, the pipe slamming down on Blane, and he grunted in pain.

A gunshot rang out, and the guy with the pipe fell heavily on top of Blane. Behind him, Blane could see Kade, holding his smoking gun.

"You hurt my brother," Kade said, turning to Willie. The gun was steady and leveled at him.

The guy next to Willie turned and ran. Kade ignored him.

"Hey, Kade, I was just lookin' out for you," Willie stammered. His gaze was locked on the gun and he swallowed.

"Give me the gun, Kade," Blane said, shoving the dead body off him. He sat up slowly, watching Kade. The sobbing child from earlier was gone. The look on Kade's face now was empty of emotion, his eyes cold.

"He won't leave us alone," Kade said, his eyes still on Willie. "He'll try again. He was going to let that guy kill you a second ago."

"I swear, this is the end," Willie said. His throat moved as he swallowed. "Me and you, we're square."

"I don't think so," Kade said, and before Blane could say another word or reach for him, the gun barked again and Willie fell back onto the concrete. "Now we're square."

The stark efficiency of Kade's actions made Blane's blood run cold, but Kade seemed unaffected as he handed the gun to Blane.

"He won't bother us anymore," Kade said, as though reassuring Blane.

Blane just nodded and struggled up from the ground. Kade took his arm, helping him. Together they walked to Blane's car and got in.

Chapter Ten

When Blane woke, he was in a small, windowless room. He was lying on the cold, hard floor and when he moved, his entire body reminded him of how he'd gotten there. His ribs ached and a headache was crushing his skull.

Getting to his feet, Blane looked to his watch, only to see they'd taken it from him. His cell phone was lying on his desk at home, so no help there. A tray of food was sitting inside the door, and as Blane glanced around, he saw a tiny camera up in the corner. It seemed they were watching.

Inspecting every inch of the walls, Blane quickly ascertained that there was no escape possible, at least not from the inside. The door was locked, the edges fitting tightly into the wall. He wasn't going anywhere until someone came through that door.

Picking up the tray, Blane flung it against the opposite wall, the crash it made not as satisfying as he'd hoped. Looking up at the camera, he flipped it the bird.

Kathleen was dead.

The realization hit him again and he had to swallow down the nausea that erupted. He'd failed. He said he'd protect her. Now she was dead.

Blane leaned against the wall, sinking down to sit on the floor as he stared at nothing. She'd been so sweet, so young. Too young to die.

Death wasn't new to him, but it having an effect on him certainly was. Blane thought he'd immunized himself to the pain of loss. War left no other option. It was stop feeling, or lose your mind. His eyes stung and it was an effort to swallow. Her death was pointless, a waste. The last thing he'd said to her had been goodbye.

Blane vowed that when he got out of here, he'd kill Frank Santini. Then he'd find whoever had the actual hand in Kathleen's death, and that person would die very, very slowly. He couldn't bring her back, but he could avenge her.

Without a way to tell the time, Blane had no way of knowing how fast or slow the day was going, or how long he'd been unconscious. The waiting began to grate on him. Forced confinement combined with his anger over Kathleen and his inability to do anything about it worked him up into a state such that he couldn't stop pacing. His long strides ate up the floor, back and forth, and he occasionally glanced up at the camera, wishing whoever was behind it was here so he could wipe the floor with his sorry ass.

His imagination kept painting Kathleen's death in his head, though Frank hadn't said how she'd died. Blane hoped it'd been quick, that she hadn't been in pain, maybe hadn't even known what was coming. Unfortunately, he doubted she'd been that lucky. What if whoever Frank sent hadn't just killed her? What if he'd hurt her first? Hit her? Raped her?

It was enough to drive him mad. Finally, when he felt like he would come out of his skin if he didn't get out of here soon, he heard someone at the door.

Taking up a spot just inside, Blane waited. Whoever it was, he'd grab him and get the hell out of here.

The keys jangled as they scraped at the lock, then the door opened. Blane seized the collar of the janitor. Hauling him into the room,

Blane shoved him up against the wall. The hat the guy was wearing fell to the floor and long, strawberry blonde hair tumbled out.

"Kathleen?"

The shock of seeing her went through Blane like an electric current. He didn't think, he just felt, and what he felt was a relief and joy that went bone-deep. Blane was kissing her before he'd made the conscious decision to do so.

She was alive. Warm and soft and unhurt. They hadn't killed her.

Blane pulled back, his gaze intent on hers as he cupped her jaw. He memorized the blue depths of her eyes, the feel of her cheek as his fingers drifted lightly over her skin. He'd been given a second chance with her. Another chance to keep her safe. Another chance to make her his. And suddenly Blane realized he wanted that. He wanted that very much.

"They told me you were dead," he rasped, still touching her as if to reassure himself that she was really there.

"Reports of my death have been greatly exaggerated," she said, her voice slightly breathless.

The Mark Twain quote amused Blane, knocking him out of his funk.

"I'm here to bust you out," she said. "Let me go now?"

Blane realized he was pressed tightly against her, rendering her nearly immobile, and he stepped back. As glad as he was that she was alive, she wouldn't be much longer if he didn't get her out of here.

"How did you get in here?" he asked.

"I'm temping here today and I saw you on the security cameras," she said, unknotting the cord that tied his hands together. Blane worked at the rest until it fell to the floor. It felt good having his arms free.

She'd been here? All day? Good God. The thought nearly made Blane's heart stop.

Kathleen reached for his face, concern etched on her features, and Blane grabbed her wrist.

"Are you all right?" she asked.

Typical. Kathleen was the one they wanted to kill, and she wanted to know if *he* was all right.

"I'm fine," Blane answered. "Though I have a serious problem with you being within a mile of this place."

Her jaw set in a stubborn line. "I don't recall asking your permission," she retorted.

Blane had nearly failed her once. He wasn't about to again. He easily took away the gun she held.

"Hey!" she protested.

"Stay behind me," he ordered, pulling her into position so his body blocked hers. He eased open the door and saw a guard lying motionless on the floor. "Is he dead?"

"Of course not! I wasn't trying to kill him. Just knock him out."

Blane shoved the gun in his pants and grabbed under the guy's armpits. "And how did you manage that?" he said, dragging the guy into his erstwhile prison.

"I hit him with a plunger."

That stopped Blane in his tracks. He gaped at her. She'd come to rescue him with only a plunger as a weapon?

Kathleen shrugged. "Then he slipped and hit his head. I got lucky."

She had no idea. "Let's hope your luck holds." He grabbed the guy's jacket, shrugging it on over his torn shirt. "Let's go."

Blane led the way down the hall to where he hoped there was an exit. Gun in hand, he eased around the corner. No one was there and he saw a freight elevator. Perfect.

Once inside, Kathleen got rid of her janitor disguise. Blane didn't bother looking anywhere else but at her as she took off the overalls. Her skirt was bunched at her waist, providing a lovely view of her legs and more before she smoothed the wrinkled fabric down. She tried to fix her hair, then gave up and let it fall around her shoulders. The fierceness of what he felt as he watched her surprised Blane and he filed it away to analyze later.

They reached what seemed to be the basement level without incident, but their luck didn't last. As they moved down a hallway toward the main elevator, a loud voice came from behind them.

"What are you doing down here? Stop right there!"

Shit. Blane grabbed Kathleen's arm and started running for the elevator. The guy behind them fired and Kathleen cried out. The bullet missed, hitting the wall instead. They reached the elevator and Blane hit the button, dragging Kathleen in front of him to shield her with his body. The guy was getting closer and fired another shot. This one hit its mark, embedding itself in Blane's shoulder and coming out the other side.

Turning, Blane fired. The guy fell and didn't move.

The elevator finally got there and they wasted no time getting inside. Kathleen jabbed again and again at the button until the doors closed. Blane leaned against the wall, taking deep breaths and trying to compartmentalize the pain.

Kathleen suddenly pulled aside his jacket. "Oh my God, Blane! You were hit!"

"I'll be fine," he said to calm her. She looked near hysterics. Her face was white and her hands shook. Blane remembered what she'd said to him when he'd seen the bruise on her face. "It looks worse than it feels."

She swallowed. "Good, because it looks horrible." She looked on the verge of tears.

The elevator doors opened and Blane concentrated on putting one foot in front of the other as they walked through the lobby. A couple dozen other people were also leaving for the day. Good. They'd blend in.

Kathleen's palm pressed into his and Blane curled his hand around hers. She was ice-cold. Two men rushed toward the elevator behind them and Kathleen's grip tightened. Blane could almost smell the fear and adrenaline pouring off her.

"It's all right," he murmured, trying to soothe her. She couldn't panic now. They were almost at the doors. "Keep moving."

With a degree of calm that belied the fine tremors Blane could feel running through her body, Kathleen walked beside him until they'd reached the outdoors and freedom. Her pace sped up and Blane gritted his teeth. Blood loss was getting to him. He could feel it oozing from the wound and coating his skin and the fabric of the coat. The pain was becoming harder to manage and he pressed his lips tightly together.

Kathleen seemed to sense that he was in trouble, wedging herself under his arm and taking some of his weight as he staggered. Blane didn't pay attention to where they were going, his focus on staying conscious and alert for signs anyone was following them. They rounded a corner and suddenly Kade was there. Blane didn't think he'd ever been so glad to see him.

"What the fuck did you do?" Kade bit out angrily to Kathleen.

"Not her fault," Blane said, moving to lean on Kade instead of Kathleen.

Kade helped Blane to the car and Blane gratefully sank into the passenger seat.

"Is he going to be okay?" he heard Kat ask Kade.

"He will be. As soon as I get him to a hospital. You coming?"

"No. I have to be at the airport by seven."

That got Blane's attention, dragging him abruptly out of the fog permeating his mind.

"Why?" He couldn't manage more than that, but he couldn't think of a single damn reason why she should be going to the airport instead of his house, where she'd be safe.

"They're going to Chicago tonight," she said. "I'm working for one of the vice presidents, Stephen Avery. I'm hoping I'll be able to find the right server on-site."

Blane looked at Kade. He didn't need to say anything, Kade knew exactly what he was thinking. She wouldn't get two feet inside the door before they executed her.

"Grab her," Blane ordered.

He saw Kade wrap an arm around a protesting Kathleen and heaved a sigh of relief. She was safe. Kade would keep her safe. Darkness enveloped him and this time he gave in to its silent embrace.

∾

When he woke, he was staring at the white ceiling of a hospital room. Blane sat up with a jerk. His shoulder reminded him of why he was there and he grimaced. His clothes had been removed and he was wearing one of those awful hospital gowns.

A nurse nearby stepped forward. "Mr. Kirk?"

"Where am I?" Blane asked.

"Indiana University Hospital," she answered, checking the drip on the IV in his arm.

"What time is it?"

She glanced over her shoulder. "After midnight."

"Where's the man who brought me?" Blane asked. He needed Kade. Kade had Kathleen. He needed to see Kathleen, needed to know she was okay.

"He left hours ago," the nurse said, reaching to take his blood pressure. "He did leave a cell phone for you. Said you'd want it."

"May I have it?"

She nodded, finishing her task before going to a corner and retrieving his cell from the counter. As he dialed, Blane said, "Please get the attending physician. I need to go."

"But you have to stay overnight for observation," she protested.

"Did the bullet hit any major organs?"

"No."

"Did they sew me up?"

"Yes."

"Then get the doctor and I'll leave my card for the cops."

Blane held the phone to his ear, dismissing her. He ignored her and she exited the room in a huff. It rang three times before Kade answered.

"Thanks for leaving me my cell," Blane said. "Are you all right?"

"Yeah, give me a minute," Kade said.

Blane heard the murmur of voices as he waited, then finally Kade came back on the line. "I'm fine. How're the nurses treating you?"

"Good enough, I guess. I just woke up a few minutes ago."

"Anything permanently damaged?"

"No. It was a clean shot," Blane said. "Where are you? Where's Kathleen?"

"Ah, yeah. About that. I'm in Chicago."

"Did you find the server?"

"Yep."

"And?"

"And it's taken care of," Kade said. "They won't be delivering any elections tomorrow."

"Good work," Blane said, relieved. He'd known Kade would come through, even if Blane had been taken out of the picture. "Did you stash Kathleen somewhere safe?"

There was a pause. "She's with me."

It took a moment for Blane to process that, then, "Are you fucking kidding me?" he ground out. "I told you to grab her, not take her to Chicago. I trusted you—"

"Relax, she's fine," Kade cut in. "Short of me tying her down, she was coming here. I came along to keep her safe."

Blane took a deep breath, let it out. There was no sense yelling at Kade. What was done was done. "Where exactly are you?"

"A motel. Outskirts of the city." Kade rattled off an address.

Kade and Kathleen were in a motel. Together. Blane tried to shake off the uneasiness that revelation had brought. It wasn't like Kade was going to do something to her. Blane trusted him. Yet he still found himself saying, "Let me talk to her."

Another pause, longer this time. "She's sleeping," Kade said. "You want me to wake her?"

A sharp pang of disappointment. "No. Let her sleep." Blane hesitated. "So you know she wasn't a plant," he said.

Silence, then, "Yeah, I know." Kade sighed. "What do you want me to do with her? Bring her back in the morning?"

A gnawing ache clawed at Blane's gut and he instinctively knew it wouldn't ease until he saw Kathleen, held her, reassured himself that she was well and whole.

"No, I'll head there soon. I should be out of the hospital here shortly and I'll drive up."

The doctor walked in and Blane quickly ended the call, telling Kade he'd text when he was on his way. After the usual cautions about the injury, the doctor signed the discharge papers. Thirty minutes later, a cab was dropping Blane off at home.

He showered, pulling on a pair of jeans and a long-sleeved shirt for the drive. Quickly jotting a note for Mona, he grabbed a sandwich from the fridge and a bottle of water, then hit the road. He should be able to be in Chicago shortly before dawn.

When Blane pulled up to the fleabag motel, Kade was outside waiting for him. The sky was just now starting to lighten in the east.

"How's the shoulder?" Kade asked as Blane got out of the car.

"It'll heal." Blane surveyed Kade, his arms akimbo. "I wanted you to keep her from coming at all and I'm pissed that you didn't. But it looks like you kept her alive, so thank you."

Kade's lips twisted. "Sounds like one cancels out the other to me."

Blane snorted in reply, but was okay with letting his anger go. It served no purpose and he didn't like tension between him and Kade. After a moment, he asked, "So are you going back to Indy?"

Kade shook his head. "I've got some business to take care of back east. I'll be in touch."

Blane nodded, hiding his disappointment. It had been nice having his brother around. Really nice. Blane had hoped Kade would feel the same, would want to stay and give up the lonely, nomadic—not to mention highly dangerous—life he lived.

"She's inside. Asleep," Kade said, handing the motel key to Blane.

"Is she all right?"

"She's fine."

Relief edged out the churning in his gut. Blane was anxious to see her, only feet from him now. As he walked by Kade, Blane clasped him lightly on the shoulder. Kade wasn't one for displays of affection and Blane hoped he understood by the gesture how grateful he was to him— for keeping Kat safe, for helping with the case, for just being there.

∼

Blane would have liked to take Kat to his house instead of her apartment, though the thought was ridiculous at this stage. No doubt she'd look at him like he was insane if he suggested it, so he didn't say anything and just drove her home.

It seemed she'd been as glad to see him as Blane was to see her, and if the motel Kade had chosen had been of a better quality, their reunion would have been decidedly more thorough.

Instead, Blane had packed her up and driven Kat back to Indy and to her apartment. Mona had brought the cat back, as Blane had suggested in his note this morning, so the feline was waiting for her when they arrived. Judging by Kat's response, that had been a smart move.

The DA had called Blane while he'd waited for Kat to dress in the motel, letting him know that the Santinis had ratted out Gage and his part in the murders of Mark and Sheila. Gage would go to prison, though his son James would remain unscathed.

The thought briefly crossed his mind that he could go now. He'd delivered Kathleen safely to her home, the bad guys were behind bars, and no one was going to hurt her. But Blane dismissed the thought as quickly as it had come. He wanted Kat, wanted her for more than just a night. For how much more, he couldn't say. What he did know was that she was the first woman he'd ever been with who was completely oblivious to his wealth or the power he wielded. She seemed blithely unconcerned with his public image or career plans, her focus solely on the man he was, without all the baggage.

So Blane stayed. He made love to her, fed her, made love to her again, talked with her, held her while she slept. She fascinated him. Kathleen had an inner strength and innocence that remained untouched, even with what had happened to her the last couple of weeks. She'd buried both her parents and made her way alone in the world. Quiet and unassuming, it seemed she was wholly unaware of her striking looks. Or maybe Blane was just seeing her more clearly now.

Blane woke when Kathleen climbed back into bed. It was the middle of the night. She moved tentatively, trying not to wake him, as she snuggled spoon-style. The feel of her curved bottom nestling against his crotch had his cock stirring to life again. Blane's hand drifted to her waist. Satisfaction flooded through him when he realized she was wearing his shirt and nothing else. A primal need to mark her, possess her again, made him lift her knee to rest her leg atop his as he pushed his now throbbing erection inside her.

Kat gasped in surprise, the sound turning quickly into a moan. She was still slick from their lovemaking earlier, the wet heat of her body like sin wrapped in silk. Blane moved slow and deep, letting her sighs drift over him. His hand kept a firm grip on her thigh, pinning her in place as he sped up, his control gradually slipping away. He thrust harder and faster, until he came in a blinding rush of heat and sensation, his cock pulsing inside her.

His hand was gripping her leg tight enough to leave marks and

Blane quickly let go, though Kat hadn't complained. She hadn't come yet, either, so Blane's hand drifted down between her thighs where his aching cock was still nestled. But she stilled his hand.

"Don't," she said softly, threading her fingers through his.

Blane lifted his head off the pillow so he could see her face better. He frowned, wondering if he'd gone too far.

"What's wrong?" he asked.

Her cheeks tinted pink and she shyly lowered her gaze. "I'm just a little sore, that's all. I'm not used to this."

Well, now didn't Blane feel like shit.

"I'm sorry—" he began, but she interrupted.

"No, don't apologize," she said with a small smile. "It's a good kind of sore." She brought their joined hands up to her breasts and closed her eyes with a sigh.

Normally after a night like this, sated and replete, Blane would already be making an excuse to leave. Itching to get home, shower, relax. But not tonight. There was something about her, this particular woman, that had him rethinking his ideas and plans for the future. The things he was feeling should have alarmed him, sent him running for the door, but they didn't.

Blane lay there watching her for a long while. She drifted to sleep, her hold on his hand loosening as her body relaxed in slumber. If possible, she looked even younger and more innocent when she slept. Guilt needled Blane. He shouldn't get involved with her any further. He should let that young pup bartender date her. Blane's track record with women was abysmal. He was too selfish and grew bored too easily. Yet even with the possibility looming that he could break her heart, Blane couldn't make himself leave her.

When the sky began to lighten, Blane climbed out of bed. Kat was dead asleep and didn't even move from where he left her. Blane took a shower, pulling his jeans on before starting a pot of coffee. After pouring himself a cup, he wandered over to her couch. A stack of books and magazines sat on the floor and curiosity got the better of him. He inspected the books. She liked legal thrillers, by the looks of it, with a couple of romances thrown in. The magazines were all various food and recipe ones, and Blane wondered if Kathleen could cook, not that he particularly cared.

As he thumbed through the stack, a manila envelope fell from between two magazines. It was thick and Blane unthinkingly opened it. A stack of cash fell into his hand.

Surprise immobilized him for a moment, then he counted it. Twenty thousand dollars. Why would Kathleen have that much money? And why would she be hiding it in her apartment?

Frowning as he thought, Blane put the money back in the envelope. He turned it over in his hand and saw writing on one side.

Buy some decent shoes.

It wasn't the words that made Blane freeze, his breath catching slightly. It was the handwriting. He knew that writing, knew it very well. It was Kade's.

~

Eleven Years Ago

Kade stared out his window, knowing it was time and yet not wanting to face it. It seemed like a lifetime ago, the day he'd first come here. He'd been so sure back then that his stay would be temporary at best. And it nearly had been, if not for Blane's persistence.

Blane had turned Kade around, given him a shot at a normal life. They'd never spoken about that night so long ago, the night things had changed between them. Blane had seen Kade at his most vulnerable, when he was weakest, and hadn't pushed him away in disgust. Blane had really meant it when he said he loved him and that he'd take care of him.

Kade felt no regret over the men he'd killed that night. He'd kept his brother safe and he'd do it again without a second thought. Blane was everything to him.

But now Blane was leaving, and he might not make it back.

∼

Blane finished packing, not that there was much to take. As a SEAL, his deployment would be for six months at a time.

Hauling his duffel downstairs, he met Mona on her way from the kitchen. Tears sparked in her eyes immediately when she saw him, but she blinked them back and smiled.

"Gerard should be here in a few minutes," she said. "I hope you don't mind my not going with you to the airport. I just can't—" She broke off.

"It's okay," Blane said, reaching to give her a hug. "I understand."

Mona gripped him tightly before letting go. She nodded, her smile thin-lipped now and tears on her lashes.

"You be careful," she managed to say. "We love you, you know."

"I will," Blane replied. "And I love you, too." He brushed a kiss to her forehead. "Where's Kade?" he asked.

Mona dabbed at her eyes. "I don't think he wants to come down," she said. "You know how he idolizes you. He's having a harder time dealing with this than even Gerard and me."

Blane glanced up the stairs with a sigh. "I'd better go up," he said.

A few moments later, he was knocking on Kade's door.

"Yeah," Kade called out.

Blane opened the door. Kade was standing at the window, looking outside.

"You're not gonna give your big brother a goodbye kiss?" Blane joked, but Kade didn't smile.

Blane sighed and sank down onto the bed. He glanced around. Kade kept the room spotless. The only area that looked like it was even used was the desk that held his computer and other electronics, some of which Blane didn't even know what they did or were for. But Kade did. He'd taken to computers like a duck to water, which probably shouldn't have been surprising since he'd tested two levels above his grade. He'd graduate high school a couple of months after he turned seventeen.

"Tell me why you're doing this again?" Kade asked.

"You know why. We've had this conversation before," Blane answered. "It's just something I feel I need to do, to give something back."

"So risking your life for a country of fools who don't appreciate it, that's how you want to 'give back'?"

Blane knew Kade well enough to know what this was really about, not that either of them would say. It had taken Kade months before he'd slept without nightmares after the run-in with Willie all those years ago. He'd wake up screaming, calling for Blane in his sleep. Blane had taken to just sticking Kade in bed with him for a while. He'd seemed to sleep better when he did that.

They'd never spoken about it, but maybe not talking had been a mistake.

"I know I may get hurt," Blane said quietly. "I may die. But that doesn't mean I don't care about you."

"Then why?" Kade cried. "Why would you do this to me?"

Blane stood, frowning as he walked over to Kade. "I'm not doing this *to* you," he said. "I'm doing this *for* you. I want you to know there's more to life than just living for yourself. And some things are worth dying for."

"I'd die for you," Kade said baldly.

Blane's smile was a little sad. "I'd rather you didn't. You've paid your dues to life."

Kade looked away, shoving his hands into the pockets of his jeans. He blinked rapidly a few times and cleared his throat.

"Well, you know I'm going to drive the Jag while you're gone," he said flippantly.

"The hell you will!" Blane retorted in mock anger. "You even touch it, I'm gonna know."

Kade snorted. "Bullshit. And don't think I don't know how to get into the liquor cabinet either. I'm going to throw so many wild fucking parties, you'll be on a plane back here before dust even coats your sunglasses."

Blane chuckled. "Just try not to get arrested or break too many hearts, okay?"

"I'm too good to get arrested, but I can't make any promises on the second one," Kade said with a shit-eating grin. "I'm pretty hot, you know."

This time Blane laughed outright. "And modest, I see," he teased.

Kade shrugged.

It got quiet then. It was time and both of them knew it.

Blane reached out first, because he knew Kade wouldn't, and wrapped him in a bear hug. Tears threatened, but he held them back. He had to be strong for Kade.

Displays of affection weren't Kade's thing, and he still didn't like to be touched when he wasn't expecting it, but his grip was tight on Blane.

Finally, they parted.

"You coming with us to the airport?" Blane asked. "Gerard is taking me."

Kade shook his head, not quite meeting Blane's eyes as he said, "Nah. Got homework to do."

Sure he did. School had always been child's play for Kade and it was rare when he had to finish his homework at home. But Blane let it slide.

"Okay."

"I'll, uh, I'll write you," Kade said, which surprised Blane.

"I'd like that," he said.

Kade glanced up at him, though by now they were nearing the same height. His eyes were startlingly blue behind the fringe of jet-black lashes.

"You know, right?" Kade said. "I mean, you know." His ears reddened and he looked away again. "You know I love you, right."

Blane's throat closed and he couldn't speak. He could count on one hand the number of times Kade had said that particular phrase to him.

"So, you know, don't get shot, or anything," Kade continued. "Or I'll be really fucking pissed."

"You got it," Blane managed, grabbing him for another hug. "I love you, too, brother."

He left while they both were still coherent and in control. Another few moments and he'd have broken down and cried like a little girl to be leaving his brother behind.

Mona met him downstairs, took one look at his face, and took his hand in hers.

"We'll take good care of him," she said.

"I know," Blane replied. "I'll be back. I promise." Grabbing his duffel, he headed out the door to the waiting car.

Kade watched from the upstairs window as Blane put his stuff in the trunk. Before he got in, he looked up and saw Kade. He raised a hand in farewell before disappearing inside the car.

Mona suddenly appeared at Kade's side. He'd shot up in the past couple of years and now was taller than she. Kade glanced down at her. She was crying, her gaze glued on the car retreating down the drive.

Kade wrapped an arm around her shoulders and she rested her head against him. His eyes were dry now. Blane had given him so much, now it was Kade's turn to give back. It was his turn to be strong, for Mona and Gerard, who loved Blane and would worry. His turn to lie awake nights, wondering where his brother was, and if he was safe. And when Blane returned, Kade would be here waiting for him.

They had each other, and that would never change.

ABOUT THE AUTHOR

Tiffany Snow has been reading romance novels since she was too young to read romance novels. After a career working in the information technology field, Tiffany now has her dream job of writing full time.

Tiffany makes her home in the Midwest with her husband and two daughters. She can be reached at Tiffany@TiffanyASnow.com. Visit her on her website, www.Tiffany-Snow.com, to keep up with her latest projects.